THE HOSTAGE PRINCE

THE HOSTAGE PRINCE

Vanessa Hannam

Fiction
Hannam

This first world edition published in Great Britain 2006 by
SEVERN HOUSE PUBLISHERS LTD of
9–15 High Street, Sutton, Surrey SM1 1DF.
This first world edition published in the USA 2006 by
SEVERN HOUSE PUBLISHERS INC of
595 Madison Avenue, New York, N.Y. 10022.

British Library Cataloguing in Publication Data

Hannam, Vanessa
    The hostage prince
    1.   Great Britain - History - Civil War, 1642-1649 - Fiction
    2.   Historical fiction
    I.   Title
    823.9'14 [F]

    ISBN-10: 0-7278-6331-2

Typeset by Palimpsest Book Production Ltd.,
Polmont, Stirlingshire, Scotland.
Printed and bound in Great Britain by
MPG Books Ltd., Bodmin, Cornwall.

Special thanks to Elspeth Sinclair for her sensitive editing. And to Elfreda Powell, Elizabeth Murray and Lady Hylton for their help and enthusiasm, Elizabeth Buchan for use of her own library and knowledge, the Duke of Northumberland and the Viscount De L'Isle of Penshurst Place. And also to the National Trust staff at Petworth House, the Trustees of the Carisbrooke Castle Museum and the London Library for their invaluable support.

Prologue

Suffolk, England 1646

Thomas Jones, a captain in the Royalist Army, owed the young soldier an answer. After all the boy had saved his life.

'To truly understand what this is all for, it sometimes helps to think of home,' he said carefully. 'We are fighting for our way of life as we have known it, as God has wished it. We are prepared to lay down our lives for those principles.' He hoped his voice carried conviction because if he made public the doubts he felt in his heart, what would this do to his men?

Although he was no more than two years the boy's senior, the war had aged the officer as time could never do. His once immaculate uniform, now worn and dishevelled, hung loosely from his tall frame.

'Come to the fire, Ned,' he said. 'It's this rain. It lowers the spirits. Sit awhile. Have some of this ale the good farmer's given us. Let me tell you about my home.'

The boy sat on a mound of damp hay and they drank together.

'So what about your home, sir?' the boy asked tentatively.

'It's a lovely place in Kent,' Tom replied. 'The house stands in a cleft in the hills leading to the sea. From the top you can see the beach, and on rough days you can hear the waves breaking.'

'I like the sea,' said the boy. 'When I was small I used to think I might like to be a sailor. But then there's the farm. We've worked hard for it.'

'Have you much land?' Tom asked.

'Before the war came we thought we might be able to rent some more land, but now that's all a pipe dream.' The boy

1

stared wistfully into the fire, and there was silence as the two thought of home.

'Has the house been in your family for long, sir?' the boy asked eventually.

'Yes, Ned, handed down for generations.' Tom hesitated, feeling in his breast pocket for the last communication he had received from his father, Sir Edwin.

Tom kicked the smouldering embers of the fire and flames sprung into life. The boy jumped up, and sprinkled water from a wooden bucket. Unlike Cromwell's men, the Royalists did not burn and pillage. They tried to leave a place as they found it.

'Thanks, you're a good soldier, Ned,' said Tom gratefully.

Emboldened by the officer's words of approval, the boy sat down again, enjoying the warmth of the fire and asked, 'How many sisters do you have?'

'Four . . . but my special sister's called Lizzie,' Tom replied, a slight smile beginning to lighten his face. 'She was christened Elizabeth Anne,' he went on. 'We were friends. We did everything together.'

'No brothers then, sir?'

'Yes. My younger brother Philip is somewhere with the King,' Tom replied, his voice trailing off as he thought about his brother. He didn't really know if he was alive or dead.

'Where d'you think the King is?' the boy asked eagerly. 'There's talk among the men, but nobody knows for certain.'

'I think he may be with the Scots, they've offered him protection,' Tom answered, unsure as to how much information he should give, even to his own men. Hiding on the coat tails of the Scots was a world away from the picture these men had of their King, the ideal for whom they had already given so much. 'But I don't know for sure,' he said quickly.

Tom was tired, fatigued beyond anything he could ever have imagined before he started the business of killing his fellow countrymen and he pretended not to see the boy brush his face with his sleeve. He knew the boy had had enough. He had seen it before, he had seen them walk away, knowing they would be shot in the back. And worse, there were tales that lone soldiers had been summarily hanged, blamed by the mob for taking food and supplies for troops, because Parliament would not grant them indemnity.

Tom looked at the boy again, so loyal and dependable, such a fine example of the many young men who had died for something they didn't really understand, and decided he would send him home, now. A life for a life.

'Where's your home, Ned?'

'Sussex, sir. So I know how you must think of your own place now, with the harvest waiting to be brought in.' He faltered, biting his lip. 'And with nobody to do it, it will soon rot in this wet weather.'

'Ned, I'm sending you home tomorrow,' Tom said suddenly. 'You'll have a horse, in fact you shall keep the horse. It deserves a better life too.'

"Home as a coward, sir, never,' Ned exclaimed in horror. 'I shall live or die with you and the men.'

'Now you listen, Ned,' Tom rebutted forcefully as he thought angrily of the young men he had seen killed in the previous month. 'I'll write out a declaration. You'll go home a proud soldier.' He thought for a moment. 'And besides, I've a commission for you.' The boy looked up sharply. 'You're to go to my family on the way. Take them some dispatches. And then you may wait quietly with your people. That's a nasty wound in your shoulder, it needs care, the sort of care you won't find here. A rest from war will do you good. One day you'll need to come forward again. We'll need men like you.'

'But, sir . . .' the boy started.

'This is an order,' Tom barked, holding up his hand.

The boy stood to attention. He could not disguise the relief on his face. 'Yes, sir,' he said gratefully. This young officer also had a home life, but for him there was no way out. 'Tell me about Lizzie,' he said quietly.

'She's very beautiful. But she doesn't know it. Please God the women don't know the full extent of the carnage and deprivation. My Lizzie is safe in my heart, Ned, as your family is in yours. I wish you God speed.'

Tom stood up and the boy jumped to his feet again. They saluted, their gazes locked together for a moment.

PART ONE

Hatherton Manor 1646

One

'I needn't wait for hell. It's here all around me,' Elizabeth Anne Jones called out in anguish.

She spoke to no one in particular, as if the walls of the great house would absorb her fears and dilute them in the happy memories of life as it used to be, before this unthinkable civil war: times which she knew, without anyone saying it, were gone for ever.

'Child, may you be forgiven. Satan prowls waiting to destroy the heedless soul. You'll be punished for saying such things.' Ruth, her old nurse, shook her head violently and then crossed herself.

'Surely God has punished us enough. I can't bear to see Mother suffering like this,' the girl retorted angrily.

'Pray to our God and saviour,' said Ruth, burying her head in her apron and stifling a sob, 'that, if it is His will, your mother may hasten to her heavenly home in peace.'

'Ruth, this can't be right,' cried Lizzie. 'Mother has so much to live for. So many people depend on her. I'm not going to accept it is God's will she should die.

Ruth was exhausted – she hadn't slept for two days. She had been aware of the onset of her mistress's labour long before the rest of the family and she had a strong sense of foreboding. Mary Jones was already worn down by the problems caused by the war and she was old for childbearing now – in her thirty-ninth year. This new assertiveness in Sir Edwin Jones's eldest daughter was worrying and could only add to the family's problems.

'I've been your nurse ever since you came into this world,' she said crossly. 'I was the first to hold you and place you on your mother's breast, and now you speak this blasphemy, first against your King and then the Almighty himself. When will you learn to submit to the will of God?'

Something snapped in Lizzie's mind. She was not going to submit to anything. From now on she would put her faith in herself and her own sense of survival. She remembered the long night when she had heard her mother's cries. She had prayed as she had never done before, had offered God her own life – anything to save her mother. But still the baby would not come. She had pleaded with her father not to summon the old woman from the village. Everyone said she was a witch and killed more than she saved with her filthy instruments and stained apron.

'What would you have me do, child?' he had answered. 'The midwife is dying of the fever. Someone must deliver your mother. We've not time to send for another midwife – she lives miles away.'

So the old witch had come, banishing all of them, while she did her worst. But now, whatever her father said, Lizzie was going to step in.

No longer able to bear her mother's cries, she pushed past her old nurse and forced her way into the birthing chamber.

Her mother was past caring about modesty, and the carnage caused by the old woman's attempts to get the baby out were all too clear. A crude cutting instrument lay soaked in blood on the bed sheet. The old woman turned to face them, her face flushed and sweating, and for a moment Lizzie thought she resembled Beelzebub himself.

'All I can do now, my Lady,' she whined with a wizened smile, 'is to pull the babe out with the birthing hook.'

Lizzie thought the old woman was almost enjoying the situation and the dreadful power she held in her hands. It was the first time she had been allowed into the manor, and if Lizzie had anything to do with it, it would be the last.

Lizzie shuddered and with a hoarse whisper which left no room for argument, she faced the old woman. 'No. You won't do that. I've heard you think nothing of sawing the arm off a child the better to remove it,' she said furiously. 'The last time you did your worst you swaddled the babe and handed him to his mother without saying what you'd done. Then you took your purse and left both babe and mother to die.'

The old woman made as if to ignore her, but Lizzie quickly moved between her and the bed.

8

As Lizzie saw the cuts the old woman had made she thought she might faint. There was no sign of the child's head. She had seen the ugly process of birth before, when she had been with Ruth to tend the wife of one of the stewards, but never in her wildest dreams had she imagined she would be called upon to see her own mother, a woman so modest and discreet, in such stark animal desperation. She set aside any forbearance and became mechanically practical.

Something told her that, against all the odds, somewhere, her mother had that final hidden reserve of strength. Lizzie was going to help her find it.

Pushing the old woman out of the way, she took Ruth's hand and pulled her roughly towards the bed.

'Look, Ruth,' Lizzie cried desperately. 'You've delivered many a poor woman in your time, and I've lost count of the animals I've brought out of their mothers. Let's do our best.'

For four more hours she and Ruth helped Mary Jones to deliver her child. Ruth gently pressing her abdomen in the way she had been taught by her own mother, who had been the village midwife.

Just when they had begun to fear the old woman might be proved right, Mary, who had begun to seem dead to the world and indifferent to her fate, summoned all her energy. With an almighty push the baby's head appeared and Lizzie held the tiny slippery form of a baby girl. All the horror of the last few days evaporated in a second as her mother stretched out her arms to receive the child.

No husband could be in the birthing chamber. Custom had it that women must travail alone. Sir Edwin had been praying in his study and trying to allay the fears of his three younger daughters, occupying them with their studies to take their minds off the worry of their mother's confinement. Ruth took the lifeless baby and plunged her into cold water, and then rubbed honey and salt on the child's mouth and gums before bathing her in oil of myrtle and roses, in readiness for the swathing bands. She let out her first reedy cry.

Sir Edwin heard it and his heart raced. He threw down his books and told his daughters to wait. He hurried down the long gallery towards his wife's chamber, feeling a mixture of relief and dread. The child had survived. But such a weak sad cry, as if it already knew something of the sinful and troubled world into which it had so reluctantly come. But what of his beloved Mary? He had heard her sufferings even with the door of his study firmly closed. He had heard the frightened whisperings of the servant girls.

Although he wanted news of his wife, he did not enter the room. He knew she would not want to see him until all traces of the birth had been removed.

The old woman heard him coming and slunk out from the shadows. She had resolutely stayed, nodding off to sleep in the far corner of the room. As she shuffled forward she whispered in Lizzie's ear, 'Her Ladyship will not live for two more sunsets, the fever will take hold. I shall tell his Lordship I could have saved her if . . . but I might be silent if I get my payment.' She gave a sly smile and wiped her hands on her soiled apron. Ruth could see the anger in Lizzie's face as she hustled her into her mother's dressing closet out of the old woman's hearing.

'Lizzie, we've done all we can,' Ruth said firmly. 'Go to your father now. Tell him he has a daughter, and that his lady isn't fit to be seen. Take the babe to him, for she may cheer him a little. I will call one of the servants to help clean the room. The old woman can't do anything now. We'd as well let her leave in her own time. No good will come of crossing her.'

But Lizzie was not going to do any such thing. All her short life she had listened to the words of her elders and, though she had often disagreed, she had seldom spoken out. On the rare occasions she had done so, she had been punished and made to wash her mouth out with a foul tasting mixture kept in the pantry for such occasions. But the events of the last few hours had shown her that she must take things into her own hands before it was too late.

'The old woman reeks of death,' she proclaimed, her eyes flashing angrily. 'She's nothing more than a butcher. I swear if Mother dies, it'll be she who killed her and all because Father would not listen to me. Then there would be another motherless child in this world. Who would feed it and love it if things go on as they are? You had better listen to me, for I mean what I say.'

Ruth was rapidly losing patience. There was too much to do to let Lizzie's temperament have its way. Life must go on. She had brought people into the world and she dressed them to meet their maker – it was all the same to her. Her blind faith in the old order was the one thing which held her together. She would have to put a stop to all this rebellious talk.

'Child, will you start talking sense!' she cautioned. 'Things will get better if we trust in God and the King, for the King is God's messenger on earth. All this will pass if we don't lose our faith. You've done a good thing today. I admire your courage, for it would not have been in me to go against his Lordship and push the old woman out, but don't let it go to your head. You're only a girl,' she went on doggedly. 'Best leave these things to the men. The King will put all to rights.'

'Oh, so you think the King will come and feed the starving tenants?' Lizzie came back quickly. 'Will he fill Father's granary and send my brothers home from this wicked war, which has divided our family and set father against son? Why, the King, not five years ago, signed his best friend Strafford's death warrant to save his own skin. He made him a scapegoat for his own folly – a good man, the voice of reason.'

Ruth gripped Lizzie's slim seventeen-year-old shoulders and stared at her. Gone was the childish innocence she had sought to preserve. Here stood a determined young woman, talking high politics and at a time like this. She pushed some stray tendrils of rich dark hair into Lizzie's cap. There was no denying she envied the girl her beauty and fresh youthful courage, but then Lizzie had always been different from the other children. A tomboy right from the start, and never afraid to speak her mind. Many a time she had been beaten by Sir Edwin for her wilful ways, although it had hurt him more than Lizzie. Ruth had found him weeping after one such occasion.

'You're wrong, child,' she said quietly. 'And you must not blame your father. He has too many burdens. He did what he thought was best. You must be a dutiful daughter and consider how much sorrow your father has to bear at this time and not add to it by disloyalty to the King he has sacrificed so much for.'

'No, Ruth, it's you who are wrong,' Lizzie retorted. 'The King has brought this on us. He's betrayed us all, even Father who's been so loyal to him. He's taken the food from the tenants' mouths to pamper his French papist Queen, with her fine palaces and pointless wars. Whatever you say, I know if my brothers had been here instead of away at the war, they would've ridden out and fetched a midwife. People've just stopped trying to make things work, they've got used to chaos. Father's as hopeless as all of them.'

'You don't know what you're saying,' Ruth scoffed. The girl was talking treason. She had to be stopped. 'I pray to God Sir Edwin never hears you talk such blasphemy,' she rounded. 'He's got enough to try him, without a daughter who doesn't know her place. Women don't understand such things.'

Lizzie understood enough to know that her brothers, Tom and Philip, were fighting for the King, and she had begun to think it was a hopeless cause. The estate was falling apart. There was plague in the village – it had already taken one of the stewards on whom her father depended. Her younger sisters Mathilda, Adela and Beatrice were always crying. Nobody appeared to be in control of anything. She didn't care what was expected of her. She was going to start imposing some order into their lives.

She shook free of Ruth and walked purposefully back to her mother's rooms. As Lizzie threw open the door, the stifling heat hit her in the face. The shutters were closed and Ruth had stoked up the fire as was the custom after a confinement. The room was dark except for a reedy light from two tallow candles on either side of a high oak bed. The thick tapestry curtains were drawn, leaving a gap through which the old woman leant, standing on her mother's beautifully worked silk footstool, soiling it with her dirty boots.

'What're you doing?' Lizzie demanded, outraged.

The old woman turned. 'Your poor mother needs bleeding. She has the poison in her.' She faltered, seeing the fury on Lizzie's face. 'It was the child. It stayed too long in her belly.'

Lizzie did not hesitate: she dragged the old woman off the stool, and threw back the curtains. Her mother lay seemingly lifeless on the white linen sheets, her nightgown pulled open, her breasts covered in bloated leaches. Incongruously, her head was bound in her best nightcap, a silk turban. Lizzie shuddered as she thought of the effigies in the church with the same serene expression her mother now wore, as if, dressed in her best cap, she was ready for her final journey.

'Take these filthy things off her, you old witch,' Lizzie hissed menacingly between clenched teeth. 'You've done your worst in this house.'

Her mother's left hand moved feebly to her breast, as if trying to cover herself.

Lizzie could see the milk was coming in, blue veins running like rivers to her darkened nipples. There was a time when her mother's nakedness would have shocked her, but not now. She turned to the old woman.

'You cut my mother as if she were no more than a haunch of venison and for no purpose. The child only needed to be coaxed.' Lizzie could not stop herself, her anger mounting. 'Just look at the blood! Why have you left those bed sheets piled on the floor?' she continued coldly and quietly. 'We must have them taken away and soaked in soda and lime. Have you not thought to restore her Ladyship's chamber to some sort of order?'

She pulled the bed curtains back and then moved swiftly to the windows, throwing back the shutters. Late afternoon light flooded the room and a shaft found its way to a wooden crib by the fire where Sir Edwin Jones's fifth daughter whimpered feebly. Lizzie picked up the bundle, its tiny limbs already bound tightly in swaddling bands.

'The baby's hungry. Have you sent for a wet nurse?' she asked, already sure of the answer. The old woman screwed up her face and shook her head in silent reply, indicating the pointlessness of any attempt to save either mother or child.

'If my poor mother can't feed her, are we going to let her die?' Lizzie cried.

'The child has had sips of gruel. Milk's a bad thing. It would poison her,' the old woman answered grimly.

Lizzie noticed her greasy hair falling from her cap and her black-rimmed finger nails, and her stomach turned.

'The child will die. Perhaps it's better so,' Ruth interjected,

13

beginning to tire of the commotion. Life must return to normal as soon as possible, babies were replaceable and the family had enough on its plate as it was.

'How can you say such things?' Lizzie replied angrily. 'The child will live, and maybe my mother will live too. If you want to pray, Ruth, pray for heaven on earth, not when we're dead and buried and being eaten by worms.'

Lizzie pushed aside the two women and leant over her mother. Holding the tiny bundle in one arm, she furiously brushed away the leeches, then covered the angry red blotches with the calico bed sheet. Her mother moaned and briefly opened her eyes.

'Here's your daughter, Mother,' Lizzie said gently. She carefully unwound the bands and released two little hands. Then she placed the baby on her mother's breast. Putting her arm around her mother's burning shoulders, she lifted her up slowly and supported her as the child began to suck. Her mother looked up from the child and smiled feebly.

'Thank you, dearest daughter. We shall call her Emily. We owe our lives to you,' she said weakly.

Through the long hours of his wife's labour Sir Edwin Jones had not slept. Instead, he had recalled the previous eleven births. Two of the babes had died within days and three of the children had been carried away by a fever which took half the tenants' children in a week. Now, like as not, he would lose his only surviving sons in the war. He had not had word of Philip for months, and Tom was somewhere with the King's army in the Midlands, having never fully recovered from the Battle of Naseby the previous June.

News of the relentless momentum of the war obsessed him and kept him awake. He felt so impotent. Mary constantly said he had done his bit for the country, it was now the turn of the younger men, but Sir Edwin had concluded that the King's men lacked sound advisers, as blunder after blunder brought the Royalist army to its knees. The King had hesitated and divided his men, some to the north and some to the south-west instead of marching to Scotland to join the Royalist Montrose. The Parliamentary New Model Army, under General Fairfax and Cromwell, had seized their chance and pounced on the divided Royalist troops, scattering the cavalry and capturing the munitions.

Sir Edwin knew there were still a few Royalist garrisons in the west and local parts of Sussex and Kent, not far from the manor, and a large one at Sandown castle, but he knew in his heart the King would never be able to consolidate the scattered remnants of his demoralized fighting force into a proper army again. It was said he was being slowly beaten back to Oxford whence he had first escaped and set up a small court.

Sir Edwin could not imagine what would happen in the next few months, but he knew that all he had fought for and believed in had come to naught. He prayed his wife would live and that he could at least salvage his domestic life from the ashes of this terrible war.

He watched his eldest daughter taking charge of the sick room, as if seeing her for the first time. Until now he had often feared that girls were nothing but a burden. To make a reasonable marriage they would have to have a portion of the family wealth, a 'jointure'. Since the dissolution of the monasteries, the days of packing them off to a nunnery were long gone, and there was Lizzie trying to save the life of this puny infant girl – another claim on the dwindling funds he had set aside for such purposes.

In the light of these circumstances, it was hardly surprising that he had long ago steeled himself against the trap of really loving any of his children with more than a kind of ambivalent tolerance. The life of a child seemed to him to be so fragile and Sir Edwin was a careful man. He would not run the risk of investing his emotions and hopes in so transient a thing as a child, but his beloved wife of eighteen years, that was a different matter. If he lost her, he would lose the will to live.

His thoughts nagged constantly, excluding any possible joy. Even the prospect of a new life filled him with gloom. There was little left to believe in now. Parliament had destroyed the old order, and had nothing with which to replace it. He could no longer look after the land: so many young men had left to fight for the King that the fields were left untended. His bounteous Kentish apples, which stored the winter like no other,

15

remained unpicked on the trees, and people starved – though mercifully not his own tenants so far, for Mary had wisely suggested he set aside stores for hard times. But these stocks would soon come to an end. He didn't blame the men for leaving. How could they refuse when they were offered four shillings a week – far beyond anything he could pay them? Somehow, though, the Judas money did not find its way to the families, and the tenants couldn't pay the rents. There was little he could do to help. Ironically it was the King's taxes that had all but finished him, the most ruinous of all being the 'ship money', squandered on a useless navy, most of which lay rotting on the sea bed. The last lot of soldiers who'd been billeted at the manor had emptied the store rooms and granaries of all that was not hidden, and he knew the debt would never be paid.

The coal supplies from the north, which used to be brought down by barge from Tyne, had been seized by Parliament. Consequently, there was no fuel for the tanners and glovemakers who took the skins from the manor cattle. His flourishing trading business in London had collapsed.

As if that were not enough, now there was a shortage of wood, as the iron smelters had heedlessly cut down all the forests. Even the quick-growing ash would take eight years to produce firewood. He felt like a man drowning. It was all so unnecessary, a nation hell-bent on in its own destruction.

He stood in the doorway of his wife's chamber, watching for a minute the scurrying maidservants putting all in order. Overseeing it all was the calm figure of his daughter Lizzie. How similar she was to her mother.

She had the same thick dark hair and wide-set violet eyes. She was unusually tall and had a brisk way of moving, somewhat at odds with the excepted carriage of a young woman of breeding.

Lizzie had taken charge of the sick room. She had thrown open the shutters and the bright light of a perfect summer day bathed the room, sweet-smelling herbs were strewn about the floors. As he stood silently watching, she lifted the child from her crib, her graceful neck bent lovingly as she smiled and cooed at her. A faint shaft of hope implanted itself in his heavy heart.

Sir Edwin advanced into the room and took his wife's limp hand.

The old woman had been slyly waiting her chance. She had seen Sir Edwin go to the room, she followed him and before Lizzie could stop him tapped him on the shoulder.

'Sir, I've not yet received my purse, and this has been a difficult birthing and . . .' she hesitated, looking towards Lizzie. 'And but for my lady's interference, I would have saved the child and the mother.'

Lizzie turned on her. 'Leave this room at once. I won't have such talk around here. Lady Mary's well, and my new sister is beautiful. Get out before my father has you thrown out.'

Seeing the look of astonishment, almost relief, on her father's face, Lizzie stood resolutely beside him. She knew she had taken a risk in speaking for her father, something she would never have done before, but it had paid off and she knew there had been a sea change in his perception of her.

The old woman turned furiously to Sir Edwin. Her voice began to rise.

'But some folk speak and do as blasphemers,' she screamed. 'This girl of yours will come to a bad end, my Lord. You listen to me . . . I see it in her eyes . . . the eyes of a hussy . . .'

'Silence, you old witch, I've heard enough from you. How dare you address my daughter in such a manner. Get out before I send for the stewards,' Sir Edwin bellowed.

The old woman angrily set to gathering her instruments and stuffing them into a soiled piece of sacking, which she hung on a hook attached to a leather belt about her waist.

'I always knew you Joneses would come to a bad end,' she screamed as she turned and shuffled from the room.

Sir Edwin gave Lizzie a reassuring pat on the shoulder. It was a gesture which expressed both his appreciation and his respect.

'Dearest Edwin, come closer, I must speak with you.' It was Mary's soft voice. Lizzie moved away from the bed and quietly left the room.

Two

The plague arrived in the village just about the time of Emily's birth and for once Sir Edwin acted quickly. The plague houses and its victims were boarded up, dependent on the parish for food and water. An unusually stifling September gave way to a ferocious winter without the usual gentle introduction of autumn. Times were hard, the cattle developed a mysterious sickness which carried them off within minutes. Some died on their feet, their bodies stiffened and they remained frozen in the sheds like strange statues. People in the village blamed the King. They said it was 'God's anger' at his secret dealings with papists. Water began to freeze in the wells, bitter winds whistled through the shutters of the manor; the ground was hard as iron and the winter root crops could not be dug.

But at least with the arrival of the cold the plague diminished and finally disappeared and the boards were taken from the houses, the survivors emerging pale and undernourished, blinking in a pale early winter sunlight.

Thanks to a diligent system of quarantine the manor escaped the plague, but Mary Jones could not shake off the child-bed fever. For weeks she hovered between life and death and only Lizzie and Ruth's devoted nursing kept her alive. Lizzie had watched the farm hands cooling their animals when fever consumed them and so she had been to the underground ice house and taken last winter's ice from the lake. It was one of Mary's own creations, a pit dug in the ground with walls stuffed with short barley straw and then packed with snow. Lizzie wrapped the ice in clean scented linen and placed it next to her mother's burning body. At last the fevers went, but Mary was seriously weakened and unable to do more than nurse her baby. For Lizzie however there was the consolation of drawing closer to her mother.

'There are things you should know about the manor,' Mary said to Lizzie one morning, aware that events might soon project her daughter into a world for which she was ill prepared. She had sent for some of her papers and accounts which confirmed her fears about the state of the family finances.

'Don't trouble your father with this for he has enough to concern him.' Mary sighed and took Lizzie's hand. 'Things are bad, Lizzie. We may have to forgo some of the servants' wages and we cannot afford to repair the cottages. If I had had the running of things they would not be as they are,' she went on.

'You should not be doing this, Mother,' said Lizzie quietly. 'Father would be furious, you will tire yourself.'

'Lizzie, I must explain something to you,' Mary replied solemnly. 'For all my learning and even though I had the good fortune to study Latin and Greek as you have done . . . Though I know that the great man Galileo tells us that the earth circumnavigates the very sun, after all is said and done I am still just a woman and I am not deemed worthy of an opinion. And I pray, dearest daughter, that knowledge will be of better use to you than it has been to me. If your brothers do not come back from this fearful war it will all fall to you and you must think of these things. You will have to make choices, Lizzie, your loyalties may be divided. Your father and brothers have not found the questions easy.'

'I have already begun to ask myself those questions,' Lizzie replied.

'My dear,' said Mary gravely, 'change is inevitable. Parliament is right to preserve the right of the people to have voice in the running of their own affairs, a right which has been theirs since the signing of Magna Carta over four hundred years ago,'

'And what of the divine right of Kings?' Lizzie asked

'That right has a responsibility perhaps the King has failed to meet,' said Mary gravely. It was a statement not a question. 'Things are changing, Lizzie, but still, you must know, your father will soon be forced to look for a suitable husband for you. Things cannot go on as they are and if anything should happen to your brothers . . .' Mary stopped for a moment. 'Well, as the eldest you would be a nice prize for any man.'

'I will not take just any husband, Mother,' said Lizzie. 'I want to be as happy as you and Father have been.' The matter

19

of a husband was something she had tried not to think about. She would not be plunged into a loveless match, only to die in childbed at the hands of the midwife.

'I did not want to marry your father, Lizzie. I did not love him, though if I were to marry him now it would be for love,' said Mary. 'But I will not support your father in this, Lizzie. I do not approve of daughters being used like cattle in a marriage market. You have done more than a man's work here and you must stand firm until you find the path you know is right. Your decisions will colour all your choices but above all they must be your own.'

That night Lizzie lay awake, listening to her sister's breathing and thought about her mother's enlightened views. She had shared her opinions with her daughter for the first time, and Lizzie realized how her gentle quiet intelligence had influenced her husband, a man who was at best more comfortable with his books. It was of course Mary's guiding hand which had been evident in the running of the estates and the family affairs. But somehow Lizzie knew in her heart that nothing had prepared them for what was to follow.

'I don't remember this kind of cold in November before,' said Lizzie late one bitter afternoon as she and Ruth sewed in the kitchen.

'Oh, I do. Some of our best times have been in the winter,' said Ruth thoughtfully. 'I often think of the times you and master Philip and Tom used to slide on the frozen lake.'

'Oh, yes, and the loveliest bit was coming back to the manor to find the fires all stoked up and having some of Father's warm ale. That all seems a long time ago now,' replied Lizzie.

'Well, it was all those new-fangled grates that Sir Edwin made to burn that dirty old coal,' Ruth clucked disapprovingly. 'It gave off a good heat but I never liked it, too much dirt and work. Give me a wood fire any day. At least we had to go back to wood with the war on,' said Ruth.

'You say that, Ruth, but remember the King requisitioned all the wood for his navy and no one is planting trees any more. People are stealing wood to keep warm. Father turns a blind eye to it, but not far from here a man was put in the stocks for stealing a few twigs.' Lizzie thought angrily of the precious wood which now lay at the bottom of the sea. 'I wonder if the fine Duke of Buckingham ever thinks about the waste? After all, he was in charge of the King's navy when it floundered off the coast of France.' Lizzie queried aloud, knowing Ruth would not offer an opinion on such matters. Lizzie envied Ruth her special brand of pragmatism which helped her through these terrible times so calmly

'Well, never mind about the likes of the Duke of Buckingham, Lizzie,' said Ruth. 'Folk make do, they count the hours until they could get into their beds and draw the curtains about them – which reminds me I must warm our own before the evening draws in,' she said, getting briskly to her feet.

She crossed the room and took down several copper warming pans and began to fill them with embers from the fire.

'I sometimes think the steam encourages the bed bugs, Ruth, even though I boil the sheets in soda as you told me,' said Lizzie, looking at her once fine hands, now red and calloused from her work in the laundry. The two laundry girls had succumbed to a fever in the lungs and were still recovering.

'Well, child, it's time you got outside and took in the sheets and the like and all her Ladyship's nightgowns and his Lordship's shirts. We will soon be out of clean ones. They've been out on those bushes for days, best bring them in and let them dry inside now, since I don't hold much hope of a break in this weather.'

Wrapping herself in a warm blanket, Lizzie struggled outside to the back of the house where the box hedges surrounding the herb garden were used as the drying area. It was beginning to get dark. The family's laundry hung frozen stiff on the bushes. It was like ghostly figures clattering together in the wind. Alone with these frozen figures, Lizzie stood quietly for a while, enjoying the brief moment of solitude, a thing hard to find in a house where each room led into the next and she shared a bed with her sisters.

Taking the arms of the first of her father's shirts, which remained firm with a form of their own, she thought of her brothers and was momentarily overcome with fear and apprehension. Holding the shirt to her body as if it were a reluctant dancing partner, she wondered if she would ever feel

21

the comforting presence of their reassuring maleness and if things could ever be as they were before the war. She could see Ruth through the window slowly lighting the lamps and the flickering flames of the fire in the glass and she could not stop herself from crying, burying her face in the freezing calico of the shirt. As the ice melted it mixed with the tears running down her face.

'Child, what are you doing? Come in before you catch your death.' It was Ruth's voice which interrupted her and, gathering the rest of the wash, Lizzie struggled back into the house.

Adversity brought with it a new kind of pleasure and later that evening the family was sitting in the kitchen with the servants. They huddled around the great hearth, drawing the hearth curtains tight shut, making a cosy tent to pull up the blaze and keep out the draught. They were playing cribbage in the light of the fire and telling each other fairy stories. A strong north wind blew about the manor.

'You can hear the Gabriel hounds hunting the devil outside the house,' said Ruth and told them the story of how the angel Gabriel came with the wind and set his howling dogs in pursuit of evil spirits.

'My turn now with *Beauty and the Beast*,' cried Beatrice.

'More please, miss,' pleaded the kitchen maid when she had finished. The girl had never heard such things in her life and much preferred this new order at the manor.

'I can do better with a real-life *Four and Twenty Blackbirds*,' said Adela firmly. 'Queen Henrietta Maria had her three-foot-nine-inch dwarf jump out of a pie on the King's birthday.'

'What happened to him?' Beatrice asked. 'Did the King eat him?'

The kitchen maid clapped her hands with glee at the idea of the King's supper.

'No, silly,' replied Mathilda haughtily. 'She took him to France to amuse her brother the French King in his wicked court, where ladies dance with their bosoms showing and they eat frogs.'

Ruth muttered disapprovingly in the flickering light of the fire, but everyone knew she relished the tales as much as anyone, while little Beatrice sat on her knee, cosily feigning terror at the stories.

'Now that's enough of all this,' Lizzie said eventually. 'Time to set the table and her Ladyship's tray.'

'What's for supper?' asked Beatrice.

'All you think about is food,' said Mathilda.

'Well, thanks to your sister Lizzie's management and your mother's work last summer,' Ruth answered, 'we won't go hungry yet. We've plenty of root vegetables, so we have a thick broth with herbs and a fine side of bacon.'

'You are right, Ruth,' Lizzie responded, pleased by the unexpected compliment. 'We must be grateful. It's more than the people in the village have. They didn't have time to preserve things in the summer and most of them have lost their one and only pig to the thieving soldiers.'

Ruth looked approvingly at Lizzie and heaved an inward sigh of relief at how naturally the girl had taken up her mother's skills during her illness. Lizzie had taken over the management of the larders and store cupboards, the contents of which seemed in abundance compared to the empty shelves in the cottages. Mary Jones's good housekeeping had seen to it that there were supplies of bottled fruits and preserves, and endive and chicory forced in boxes of compost in the cellars. Root vegetables dug in the summer remained fresh, buried in compost in the cool of the cellar for many months, and sides of salt meat hung from hooks in the larder. She was an expert in drying herbs and berries and her cheeses were renowned in the area.

'We must say a prayer for there are many families who are starving,' said Ruth gravely.

'So where has all the food gone?' asked Adela, starting to cry. 'I don't want to eat while they are starving,' she wailed. 'Is it our fault?'

'No, darling,' said Lizzie, putting her arms round Adela. 'Soldiers were billeted on them. First Colonel Fairfax's unruly mob, and just as they had managed to scrape a reasonable harvest with every able-bodied woman and child working until after dark . . . the King's men . . . the worst of all, with empty promises of repayment when the war was over. And so they resigned themselves. But tomorrow we will take a

23

cart and load it up with bread and take it to the village.'

'Oh, you mean that horrible black stuff you make all the time,' said Beatrice, wrinkling her nose. 'I thought it was for the pigs.'

'A fine thing if you can afford to be fussy about your bread,' said Ruth crossly. 'There may come a time when you will be as grateful as they are for Miss Lizzie's coarse bread.'

Lizzie caught Ruth's eye and a shiver of fear went down her back, as something told her that things were going to get harder for all of them and there might come a time when she would have to put her family before the villagers.

Three

Sir Edwin looked about him with a certain trepidation. He had been absent for some days on what Ruth called 'the King's business' and had had no news of his wife. Sam the steward had taken his greatcoat but none of the family seemed to have heard his arrival.

Since his wife's confinement and in view of the family's straightened circumstances the family had abandoned the great hall. It was impossible to make any impact on the bitter cold. The vaulted ceilings siphoned any warmth from the hearth, however much it blazed, and draughts whistled and snaked about the stone floor. Even the mice had taken to their nests behind the oak panelling and not a living thing moved in the still and petrified air.

It was hard to believe that this empty unloved space had once been the scene of vigorous gatherings, when the rafters had echoed to the sound of lutes and viols and the voices of the children singing the madrigals of John Dowland and reciting the words of Andrew Marvell. Mary had taught her daughters well in the art of entertainment, as befitted young girls of their station.

24

But it was not the grave state of their mother's health and the unprecedented winter weather alone which contributed to the air of desperate gloom which had combined to envelop the house. Things had gone badly for the King – ever since he had fled his London palace at Whitehall and set up Court in Oxford, a city always loyal to the Crown. Stories were rife. Simmering resentment toward the Royalist cause was beginning to emerge in unexpected quarters. One favourite rumour in the neighbourhood was that the King and Queen left the Palace at Whitehall in such a hurry that they forgot their two youngest children Henry and Elizabeth, who had been the prisoners of Parliament ever since

There was news of a Parliamentary army in the area and many local families had switched allegiance in order to survive. Nonetheless Parliamentary forces had plundered local farmers; food and horses had been sequestered from Royalist houses; husbands and sons had fled for their lives, or were fighting for the King. Royalist women had to fend for themselves, often without the support of their stewards who had also joined up or switched allegiance. Sir Edwin pondered these things in his mind, and wished that his sons were there to support him in this house full of vulnerable women.

When she saw her father, Lizzie let out a cry of joy. For once there was good news and it had already been decided that she should be the one to give it.

'Father,' she cried excitedly, 'you must go at once to Mother. She is much better. The fever is gone and although she is still weak as a kitten and must remain in her chamber, she is not going to the angels.'

'If my Lady is spared, Sir Edwin,' Ruth broke in, 'you have your daughter to thank. She has the healing gift. Most folks would have let her Ladyship go to her maker, as she herself was set on doing. But Miss Lizzie would have none of it. Why, she even kept the babe nursing and found milk for her Ladyship to sip from the silver pap cup used for infants. Lord knows where she gets the cow's milk from, when there's plenty in the village a-dying for want of it.'

Sir Edwin put an arm about his Lizzie's shoulders.

'Come sit with us, Father,' Lizzie said. 'It's been our secret.

We wanted it to be a surprise, and besides, at first, I couldn't believe it.'

'So tell me, daughter, when did you see such an improvement?'

'When the fever was high,' said Lizzie breathlessly, 'I took to bathing her in cold water and I cut chunks of ice from the ice and wrapped them and placed them on her limbs, especially the back of her neck where she felt such pain. I never gave up because I knew she wanted to come back to us.'

'Come, Lizzie,' said Sir Edwin warmly. 'You deserve all our thanks. And I should rightly receive all your rebukes for I have not been myself. While your mother has been ill,' he gulped, overcome with emotions he had not allowed himself to face, 'and with your brothers away, I don't know what we would've done without . . . our Lizzie.'

In unison the children rose from the table. Sir Edwin gathered their heads to the shabby velvet of his coat, but as for his eldest daughter he had something to say. He took her roughened hand and with a deep bow lightly touched it with his lips.

'You're a fine young woman,' he went on proudly. 'My very dear daughter, you've restored to me that which is most precious and for that I can find no words sufficient to thank you. Let's talk for a moment. Pour me some of that ale, my dear, and let's warm it with the fire iron for it's a cold night.'

After a moment, however, Sir Edwin hesitated and put his sleeve to his brow in a gesture of despair. 'Dear Father,' said Lizzie quietly. 'I know what you're thinking. It's about Tom and Philip.'

'Yes, it's hard,' Sir Edwin replied hesitantly. 'Hard for us all. Your little sisters too . . . they're too young to understand this horror we've brought on ourselves.'

They drew away from the fire and sat on a bench, their feet on two stools normally used by the kitchen girl, who was too short to reach the top shelves in the pantry. Sir Edwin cupped his warm ale in his hand, drank and then handed it to his daughter.

'Father,' Lizzie said seriously. 'It is wrong to try to hide

26

things from the girls. It's worse if they don't understand what's going on. Tell me about Tom and Philip, for you must have had word.'

'You're right. I have,' said Sir Edwin cautiously. 'You had best tell the girls some of the truth . . . I've had word of Tom . . . things aren't going well, I fear, but it will quieten down, for when winter's set in men can't fight. The land is frozen. The armies will regroup. Men will recover from their wounds and some, God rest them, will die. But Tom is well. I give you my word on that.'

'And Philip?' Lizzie asked, trying to conceal the anxiety in her voice.

'I can't say,' Sir Edwin responded carefully. 'I've not heard . . . He may be in France – there's a great deal of diplomacy: the Queen needs support, her relatives have a role to play. No, there's no more I can say.'

Sir Edwin looked at her fixedly. She knew there was more, but he wasn't to be pressed. She sensed that her brother was somewhere on a very big stage far away from the manor. 'And now I must go to your mother and see my latest child. You know, Lizzie,' he said, taking Lizzie's hand, 'daughters are not such a bad thing. In fact they are a blessing, as your mother has always said.'

Chapter Four

As Mary slowly regained her strength, she realized how much her elder daughter had taken upon her shoulders and was amazed at her grasp of the running of the large household. Mary thought of the manor a few years before, when there had been more servants than family. Scullions slept under the sinks, two good spit boys managed the bellows and kept the meat the right distance from the fire. Now the meat was cooked by the scullery maid who found it hard to get it

27

cooked on the inside without burning the outside. The previous week one of the kitchen maids had been badly burned but Sam had saved her by dowsing her with water from the bucket kept by the fireside. Mary remembered that half a dozen or so had died that way in her parents' day without much comment. She saw that there was perhaps a certain inevitable justice in the way things had turned out.

One afternoon in mid December, when an unusual burst of fine weather melted some of the ice from the windows and took the chill off the air, the family arranged a surprise for Mary. Supervised by Lizzie and an anxious Ruth, fussing and muttering as she wrapped the invalid in her winter fur-trimmed cloak, the children took her to the great hall. The fires had been burning for the last two days and there was a sweet smell of apple-wood. Lizzie had arranged for some of the old trees to be felled and boughs of it had been drying, stacked up in the corner of the stables. Beatrice was dressed as an angel in white and silver in a *tableau vivant* in the gallery, with candles behind her head as she leaned over a crib to depict the birth of Christ.

Mary gasped with pleasure. The hall was decorated throughout with winter greenery and the long oak table was set for a meal. There were thick wooden platters spread with figs, sweetmeats and sugared almonds. Lizzie had laid out the best damask cloth, a present to her parents on their wedding day: a full forty feet long. The family coat of arms could be seen in the weave with her parents' names repeated amongst garlands of flowers. Lizzie had sewn swoops of ivy and holly on to the cloth, mixed with hellebores which she had brought on under piles of straw in the kitchen garden. Candles had been set in profusion, awaiting a taper to plunge the room into light when darkness fell.

As her mother collapsed happily on to a wooden high-backed bench by the hearth, Lizzie went to her and knelt at her feet, to remove any thoughts her mother might have that she was no longer the mistress of her house and deserving of respect from her eldest daughter.

'You've been so ill, Mother,' said Lizzie, her voice cracking with emotion as she saw her mother's tears of happiness. 'You'd forgotten, it will soon be Christmas, and today, although the sun is shining, it is the shortest day, and we're going to celebrate.'

'My dearest daughter,' cried Mary. 'It is a wonder! I had begun to think we would never use this room again.'

'But wait, Mother, this is not all,' Lizzie interrupted. 'We've another surprise for you, later, when we've all put on our best gowns. Father's coming back with more sweetmeats, figs, and chocolate from London, and ribbons for us all, just like it used to be. All the servants are coming and we're going to dance and sing and the girls have prepared a poem for you. Best of all I've found some of Father's favourite tobacco smuggled in from a traveller who supplies the King himself!'

'Oh, my dear,' said Mary with tears in her eyes. 'It'll be quite like old times with the smell of your Father's pipe and the sounds of music. If only . . .' Mary stopped, seeing a shadow pass over her daughter's radiant face.

Later that afternoon Lizzie took her mother's hand and led her to one of the tall windows that looked down the twisting drive, silver with evening frost.

'Look at those leafless skeletal trees pointing towards the house in the cold north wind from the sea,' said her mother thoughtfully. 'They look like so many figures signing the way to the traveller.'

Then, just as she spoke, she saw in the distance the lodge keepers running, heavily clothed against the cold, and with a sense of urgency pull open the heavy iron gates. She was expecting the red and blue plumes of Edwin's hat, but she saw not one, but three horsemen. Slowly, as the children could no longer keep their closely guarded secret and shrieked with joy, she cried out, 'My Tom, my Philip,' in a voice which even roused the kitchen maid who had been drowsily watching over the suckling pigs on the spit, and sent everyone hurrying to the galleried entrance to line up as they had been carefully rehearsed by Lizzie.

Lizzie and Tom finally talked together the day after Christmas. They sat in a cosy panelled room leading off the gallery. It had been closed up after their grandmother had died. She had used it for sewing and embroidery. In it she had created most of the magnificent work which had adorned both the manor and the church, although the exquisite altar cloths and robes were now hidden for fear of the Puritan purge. Since the news of her brothers' return, Lizzie had set the housemaids to polishing and scrubbing, and now the room shone and sparkled.

Sam, the head steward, had also restored the panelling, and it was in the course of this work that Lizzie had made a discovery. She had been standing on a chair, holding up a tapestry to sample its suitability for the room, when she had slipped. Reaching out a hand to save herself, she'd fallen against a carved eagle head in the ornate cornice. The panelling had started to shift away from her and without its support she'd fallen to the floor. As she'd picked herself up, she'd seen what appeared to be a door. She'd pushed and as it opened, there came a strong musty smell. It had been late in the afternoon, and the light was poor, but she could make out a small room with what appeared to be an old bed and a table. Before she could inspect it further, she had heard voices. Some instinct had made her close the door quickly and conceal her discovery.

But now she was alone at last with Tom. 'I want to show you something,' she said excitedly.

'This was obviously a hiding place used by the family before they converted to the Protestant faith,' exclaimed Tom, aghast, when he saw the room. 'Apparently we hid many a Catholic from the wrath of King Henry's fearful persecution of families still loyal to Rome,' he continued.

Lizzie shuddered as she saw a similarity in the folly of Kings and the crimes they committed for their own ends. She asked herself if much had changed. Blood was still spilled in the name of the King's peccadilloes, for King Henry's desire to cast away his barren Catholic wife, and for King Charles. Surely the voice of Rome sought its redress through the advice of Charles's Catholic Queen, who, it was said, would bring back papery to the Royal family and its heirs.

'Tell no one of this,' said Tom urgently. 'It will only serve its purpose if it remains the secret it is meant to be. Let us close it up and speak of it no more.'

With that Tom took a seat by the fire and Lizzie sat on a footstool at his feet, her head resting against his knee, just like old times. They talked of trivialities for a while and then

Tom got up and sat facing her. He loved his sister as he loved no other woman. He had had no time in his short life for courting and neither was it the custom for young men of property to marry too soon – there were economic reasons for that. His father did not wish to move out of the manor with his family in favour of a new bride, and besides there were not many local girls with the necessary means to make the proposition attractive. The manor was short of funds and a new bride must bring with her a considerable dowry. Tom was the family's greatest asset and would be saved for a rich prize, war permitting.

'So how's my little sister?' he asked eventually.

Lizzie thought carefully before she answered. She didn't want to add to her brother's burdens.

'It's as if I've missed out on a bit of growing up, Tom,' she said. 'Before Mother got ill, I was a child and treated like one. Now, suddenly, I feel like a woman having to be a man. It's a difficult world for women, Tom. Mother was so clever. She let Father think he ran everything, but she was always there in the background. I've tried to take her place, but it's only when someone doesn't do their job that you know how much they did and . . .' She faltered.

Tom could see she looked drawn and tired: it made him feel angry with the world in general. After all he was the eldest son: he should be here at the manor fulfilling his responsibilities. He had been shocked at the hardship he'd found on his return. Lizzie had done well in helping the family to adjust to the deprivations which had begun to topple the established order. Although the house had not suffered as he had feared, he saw the darns in his sisters' gowns, the depleted shelves in the still rooms, and felt the atmosphere of apprehension. As he had ridden round the estate that very morning when the sun had shone crisply on a fresh fall of snow, the poverty and hardship in the tenants' homes was evident everywhere. The rents were not paid and the farm steward pointed out the empty chicken coops and ghostly barns and the sullen faces behind the blackthorn slats of the cottage windows.

'I know it's difficult for you to keep faith,' Tom said encouragingly. 'But you must have confidence in the King. We will regroup and, with the help of the Scots, we'll win the war.

The peasants are ignorant, and when you think how we have cared for them, they're disloyal.'

Lizzie felt a stirring of anger, something she had wished to keep out of their conversation, but before she could stop herself she rounded on her brother.

'Can you blame them, Tom?' she asked. 'The little food they have they've hidden because they know the troops will come back. The Levellers are the worst. They claim to be Parliament's men, but they're a band of madmen. They want everyone to be equal. They burn and murder anything that looks like privilege, without thought for who'll look after the poor people, when nobody's left to care for the estates.'

'Come, Lizzie, it's not as bad as that,' Tom replied quickly. 'Father's constantly helping people way beyond the call of duty in my view.'

'Of course he is, and it *is* his duty,' Lizzie answered promptly. 'But they don't know how Father's turned a blind eye to the poachers who steal our deer. When the rangers catch them and bring them to the bench, Father dismisses them with a pint of ale all round. But now all that trust's been abused and muddled.'

'I must say I've seen some sullen faces about,' Tom agreed.

'They think you've come back to collect the rents and throw them out,' Lizzie answered sharply. 'They know Father wouldn't do so, but you come back as the King's man, and they've come to distrust their King. They'll go whichever way the wind blows, Tom. I'd do the same if I were in their shoes.'

There was a pause while Tom thought. His face hardened as he answered.

'The King is God's Regent on earth: we mustn't forget that. Have you thought about republicanism? What it could mean? The end of centuries of tradition? I can and I must remain loyal. That's all I wish to say. You mustn't question me further.'

Lizzie saw a frightening coldness in her brother's eyes. Pondering it, she realized that he had been forced to do terrible things in the name of the cause. He had aged a thousand years. Gone was the carefree young boy; before her stood a man at odds with his deepest conviction that life was sacred. With so much blood on his sword now – when before the war he'd done no more than nick the shoulder of his fencing master – he could not afford to let his conscience undermine his mission. If he did, he would hate himself. Then she thought of Philip, just sixteen. Was he a better man for his brutal initiation into the world of men? She doubted it: she had seen him going to the stables with Mathilda and Adela, talking happily about Lizzie's mare Snowdrop, who was in foal. Had he thought of the appalling injuries inflicted on the horses taken for battle? Philip loved animals. How he must have had to harden his heart as he heard their screams . . .

'I'm torn, sister,' Tom said presently in a troubled voice. 'You know when the weather improves, the troops will be active, and Philip and I must go and join our men. Also, I must warn you, Father's determined to fight again.'

Lizzie cut him short with a gasp of horror.

'You can't mean it, Tom. We're a household of women. I'd be the only one with any authority. How would we fare if the Parliamentary troops came here? Everyone knows we're a Royalist household! You know I couldn't depend on the men on the estate to defend us. Why, they've already stopped locking the gates at night, and the perimeter walls are falling down. We'd be powerless.'

'The sad truth is,' said Tom, 'you might have as much to fear from our own troops. Of course I agree it would be better if Father was here. I'm afraid the days of chivalry are gone. And that's what we're fighting for: trying to preserve something we all believe in.'

As she sat quietly listening to Tom, Lizzie began to feel even more confused and frightened. She loved Tom more than any other human being on earth. Sometimes when he'd been away fighting, her fears that she might lose him had been unbearable.

'There's no greater honour than to lay down your life for your King and your country,' Tom replied evenly. 'I would expect no less from one of our family. You must give your fears and prayers to God. It is in his hands.'

It occurred to Lizzie that this blind faith was in fact apathy. Why hadn't anyone spoken out? For all these years, while events festered and their lives continued in the same order, had they not heard the voices of change?

The sullen faces on the estate were a legacy of that unwillingness to welcome the inevitable. She thought of Queen Elizabeth who had made England great. She had looked beyond the island shores to the world outside, brought vigour and confidence to her people with clever diplomacy rather than with the spilling of blood. Since her death, subsequent Kings had weakened themselves in a moribund complacency. It was not enough to believe in rights, what about responsibilities?

Lizzie rose abruptly and walked to the casement window. Her mother's garden lay dormant, waiting for the spring to tease the first green shoots of the tulips, brought to her from Holland in the new trade routes now lost in the chaos of war. Then there were the many trees and shrubs her mother had acquired when her parents travelled to similarly wealthy relatives. She never returned from a visit without her plant box full of cuttings preserved in damp felt. Lizzie briefly recalled the smell of the roses imported from France as she nervously fingered some of their dried petals set in a Chinese porcelain bowl on the table by the window. It was warm in the room and in an hour or so Sam would peal the bell in the hall to call the family for their evening meal.

'At least there are some aspects of their lives which remain intact in a way that the families in the village could never even dream of,' she said flatly. She was filled with doubt not only about the perceived wisdom of her parents and their like, but also about the allegiances which were expected of her, as if she had no right to question the preconceptions which had given birth to the upheavals which surrounded them all.

'D'you know what it's like for the people on the estate, Tom?' she asked. 'They don't have glass in their windows. They huddle in front of meagre fires, and hang oiled rags over the window or just twigs even, to keep the bitter cold from their homes. Their children have no boots, and they've no meat. They live off roots and unleavened bread. The Church has preached a morbid acceptance of their lot. They're put in the stocks if they miss a Sunday service when they have to listen to the clergyman indoctrinating them with talk of hellfire and damnation. It can't go on, Tom. No wonder they want something new. I have to speak out, I am entitled to my opinion,' said Lizzie, suddenly pulling off her cap dramatically as she was prone to do when she became agitated. Her dark hair, almost blue-black in the light from the snow-covered landscape filtering through the smoky glass of the window, sprang out in rippling waves.

Tom had not realized quite what a beauty his sister was. There was a moment when he felt a pang of apprehension at the thought of such a prize alone at the manor without protection. But he quickly dismissed it.

'I don't care if you're angry or not,' she blurted. 'I wouldn't go to the stake for the King. I think the country needs a different form of rule. The King won't compromise and he has blood on his hands.' She could not disguise the challenge in her voice.

She looked Tom fiercely in the eyes and then she said the words she had resolved never to utter.

'I don't believe in the Cavalier cause any more. The people have rights, especially as the old order hasn't accepted that rights bring responsibilities with them. They shouldn't send the people down the path of needless bloodshed. That's what Parliament's for, to rule with the mind and not with the sword.'

Tom rose slowly. He had already warned his sister but she had not listened. His voice shook as he answered her in measured words over which there could be no misunderstanding.

'I shall forget what you've just said, sister,' he said icily. 'I hope, for your sake, these walls do not have ears. I can't talk to you again about this. You don't understand the world of politics. I shall excuse you now, madam. With your permission I shall withdraw and leave you to contemplate the gravity of your misguided thoughts.'

With a bow Tom left the room. The air was still and cold and so was Lizzie's heart. She had never felt more alone.

Lizzie sat for some time alone in the room, hardly daring to acknowledge the terror she felt. She had lost the best friend she had ever had and all because she spoke her mind, said what she truly believed. She wondered if Ruth was right, if her outspokenness was inappropriate for a woman and would be her undoing.

She did not hear the door open as Philip came quietly into

35

the room. Philip was not as tall as Tom and did not have his conventional handsome face. His characterful face and distinctive features perfectly complimented his cheerful nature which radiated consistency and dependency. Often, when Tom had excelled, Philip simply did well, he had been modestly content to succeed quietly and be there to pick up the pieces when, as often happened, Tom overreached himself.

Philip knew at once that the interview between Tom and Lizzie had ended unhappily. Tom had passed him in the hall looking cross and piqued, muttering under his breath something to the effect that women should know their place.

'What on earth is the matter, Lizzie?' Philip asked, finding her clearly distressed.

'I've quarrelled with Tom,' she answered, wiping away her tears.

Despite the fact that Lizzie idolized her elder brother and Philip had often felt left out, he was concerned by his sister's obvious unhappiness. He had begun to realize how much strain had landed on her young shoulders and he was genuinely worried about her. That Tom could have added to that stress was in his view predictable, but that is not what he would say to Lizzie.

'I cannot imagine you two disagreeing, what was it about?' he asked.

'It was about the war. I find Tom very changed. He used to be so open minded but it was as if he couldn't bring himself to reason things out, consider an alternative to all this mindless violence.'

'Lizzie, my dear sister,' said Philip gently, 'you must surely understand that Tom left this house at the beginning of the war as one person and came back as another. He is a soldier now, he must obey without question, that is how it is. If you undermined his convictions, his dedication to a cause, he would be angry. He cannot afford the luxury of asking "Why".'

Lizzie looked up at him from her chair, taking the handkerchief he offered her to wipe her eyes, and thought Philip too had changed. He had left the house a boy and come back a man.

Philip looked at his sister and felt an overwhelming love for her, a desire to protect her. She sat looking so injured, he could see that she feared that nothing would be the same between her and Tom again.

'It's difficult to imagine what men have been through, Lizzie,' he said at last. 'War brutalizes them, things are not as they were . . . but . . .' He hesitated before putting his arms about his sister. He had never done so before.

To his surprise, she did not resist his offer of comfort and allowed her head to fall on his shoulder. He felt her whole body rack with sobs and was sure it was the first time she had given in to her emotions since her brother's return.

'Never mind, Lizzie, you have me,' said Philip.

The next day her brothers left the manor on fresh horses. With a flourish of his feathered hat, Tom waved as they set off down the drive. He never looked at his sister. She ran, as she had always done, to the topmost window of the clock tower where Sir Edwin had installed his revolutionary water clock, to get a last sighting as the horses rounded a curve in the road outside the gates. But Tom didn't turn, as he had always done, on each occasion of their parting. Lizzie fell to the cold stone floor and cried for the friend she had lost and the final act of her childhood. Later she found a long and comforting letter from Philip left under her pillow.

Five

One bright morning in March when the cold winds of February had been replaced by an unusually sunny period, Sir Edwin felt his spirits rising. Although she was still confined to her chamber, his wife was almost restored to her old self and under Lizzie's supervision the house was running smoothly. Added to which the coming of spring brought hope and he had a feeling the tide of events might turn in the King's favour.

But his optimism was soon dashed with the arrival of some unwelcome information.

Sir Edwin received the news in his study, when a rider came with the papers concealed in his tobacco delivery. 'The King has been taken prisoner.' The words filled Sir Edwin with horror and as he soon discovered the news was already fluttering from town to hamlet like Chinese whispers. The King had fled north with the fall of Oxford, and thence to Scotland where he had mistakenly thought the Scots would protect him. Sir Edwin thought this sounded reasonable. After all Charles's father, James, was created King of Scotland before he was ever King of England. But at the back of his mind Sir Edwin thought Charles had 'sold his principals for his life' to strike a bargain with the Scottish Presbyterians who, Sir Edwin thought, were no better than the 'tall-hatted Puritans'. But then, as Sir Edwin conceded, many rumours circulated against the King. Some said he was not the legitimate grandson of Mary Queens of Scots and that his father James was a bastard by her paramour Rizzio, whom she brought with her from France. Along with the popular opinion at the time, Sir Edwin believed that although of noble blood, Rizzio was still a rogue and a Papist.

Sir Edwin remembered with a shudder how they had settled the matter of the Queen's lover – the Scottish nobles had murdered him in front of her, while King Charles's father, James, was still in her belly. His blood had spilled over her as she pleaded for his life. Sir Edwin thought the murderous history of the Scots did not bode well for the King's safety and recalled how these, what he referred to as a barbaric people, had even managed to taint the judgement of their Queen and driven her to sanction the murder of her own husband. Perhaps, he thought, the King's lack of judgement was explained by his dubious ancestry. He asked himself for the first time: was this man fit to rule?

Sir Edwin forbade the seditious pamphlets that recounted these and other stories, but the feeling was about: the King's reputation had become contaminated by rumours. Sir Edwin had one of the kitchen boys beaten for repeating the stories and claiming that 'if the King lay down with dogs of Covenanters he would get up with fleas', and that 'the Scots had sold the King to Parliament for forty thousand pounds to equip their army'.

Sir Edwin put these doubts from his mind and wrestled with his conscience. He must take action, and for one last time give the King the benefit of the doubt.

Later that evening Sir Edwin summoned the household to the great hall for the usual family prayers. The stewards stood respectfully holding their caps and the maids donned clean aprons. They stood silent and apprehensive for he had warned them that he had something serious to tell them.

His announcement shocked them all. He would be leaving to rejoin the Cavaliers. They would now be answerable to the Lady Elizabeth Anne until his wife Lady Mary was completely recovered.

This was a decision which had come to Sir Edwin slowly and now he knew that if he were to leave his family he must establish amongst his retainers a blind loyalty to the cause to which he now must rally even though, God forgive him, his own heart was riven with doubt. He would fight not just for this pale weak King but for the principle of the monarchy. The alternative was unthinkable.

'If any one of you will not speak out for the King,' he told them, 'you must leave the manor now, and you will be given a small sum in recognition of your past service.'

There was an immediate consensus and not a voice spoke out. Sir Edwin continued: 'Those of you who feel you are in my family's service as bondsmen are to be absolved from that obligation forthwith. I will have no man or woman here save from the dictates of his own conscience and loyalty to his King and country.'

There was a murmur of approval. Sam stepped forward and the room fell silent again. Nervously feeling the rim of his cap, he bowed to his master and asked permission to speak.

'I speak for us all, my Lord. We are loyal to the Crown and my Lord may ride to battle knowing we will serve your Lordship's family and defend the honour of the King and pray God he will soon be delivered back into our hands.' At which Sam turned to the room and, throwing his cap in the air, led the cry of 'God save the King.'

*   *   *

Lizzie tried her best to reassure her sisters as they lay in bed that night. She dreaded the dark, as she knew she would not sleep. Candles were a luxury now, so before the flame of the bedside candle was extinguished, she pulled back the heavy velvet curtains to let in the moonlight, now so bright she could read by it. There were two large four-posters in the room. Lizzie shared one with Mathilda, and Adela and Beatrice shared the other, although Beatrice had a habit of ending up in Ruth's bed. Tonight they all lay together. The gravity of their father's announcement had affected them greatly. So far the events of the outside world had had no more than a marginal affect on their lives. Lessons had gone on as usual, but the old tutor had relaxed some of his draconian regime and now that they ate with everyone else in the parlour off the kitchens they had made friends with the servants. In short, life was cosier and in some ways better. They did not have to wear caps and gloves and layers of velvet overskirts with long sleeves and tight embroidered bodices, stiff and board-like, so restricting that sometimes they felt they couldn't breathe. Instead, they wore simple grey dresses with white aprons and a delicate white cap which tied under the chin, a great improvement on the elaborate wimple which rubbed on their cheeks and restricted their hearing. Now they rushed about the house like kittens, instead of gliding like miniature warships. The most marked improvement was better food.

'Do you always eat like this?' Mathilda had asked Ruth after the first week, tucking into roast peahen and fig pudding. Ruth had long suspected that the nursery food had been much depleted by the time it got to the children in the north wing of the house. While the children remained pale and thin, the nursery maids and kitchen boys were sturdy by comparison. Rickets was not nearly so prevalent in the lower orders. Ruth remembered her own diet as a child in the village, where vegetables and coarse gruel kept them strong.

'Lizzie, if Father's going away, who will look after us?' Mathilda asked.

'Why, Lizzie, of course,' Adela replied. 'You are so foolish. You heard what Father said.'

'Lizzie, you won't make us wear our wimples again and

stop us playing in the gardens, will you?' Mathilda asked anxiously. 'Mother says we'll never find husbands if we have dark skin like the village girls, and that high-born ladies must be covered from the light. I hate it in the dark schoolroom. Why is it that the sun never comes in our windows?'

'You know the windows face north,' said Lizzie. 'That's because the plague comes from the south over the sea.'

'If Father and Philip and Tom are fighting Colonel Fairfax's army,' Adela asked, holding Beatrice tight under the covers, 'who's going to stop the wicked Spaniards coming over the sea and bringing the plague?'

As Lizzie lay with her sisters, listening to their childish fears, the awesome responsibility that had fallen upon her made her feel sick with apprehension. Eventually the girls fell asleep and Lizzie alone heard the clock strike through the night. She knew her father would be leaving at first light. She would hear the stable lads bringing the horses round to the front of the house. They had said their farewells. Sir Edwin's lips had been grimly set in an effort to keep the parting as unemotional as possible.

Lizzie was unable to sleep that night. Sick with apprehension, she heard the clock strike four. She thought she heard the faint sound of horses shuffling in the drive below. Her heart thudding, she slid out of bed and crept quietly across the room to the window and peered round the curtains.

The moon had sunk low in the sky, the yew hedges of her mother's formal garden cast long and sinister shadows across the lawns. Two man-sized urns marked the entrance to the rose garden and her eyes went to them. She saw several shadows, then heard distinctly a horse coughing followed by a stifled oath.

She leaned forward over the sill. The moon caught something silver which moved. With an involuntary gasp she saw helmets, perhaps twenty or more. The Parliamentary army had come to the manor, stealthily, and at night. Lizzie knew before the thought became articulate, that could only mean one thing: they had come for her father.

She didn't stop to put on slippers, or cover her nightdress. She ran like the wind down the gallery to her father's room.

41

He was asleep, his clothes for the next day hanging on a clothes stand, crumpled boots on the floor, sword and musket on the table beside the bed. Without a sound she touched his shoulder. He woke with a start, sitting upright and automatically reaching for his sword. She put her hand to his lips before he could speak.

'Father, don't argue,' Lizzie whispered urgently. 'The Roundheads are here. You don't have a minute to lose. Come with me at once. Gather your clothes. Trust me. I know where you can hide. Come.'

Still dulled by sleep, her father gathered his clothes and equipment and followed her quickly along the gallery.

As they approached the parlour door, there was a great banging on the main door, and cries of 'Open up in the name of Parliament.' Lizzie heard the steward calling, 'Wait on. How do we know you're not common ruffians, come to murder us all in our beds?'

'Quick, come inside,' Lizzie whispered, pushing her father into the room. 'Father, I can't reach. Do you see the scroll, there, on top of the panelling by the hearth?' she whispered, her heart beating so fast she thought her chest would burst. 'Push it hard and a panel will open.'

Sir Edwin reacted at once and the door opened and again there was the musty smell of undisturbed air.

'Why, daughter, you're a miracle,' Sir Edwin said in amazement. 'How did I not know of this and in my own home? It must be the priest hole we could never find.'

'Say nothing, Father.' Lizzie was apprehensive. 'We've no time. There's a candle on the table and a taper. The coverlet is clean. I've prepared it in readiness, for I suspected it would be needed before long . . . When I tap three times on the panel, you'll know they have gone.'

'Tell them I have gone to London to see the moneylenders,' Sir Edwin said, catching her arm. 'That the estate's in debt. Now, *that* they will believe.' He clasped her hand. 'I know you've been hiding the stores, Lizzie. I thank God for you – a daughter with a man's courage. Give nothing away. Say you're faithful to neither King nor Parliament, just to God.'

Lizzie didn't have time to answer. Shutting the door, she

moved swiftly back to her bedroom where her sisters were still asleep, oblivious of the noise outside. She slipped into the bed beside Mathilda. She would pretend to be asleep. But within what seemed like seconds, the door opened and Ruth burst in. She began to shake her violently.

'May God have mercy on us. Roundhead soldiers are here. His Lordship's nowhere to be found. His sword's gone,' Ruth cried, wringing her hands. 'If Sam doesn't let them in, they'll break down the door. What shall we do?'

A long plait of hair hung from the back of Ruth's nightcap. She had covered her nightdress with her large grey outdoor cape, and in her hand she held one of the implements from the bedroom fireplace. She looked formidable.

The girls had awoken and were silent and apprehensive. They knew this was no time for tears. 'Father's safe,' Lizzie reassured them all. 'Listen carefully, Ruth,' she went on. 'Tell Sam to unlock the door. Here, take my Bible with you and put down the fire tongs. We shall be calm, my father left last evening to go to London to raise a loan for the estate . . . We don't know when he'll be back.'

Ruth nodded, as Lizzie continued.

'You may tell the gentlemen that we're a household of defenceless women, and that the Lady Elizabeth will attend them shortly, when she's had time to dress, as any God-fearing woman would wish to do in the presence of such ruffians.'

Lizzie's command was absolute. Repeating the words, as if to learn them by rote, Ruth busied from the room. There was the sound of breaking glass and the rough male voices became louder.

Lizzie put on her dark-red velvet Sunday gown and a wimple set on a high mantilla embroidered with pearls. The dress hung loosely as she had lost weight since she had given up the life of an aristocratic lady of leisure. She looked at herself briefly in the looking-glass and took a deep breath. Clasping her grandmother's crucifix, which hung on a thick gold chain to just above her waist, and fastening the household keys which jangled from a silk ribbon to just below where her apron would have been, she walked slowly along the gallery.

Below her, between the banisters, she could see the entrance

43

hall had become a seething mass of activity. Angry voices joined in a cacophony of sound.

'Where are your manners?' she heard Ruth ask. 'And what do you mean by coming into this house with your heads covered? Take off your hats this instant.'

There followed a communal jeer and a comment which provoked Sam to intervene. 'Who's your officer? You shall be reported for using such foul talk in the presence of a lady.'

'If that's a lady, I'm the King of France,' sneered one of the soldiers. 'And we know what he likes doing. Mind you, you'd need a blindfold to do it to her.'

Lizzie could feel the anger rising. It superseded all caution and her resolutions for dignified cold disdain disappeared. These were men who looked no better than common thieves and criminals, or the tinkers who came to the village, forcing families to bar their doors and lock up their daughters. Years of tradition must surely have taught her to bring some order and respect into this intrusion. She knew she must do it with her entrance, her first words. She had never been faced with such a challenge, but she felt the adrenaline of her fury arming her. She was glad she had put on her boots with the high heels so fashionable at Court. They made her taller and more imposing. She put the crucifix to her lips and briefly said a prayer to anyone who might be listening, and descended a few steps of the wide oak staircase.

'Silence at once.' It was her own voice, clear and commanding.

The effect was instantaneous. All heads turned towards the staircase. Lizzie remained imperiously half-way down.

While she had the advantage, she came in quickly on the attack. 'Who's your commanding officer?'

The men shuffled awkwardly. In the commotion the front door had been left open and a figure appeared.

'Captain Mildmay at your service, madam.' The man gave a stiff and more formal bow than would have been expected from a gentleman of breeding in such circumstances.

'I am Lady Elizabeth Anne Jones. My father is away and I'm in authority here. On whose orders do you behave like this, forcing your way into our home, when decent people are in their beds, and insulting our retainer? You shall be informed of the words used towards the women in this house, and be shamed if the wretch is not punished. Is this rabble what you call an army?'

The man stood very still, his gaze fixed upon Lizzie.

He was of middling height, not as tall as her father or brothers, but his stance gave him a presence both engaging and unnerving. He stood with one leg slightly forward, his body leaning back, chin lifted and expression arrogant. He had removed his helmet. He wore no long curls as was the custom with the Cavalier soldiers. His hair was cut short which made his look deceptively youthful but it was not cut in the unattractive pudding-basin bob which gave birth to the title Roundhead, a name if used now punishable by law. His eyes were slate grey and they travelled up and down her body slowly, unblinking. His lips held a faint half smile of approval. She saw one of the men give a lewd nudge to the man beside him. No man had ever looked at Lizzie in this way, and a deep blush began to spread over her neck and face. His eyes returned to her bosom and rested for a second. Involuntarily she moved her hand to the top of her bodice.

Her confidence was briefly undermined by his undisguised interest in her body. She felt a flashing kind of shame, as she felt a mixture of confusing emotions entirely new to her.

'Upon my word, my Lady,' he said languidly, 'we meant no disrespect, and I apologize for my men. They are fatigued and hungry after a long ride.'

Turning to face them, he barked a series of orders. 'Stand to attention, the lot of you, and remove your headgear. Her Ladyship will submit a full account of your conduct before my arrival. Such ill-discipline will be punished. I will not have it in my men. Do you understand?'

The men stood to attention resentfully and removed their helmets. The smell of unwashed hair filled the room, and Ruth ostentatiously produced a handkerchief and covered her nose, a gesture which did not escape the sharp eyes of Captain Mildmay. He fixed her with a challenging gaze but she boldly held her ground, dabbing her nose and giving a loud sniff.

'My Lady, this is not a pretty business,' the captain said

formally. 'It grieves me to have to impose it upon one so charmingly innocent as yourself.'

'You've yet to explain yourself, sir,' Lizzie replied, still blushing furiously. 'Please do so at once and do not mistake my natural courtesy for frailty. I do assure you of my competence in the position I hold in my father's absence. He has schooled me well in the matter of spotting the difference between a knave and a gentleman.'

'My Lady,' the captain replied, 'I stand corrected before you. But, alas! I have my orders, and it is with regret that I must now insist on your obeying them. We have come for your father, Sir Edwin, and much as I wish no disrespect to you, I cannot accept your assurances. My men must carry out a search at once.'

Six

Lizzie came down the stairs swiftly and proceeded towards Captain Mildmay. 'Sir, a word in private, please. If you would be so good as to come into the great hall with my steward.'

Lizzie swept purposefully out of the room, giving no indication that there might have been any doubt whatsoever in Captain Mildmay's co-operation with her wishes.

Dawn had come, and a grey watery light filtered through the tall stained-glass windows. The room had not been used for many days and the cold clung in dampened swirls, catching Lizzie's breath. Without turning, she knew Captain Mildmay was standing close to her, closer than she would have liked. She could smell the pungent odour of horses and male sweat. The nearness of his presence, and the knowledge that his eyes would be upon her when she turned, made her colour again. She put a kerchief to her face as she turned to face him in an attempt to disguise her blushes.

'So, madam, are you playing for time?' he enquired coolly. 'Or have you something of importance to add to the proceedings?'

'No, sir, I am not playing for time as you put it, for I have nothing to hide,' Lizzie said defiantly. 'If my father were here, I would not presume to parley with you or any soldiers. Whether they be loyal to the King or to Parliament I care not, my concern is for my household. I must tell you that my mother is lately brought to bed of a child and is confined to the privacy of her chamber and I would ask you to respect that privacy.'

'Now, madam, do you take me for a fool?' the captain replied with surprise. 'Where else would a husband be found than in his lady's chamber? If that is all you had to say to me, I must warn you that search the house we must.'

'Captain Mildmay, if I gave you my word as a gentlewoman that my father is not in my mother's chamber, would you feel inclined to take it, and let my poor mother in peace?' Lizzie asked gravely. 'And would you give me time to assemble my sisters and allay their fears, for they think your soldiers are from the devil himself . . . if their conduct this day is a reflection of the Puritan ethic?'

'Madam, let me take your hand on it,' said the captain seriously. 'I would not doubt the word of one so beautiful and untouched by the mendacity of the world outside your noble family, for I understand your family are an ancient noble line, and not of the recent batch of knights forced by the King to buy the title if they owned more than two thousand acres, and I know that is why you are accorded the title of Lady as your father's daughter.'

In response to his gesture, Lizzie proffered her hand, holding it high and limp as she had seen her mother do. To her confusion he took it but did not release it. Instead he lowered it and in so doing reduced the space between them, as he took a step forward. Looking straight into her eyes, his own narrowing sardonically, he gave a faint almost imperceptible laugh.

'I will trust you, madam, and the search will be perfunctory, compared to the norm . . . but you will remember this does not come without a caveat. These are terrible times, and I am mindful of the delicacy of your position. We shall meet again, madam, but for now will you be so good as to take me and my men about your house and nothing shall offend you. But remember . . . this is not lightly done, nor will it escape the notice of others in high places.' He paused a moment and she felt his grip tighten. 'There are many families, madam, where divided loyalties have proved an advantage.'

The enormity of the captain's words slowly penetrated Lizzie's consciousness. What could she have said to give him the impression that she was at odds with the Royalist cause? True, before he came she had personally instructed some of the men on the estate to pull down the fences which the neighbouring squire, Sir Oswald Molyneux, true to the King, had erected on common grazing land on the heath outside the village.

Of course she had lost the battle and now some of the displaced families had settled on the land behind the manor. She had persuaded Sir Edwin to look kindly on them and their gratitude had been apparent in many different ways. Fences had been mysteriously mended and the barn roof repaired, and where once the winter stores would have rotted they remained dry. It was because of this that Lizzie had been able to over-winter some of the cattle and provide milk for the household and some of the most needy villagers.

Lizzie pulled her hand away. Captain Mildmay resisted briefly and then, with a formal bow, asked her to lead the way, as if the matter were settled.

'Madam, I'm at your service,' the captain said with almost exaggerated courtesy. 'Will you lead the way with all speed that we may finish our business here today as swiftly as possible?'

As Lizzie looked at him, she felt something between fear and a compelling attraction. She had to admit that Captain Mildmay was by any standards a handsome young man, with his vigorous head of dark hair swept from his forehead and his eyes so vibrant and compelling as he fixed her in his gaze. Lizzie decided he could be either very good or very bad, but definitely nothing in between.

Life at the manor had not exposed her to such worldly

men as Captain Mildmay. She had seldom ventured outside the county, and had never been alone with any man except for her father and brothers in all her seventeen years. Her knowledge of the county and the cities beyond its boundaries was confined to the conversations of her parents and the neighbouring squires. Further information was relayed in the royalist news sheet which Sir Edwin occasionally left lying about. For most of the population the only information about current events they had was gleamed at the obligatory Sunday church service, but Lizzie had long ago tired of the ignorant ranting of the ill-educated parson Jeeps. He appeared to have no convictions of any sort save the repetitive warnings against Popery, the devil and the sins of the flesh.

She thought about the sins of the flesh now. She had often wondered how such things could destroy natural feelings of modesty. The presence of Captain Mildmay had opened the door to a room she thought she would never enter and it was as if it were a room full of looking-glasses. She saw herself now in the glass, a different Lizzie Anne flushed with a heedless anticipation of the next time she would see him, as he had promised.

But Ruth had also entered the room without her noticing.

'I shall come with you, my Lady,' she insisted. 'It isn't seemly for you to be with the captain alone.'

'Upon my word, madam, the servants in this house are a bold and outspoken lot,' the captain flashed. 'Your serving woman would be better employed offering refreshments to my men, not to mention myself, for I've a long ride ahead of me when I leave here without my prisoner.'

'I would as soon give alms to the lepers in the huts outside the village than give his Lordship's wine to turncoats such as you, saving your presence, my Lady.' Ruth spat the words between clenched teeth.

Lizzie saw the expression on Captain Mildmay's face rapidly change from benign indulgence to cold anger. Before he had time to speak she hustled Ruth out of the room, asking him to wait a moment. As they left, she heard Captain Mildmay mutter under his breath, 'God's teeth. I'll have that woman flogged.'

While he was instructing his men, Lizzie pushed Ruth into a store room.

'What possessed you to speak like that?' Lizzie said furiously. 'Do you know what danger we are all in? People have been arrested for less.'

'They think we're just a bunch of ignorant country folk,' Ruth retorted. 'But not us at the manor . . . You know your mother taught me to read and write, when I was a grown woman too, and what's the use of learning if you don't use it?'

'There's such a thing as a little learning being a dangerous thing, Ruth.'

'I've read about that man,' Ruth sneered, ignoring her comment. 'In your father's news sheet, the *Mercurias Politicas* . . . he must be the Mildmay who betrayed the King. He was part of his Majesty's retinue . . . no less than the Royal Carver, and then he turned to the other side. We are in the presence of a traitor. I would no more pander to him and his like than trade with the devil.' Ruth crossed herself vigorously.

'Listen to me, Ruth,' hissed Lizzie. 'We have to learn to dissemble. I'll do anything to spare us all the terrible things we know are going on in the name of Parliament.'

'I must obey you here, my Lady, for it is your father's wish, but you should obey your conscience, for at the end of your days you'll be answerable to it alone.'

'When that day comes,' said Lizzie vehemently. 'I don't want blood on my hands. Most decent people want peace. Everyone seems to have forgotten that.'

Ruth had gone very red. She fiddled with her apron and for the first time in her life Lizzie saw a frown of doubt on her old face. Lizzie loved her old nurse. Her wise and constant presence had been the most important thing in her memory. Now that Lizzie had become the mistress and Ruth had begun to call her 'my Lady' instead of 'child', she felt it as a kind of bereavement. She knew that Ruth felt it too and in a moment of deep compassion she put her arms about the old woman.

'Don't worry, Ruth. No harm will come to you. But trust me. Remember, I am what you've made me.'

'Aye and until today I didn't realize you were a woman ripe for the eyes of men such as that captain, who would be the ruin of you,' Ruth warned darkly. 'Remember that your virtue is all you will have in the sight of God. I saw the way he looked at you.'

'You need have no fears in that direction,' Lizzie retorted crisply. 'I'm too busy protecting my father to give his loose glances a thought. Give the men ale and bread and some ham from the carcass in the larder,' she continued sturdily, not wanting Ruth to see how the presence of the captain had affected her.

Ruth gave a sullen nod and was about to turn on her heel, but Lizzie caught her arm. 'Do it with grace,' she added. 'And offer them shelter from the wind in the old barn. Then perhaps we'll not be burned down like some poor people we've heard about.'

She felt Ruth's shoulders stiffen.

'It's just that I am an old woman,' she replied tearfully. 'And I don't understand the world any more.'

Captain Mildmay's soldiers moved through the house in a token search, and Ruth kept her silence. When the men came to Mary's bedchamber, only the captain was granted admittance. Her mother, willingly distanced from the night's events, was fully dressed and groomed, the room set in perfect order, the baby asleep in her crib.

'Your humble servant, my Lady,' he had said with a bow, delivering some placatory apologies for the disturbance. He left as quickly as he had entered.

'Believe me,' the captain said to Lizzie as they emerged on to the gallery outside the room, 'it grieves me to see gentlewomen such as your mother so put about by the intransigence of those who should know when defeat must be followed by progress.'

Lizzie had hoped to keep him talking, thinking he might miss the parlour where her father was still hiding, but to her dismay the captain paused, pointed to the closed door and issued a command.

'I think we've missed a room,' the captain barked. 'Men, jump to it.'

Lizzie's heart pounded as the men burst into the room and started their search.

Seven

When Sir Edwin first entered the hiding place, it had seemed in total darkness. But as his eyes became accustomed to the gloom he saw a small chink of light in the far corner of the tiny space, which was about the length of a man's body and wide enough to accommodate the bed, a small table and a chair. There was not quite enough room to stand upright, for Sir Edwin was a tall man. He felt his way gingerly to the chink of light and peered through. It gave him a keyhole view of the great hall.

Sir Edwin felt about for the candle and lit it with the taper, being careful to block up the spy hole with the Bible, which lay on a small three-legged stool. He was sweating and he took steady even breaths and tried to calm himself.

Sir Edwin had experienced fear before, always before a battle, although since the first great disaster at Edgehill, some six years ago, except for some minor skirmishes, he had not taken up arms for the King. He had not forgotten what fear felt like but this was an entirely new kind of emotion because events were beyond his control. He knew for certain that if he were caught he would be conveyed to the Tower and summary execution would follow within days. Parliament dealt with the weakened residue of the King's supporters swiftly and with no mercy. He knelt down on the floor and prayed silently, not so much for himself but to be spared in order to protect his defenceless family.

Time seemed to pass slowly. He heard nothing for what seemed like an eternity and then muffled sound of feet. He extinguished the candle and gently pulled away the Bible. He could see Lizzie and a man, some sort of officer. The man was seated at the table being waited on by Sam, but he could barely hear what they were saying. Sometimes he could make out the odd sentence and the little he heard made him tremble

52

with anger. He clenched his fists so hard that his nails cut into his flesh.

Lizzie and the man were joined by soldiers with drawn swords, and Sir Edwin found himself seething with rage.

'Drawn swords in a house full of women and babies,' he whispered to himself. If I live I will not forget this day and I will have my revenge, he vowed silently, as a mouse scuttled across his feet in the direction of the entrance to his hiding place. What if it ran under the panel and into the room, attracting the soldiers' attention? He saw it stop in the dim light of the candle and look up at him. He would never catch it and, if he tried to, the noise would betray him. He willed it to return to its home, and, as if reading his thoughts, it turned and scuttled into a hole beside the far wall.

The mouse had distracted him, and when he looked again he could see the group had made its way to the staircase. He saw the men banging the panelling with their swords. But as they went up they were lost from view. All went silent for what seemed like a lifetime, happy memories of times gone by flashed through his mind and he clung to them like a drowning man as he resigned himself to the possibility of discovery. His fate depended on so many things, but not now his own skill or courage; even so he felt for the hilt of his sword.

But the spilling of blood in front of his wife and daughters was unthinkable, he would just have to put his life in the tender care of God almighty.

Sir Edwin was about to need all the self-control he could muster. He heard the door open into the parlour. At first he could not hear voices, just a banging and clattering of metal on wood which grew nearer. It was swords hitting the panelling, testing for a cavity behind.

'And so, madam, what better place for concealment than in this fine room behind such exquisite panelling,' came a man's voice. It was taunting and disrespectful. The villain must be talking to Lizzie. Sir Edwin had to control himself. He felt a desperate desire to burst out of his hiding place. What right did these knaves have to burst into his home and question a young woman like Lizzie in such a manner? Then he recalled the recent rape of a young noblewoman in just such circumstances. He had his hand near the door. Then he heard another voice, rough and ill-tutored with a country accent he did not recognize.

'So will we rip out the panels like we did in the last place, sir?' came a course male response. And then he heard a calm, strangely familiar, woman's voice.

'I should hope you will not waste your time vandalizing a lady's sewing room. We look for more in Cromwell's New Model Army, do we not, Captain?'

At first Sir Edwin could hardly believe his ears. It was Lizzie. Her words resonated authority when she spoke . . . she did not ask or suggest, she commanded. Sir Edwin felt a burst of pride and a stab of fear. How would her comments be received?

'You're right, madam,' replied the first man. 'We'll leave this beautiful room undisturbed and your expectations of the Parliamentary army unsullied.' The voice was educated and full of authority. Sir Edwin assumed it belonged to the man who had been sitting with Lizzie in the great hall. He sat down heavily on the bed and pondered how he and Mary had produced such a daughter.

When Captain Mildmay and two of his men had completed the tour of the house, the captain raised the inevitable subject of supplies.

'One last thing, madam,' he asked finally. 'Be so kind as to summon your bailiff. My men will nccd food and ale. We ride for London as soon as we can.'

Lizzie felt herself going hot and cold. She knew the bailiff had been hiding food for weeks in preparation for just this situation.

With immaculate timing, Ruth swept in. She gave a brief curtsey.

'My Lady, we've prepared some food for the captain and something for the men in the barn.'

'Thank you, Ruth,' Lizzie said hastily, before Ruth could spoil the gesture.

'You may remain quietly until the captain has finished,' she continued formally, gesturing to the carver chair on the top right of the table, where food had been laid out.

She would not have Captain Mildmay sitting in her father or mother's place. Ruth took the point and quickly moved the place round with a barely concealed smile, nor was this lost on the captain, whose mouth tightened.

'Well, mistress, we shall see if your victuals make up for the carelessness of your tongue,' he said to Ruth menacingly, as she held the chair out for him. 'Which could,' he continued, 'have been cut out for less, had I not had consideration for your mistress.'

He fixed Ruth with a steady stare, tapping the hilt of his sword. Lizzie saw Ruth's ruddy complexion whiten and felt as if she were in the presence of something frightening and powerful.

Sam stood behind the chair with a ewer of hot water and a linen cloth so that the captain might wash before he tucked into the cold venison, some of her mother's cheese, fresh bread and the manor's ale. The atmosphere in the room hung heavy with apprehension. Sam fixed Lizzie with a long steady look which urged caution.

Lizzie sat politely as the captain ate.

She was surprised by the delicacy of his hands since the life of an active soldier had left her brothers with rough skin, broken nails, and the tell-tale blue patches left by chilblains. As she watched him ever more closely, she came to the conclusion that there were many things about the captain which disturbed her. As he ate he seemed quite at ease and soon they began to talk on a wide range of subjects. Occasionally, he broke into Latin in which he was clearly surprised to find Lizzie more fluent than himself. She sensed he was summing her up and that the easy dialogue was a cover. She wondered if he would bring up the matter of supplies again. But just when she thought the time had come for her to rise from the table and see him to the door, he asked her to dismiss the steward, there were private matters he had to discuss. She knew the wisest thing was to comply with his request, knowing that Sam would not be far away, for he was as alert to the danger the captain represented.

The captain wiped his mouth with the linen cloth and leaned towards her, taking her hand. She had been nervously toying with some crumbs on the table. This was the second time he

55

had touched her and a sensation altogether new to her swept through her entire body. It was both delightfully pleasant and at the same time unnerving, rather as she had once felt when she had drunk too much wine on her Saint's day.

He had her eyes in a look which she could not break. For one moment she thought he might be going to kiss her. But he did not, instead he put a finger under her chin and looked at her searchingly.

'Sit for a while, Elizabeth, with your permission I shall call you that. There are things I want to say to you for your own protection. I am bothered by the position you are in, and I fancy your father has concealed from you the reality of the situation.'

He continued to hold her hand, and for a moment she would have pulled it away but then, whether because she was overcome by fatigue or fear she did not know, she felt herself on the verge of tears. She bit her lip to conceal the fact, but Captain Mildmay, being a perspicacious observer of women, knew he had defeated her and caught her off guard. He seized his moment.

'Did you know that Parliament has the power to confiscate your estates, and might well do so if the household is not sympathetic to the Parliamentary cause?' he asked casually. 'Indeed, might already have done so,' he continued, 'if it had not been noted in the area that your father is a good man and has many supporters on both sides. He has looked kindly on the victims of the King's profligate mismanagement, and has not pressed your tenants for unpaid rents. And he has not forced the men into the King's army as have some of your neighbours.'

'My father is loyal to God, Captain Mildmay,' Lizzie said, remembering her father's words. 'His tenants are God's people; they know they can come to him. We have been brought up to feel an obligation to their welfare. I did not agree with the suffering caused to the common people by the wicked seizure of their lands and I see no reason to shed innocent blood to fight the Scots over their religion.'

'Indeed, you have strong views and are cunning enough not to label them. There are many statesmen who could learn from you,' the captain said.

'We're simple country squires and there is but one God and he's not interested in the clothes men wear. It's what is in their souls that he takes an interest in,' Lizzie replied.

She realized that Captain Mildmay was listening intently to her, instead of dismissing her, as had the men of her own family. She went on to tell him how she had learned well how to manage the estate, and the burden she had taken on. He asked her about stores. She explained the situation whereby there was barely enough food for the villagers, let alone for a battalion of hungry men and horses. They had already been cleaned out by the King's soldiers when they victualled on the way to Oxford and without hope of repayment.

As she continued, she gradually let her guard down, revealing the truth of her convictions. She had seen her family ruined, and she wondered if indeed Parliament could restore the country to order and prevent it from sliding further into anarchy as she had read in some of the pamphlets which had been circulating.

Seeing the pensive look on her face, Captain Mildmay took his advantage. 'My dear,' he said seriously, 'you and your family stand on the edge of an abyss. The King's army is fighting a lost cause, so look to and see how you may best save yourselves.'

'And how, sir, are we to do that?' Lizzie asked.

'I can protect you,' the captain replied quickly. 'But you must consider where you stand in this.'

'I, sir,' said Lizzie, 'I've no experience in such things. How can I take the conscience of my entire family upon my shoulders when my own is burdensome enough?'

'Fiddlesticks,' the captain retorted sharply. 'You're no simpering maid. You're capable of making up your own mind, and . . . if needs be . . . deciding what's best for your remaining family.'

'Tell me first what will become of the King?' Lizzie asked.

'The King will be charged, I fancy . . . with treason,' the captain answered guardedly. 'It's known that he's been looking to France for foreign mercenaries to spill the blood of his own people, instead of accepting the compromise he's been offered by Parliament.'

'Oh, no, I didn't know,' Lizzie gasped, looking white and

shocked. 'How could such a thing be?'

'Think of your father and brothers and the young men on the estate. They were commissioned and given nothing but a farm pike to fight Cromwell's modern army. The finest fighting force this country will ever have,' the captain said, seizing his advantage again. 'They've been used by a stupid man,' he went on. 'And his cowardly braggart of a foreign nephew. And when the battle was lost, he abandoned them without food or clothing. Many of them died trying to get back to their wives and families in bitter cold so far from home.' He paused for a moment, looking thoughtfully down at the table and then raised his eyes with a bright flash towards Lizzie's.

'Now they're all dead and for nothing. But he doesn't learn from his mistakes. He's trying to import foreign mercenaries to kill his own people. For him it's simple. He doesn't value the life of the individual,' he said finally.

'Surely Prince Rupert was a brave and talented campaigner?' Lizzie asked in a measured tone. 'He thinks of himself as an Englishman.'

'If he were a true Englishman, he wouldn't have been so careless with the lives of his countrymen,' the captain said.

'It's true,' Lizzie replied. 'I've seen bitter tears shed by the widows and orphans here at the manor. And I've seen the land untended for lack of men. Now we're left to fend for them. I don't know who'll plant the fields for next winter. And I must kill the geese in the pens before they're fattened, and the pigs are hungry, for there's nothing to spare from the table . . . and what if my father and brothers should die, for what, for what?'

Lizzie could no longer control her desperation. Her shoulders began to shake.

Captain Mildmay did not put a comforting arm about her, but kept hold of her hand.

'I hate the King,' Lizzie burst out. 'And all his family and the Scots and his dwarf Catholic Queen. I'd give Cromwell or Fairfax all my support if he could stop this wickedness, and give us back the life we used to have before the King taxed us all to ruin.'

'These are strong words, my dear. Am I to believe them?' the captain enquired gravely.

'Yes, sir, you can believe them,' Lizzie assured him. 'For

58

it's not the first time I've said them, Indeed I've fallen foul of my own brother in the argument.'

Lizzie looked intensely at the captain, unnerved by her own sudden lack of reserve.

'Elizabeth, I'll send word that the Parliamentary army are to spare you further intrusion, for I believe you're like many others disillusioned with your King.'

'Sir, I don't know what to say. I can't vouch for my father . . . but I'll speak to him if he should return.'

She knew as she said the words 'if he should return', by the fleeting look he gave her, that he knew full well that her father was concealed in the house, but she could not fully understand why he would walk away without his prisoner.

'It's enough for the moment that I know of the many good deeds you've done for the common people. It's our business to know these things,' said the captain quietly.

'Sir, I can only tell you,' said Lizzie simply, 'with the men folk away I must do all I can to protect my mother and sisters.'

'I'm glad to have been of service,' the captain said. 'But I must warn you that you've much to fear from the army still loyal to the King. They're desperate. They'll take captive even their own supporters and ask a ransom for their return. And they'll take whatever they've a mind to, even from your father's estates while he's fighting the same cause.'

Lizzie sighed and wrung her hands. 'Where has honour gone? I can't believe what you say and yet I sense that I must,' she said desperately.

'My dear, hunger and honour don't mix,' said the captain. 'As a soldier you find that out very quickly. Have you never heard that an army marches on its stomach? Feed your soldiers and you'll have their honour, but neglect them at your peril. Your father sounds like a thoughtful man. Where does he really stand in all this?' he went on.

'He is not a fighting man. He prefers to spend time with his books,' said Lizzie pointedly.

'Elizabeth, I've been struck by your dilemma. Unless something is done it's only a matter of time before your father's estates are sequestered by Parliament. For I know he's in debt. Supporting the King in his folly has not only spilled needless blood but has ruined landowners such as your father. I could help you . . .' Captain Mildmay's voice trailed away, while he gave Lizzie a chance to digest the message he was giving her.

'Sir,' she replied cautiously. 'We've heard many fearful stories about the conduct of General Fairfax's soldiers under the leadership of this man Cromwell.'

'He's a fine officer and leader,' the captain said sternly. 'He has a vision of England with a trained disciplined army and proper roads. As you know, the country's virtually impassable from north to south. But more than that, we need law and order. The present system of the local squire administering the law must end.'

'All this may well be so, but I must think about what's happening now, under this so-called new order,' Lizzie said quickly. 'Why, in Hampshire, we heard of a family burned in their beds, and all because they were loyal to the King. Must I think we would be safer in the hands of men like this than in the hope that the Cavalier army will send a magistrate and men to protect us? I don't know which way to turn. I think we're lost whatever we do. You're all Levellers at heart, even you, with your fine clothes and gentleman's ways. How can I trust you?'

'I know that was a terrible thing, and there are many stories on both sides,' the captain said gravely. 'What you saw in your house today was as nothing compared to what you may expect. In Cromwell we have a new general who's taking a firm hand with the Parliamentary army. It's to become the first army to be in the pay of the government. It'll be fed and disciplined and trained as no army before has ever been.'

'And what about the Levellers?' Lizzie asked. 'The very name has become a byword for fear. I have read about them continually in my father's pamphlets.'

'General Cromwell's dealt with the Levellers who were responsible for the deeds you have read about,' the captain countered. 'And now he must deal with the King and his henchmen. Take your infamous Prince Rupert. What can you expect? He learned his behaviour at the knee of his barbarian mother, the Winter Queen. You've heard of what happened at the battle at Marston Moor only three years ago?' the captain asked.

'Of course I have. It was just bad luck,' replied Lizzie.

'It was no such thing, it was bad soldiering,' the captain

came back quickly. 'The Prince lost four thousand men in three hours. He sent them off in a disorderly gallop. Cromwell's men took it at a slow trot, and were able to regroup. And when he saw the battle was lost, the prince didn't wait to save his men, but rode back to Whitehall to save his skin.'

The more she heard, the more Lizzie began to realize that her sympathies no longer lay with the King, who had brought this unimaginable horror upon them. Could it be that he could be guilty of betraying the Crown by his intransigence and refusal to acknowledge the rights of the people? Did he really have a right to send so many young men to their deaths to fight for the very thing which deprived them of their lives and livelihoods, since the destruction of a whole manorial way of life had left hundreds starving?

The captain's voice broke into her thoughts. 'This is an important moment in your life, you must make some decisions,' he said firmly.

'I am well aware of what you are offering,' said Lizzie quietly.

'You must think very carefully,' the captain replied. 'Your home and your family depend on your answer.'

Lizzie knew that her decision would for many reasons change her life for ever. There was something intangible in the air and the captain had brought more than his soldiers to the manor.

When it came to it she only had to think for a moment. She realized she did not have time to procrastinate and that she did not have a choice.

'I give you my word I can no longer support the King,' she said clearly. 'I am responsible for my family now, and I ask for your protection. No King's men will be harboured in this house. I will find food for the men on this occasion if we can in the future be left alone.'

'That is all well and good,' said the captain, 'but words are not enough. You must show that you mean it.'

'I will speak to the parson and have the altar moved to the middle of the church. That will demonstrate our allegiance, that will be a start,' said Lizzie, thinking about the fine altar and the silver and gold candle sticks already hidden in a trunk deep under the copper beech at the far end of the orchard. That would remain where it was!

But all the time Lizzie knew that she must play a double game. She suspected the captain was as fickle as the wind: she had a nagging doubt that he did not truly believe in the so-called Puritan ethic at all. It was little things like the bows on his stockings when he'd loosened his boots at the table, the jewelled scabbard to his sword, the exquisite French lace that peeped from the cuff of his dull grey uniform and his surprising omission of 'Thanks be to God' before he ate.

But most of all it was the way he looked at her, the way he came so near to her. He had established a kind of intimacy, which against her better nature she not only encouraged but enjoyed.

When Captain Mildmay rode away from the manor, it was a fine morning and the sun glittered on the soldiers' helmets. The servants busied themselves in clearing up the dozens of horse droppings around the drive and gardens, and Sam muttered that had it not been for the hard frost the gardens would have been destroyed for ever.

No food was taken from the estate and Lizzie knew her actions had saved the manor and the tenants, but although he had not said so, she also knew that the captain rode towards their neighbours, the Molyneux, who had had little mercy for the commoners. The reprieve she held in her hand, signed by the captain, fluttered uneasily in the icy north wind. As she stood in her warm velvet cape watching the departure from the big stone steps at the front of the house, she felt a deep and profound unease.

'I shall be back, aye, and before you know it, my Lady,' the captain called over his shoulder as he turned his fine black horse to ride away. 'Never fear. You've done a good thing today, even though I can see by your face that your heart may tell you otherwise. It's your mind you need now, Elizabeth, and of that you have plenty.'

Lizzie set about clearing up after the unwelcome visitors, grateful that they still had a home, said her Pater Noster to herself, and went slowly to release her father. There was another battle she would have to win.

* * *

As Captain Mildmay rode towards the Molyneux estate he sensed the murmuring dissatisfaction amongst his men. They had been deprived of sport in the Jones household and they were bored. Their blood lust was up and their mood was ugly. He would have to be extra careful or things could get out of hand. He would have to allow them some satisfaction – perhaps the odd beating or two, and maybe some roughing up here and there, and certainly they would not leave without their prisoner.

If the women put up a fight it would be difficult. Royalist women sometimes fought as bravely as any man, and the squire's lady was said to be handy with a musket. Then his men would have an excuse to fight like with like. But there was to be no rape this time. He had made himself clear on that subject, despite the lewd winks and nods from his sergeant. They would clear the barns and fill the supply wagons and if the stewards put up a fight they would come off the worse for it.

The squire did not put up a fight. He traded on a clear passport for his wife and children. The captain allowed them time for some touching farewells and the family were given a few hours to pack what they could in two coaches, for there were six children.

The crying and weeping began to get on his nerves. He left his sergeant in charge and went outside to the barns. On the squire's orders the stewards opened the barns and loaded the wagons. He was in the middle of supervising the operation when he heard a shot.

The captain rushed inside to find a scene of mayhem with a girl lying on the stone floor of the kitchen, her skirts above her waist.

Next to her a man lay dead – one of the stewards, he recognized. The girl was whimpering quietly. When she saw the captain, she pulled down her skirts and huddled over her knees, trembling wildly.

'I shot him, sir, in self-defence. He attacked me,' blurted one of his men.

A large woman appeared from behind the gaggle of people filling the room.

'Not so . . . He was trying to defend the girl, while your

men had sport with her, and he paid with his life,' she said defiantly.

'Sergeant, what's the meaning of this?' the captain barked.

The man was sweating profusely, and the captain knew full well that his explanation of events was not even an approximation of the truth. But then, what was one more dead man among so many?

The squire's lady came as if from nowhere, commanding and imperious. She pushed the men aside and knelt beside the dead man, feeling his pulse. She looked Captain Mildmay full in the face, and spat at him.

'You call yourself an officer? You're not fit to lick this man's boots. Your men did this. May you all rot in hell, and God save the King,' she screamed.

It was later as he rode away with his prisoner, leaving his men to bring on the contents of the looted barns and whatever else they took a fancy to, that he turned and saw the first flames lighting the darkening sky.

He hoped they had got the children away before the fire took hold, the smell of burning flesh was sickening. He remembered it from the month previously. This time it would not be on his conscience . . . On that occasion he was not to know the children were hiding with their mother in the cellar.

The squire turned and looked at his burning home and wept; large tears swilled down his face.

'May God in his heaven forgive you,' he said in a voice hardly audible above the clatter of the horse hooves.

Eight

Nobody had been more surprised than Mary when her husband ran into her room and took her in his arms. She had resigned herself to his dawn departure, having no idea that he was secreted in the priest hole whose existence she'd forgotten. The arrival of the Parliamentary troops had terrified her. The fact that the troops had dispersed in an orderly way, leaving house, estate and occupants intact, was something she could not explain until she had heard what her eldest daughter had to say.

Lizzie's arguments were delivered with a conviction which belied her inner turmoil. She knew she had but one chance to persuade her parents to do what was both expedient and necessary. Her father exploded with venomous anger when Lizzie told him of the indemnity from Captain Mildmay. Mary calmed him, and begged her husband to give his daughter a chance to explain.

'At forty-five you are no longer able to fight in a hard and mismanaged campaign. Haven't you done enough already?' Mary asked. 'After all, we have sent both our sons to a likely death.'

'Surely the wise thing to do would be to get word to the King,' Lizzie intervened quickly. 'He must compromise before more blood is spilled in a hopeless cause. Couldn't men like you be of more use as negotiators?'

'You two women have taken leave of your senses. I will never accept the concept of Republicanism, never, do you hear,' Sir Edwin thundered. 'All these semantics are a disguise for the real truth of the matter,' he warned.

'No,' Lizzie argued vehemently. 'You're wrong. The King's being given the opportunity to negotiate. If he won't, he'll have to abdicate and his son will be appointed in his place.'

At this Sir Edwin guffawed and asked sarcastically, 'Perhaps the Catholic Queen should be made regent while they're at it?'

'Father,' Lizzie replied, 'you must see the country can't be governed without Parliament. The King was wrong to abolish it for so many years just because it wouldn't grant him money to raise an army against the Scots. Look what that led to. The people were taxed into ruin, and all the time the bishops, whose war it really was, became more powerful. They even taxed our own curate for half his stipend.'

This got her father's attention. She knew that even he could not quite identify with the religious dissension between the Protestant Church of England and the Presbyterian Scots with their phobic loathing of Popery.

But the argument which gave Lizzie time to continue her onslaught was most definitely his worry at abandoning them all at such a dangerous time. His near escape from the Parliamentary troops had shocked him into considering the very real danger his wife and daughters were in.

Lizzie was right. He was not a young man, and he was certainly beginning to feel his age. The last campaign had brought on pains in all his limbs and he could not mount his horse without a mounting block. He was tired of the war, he wanted peace. But still he had the nagging feeling that his daughter's over-simplification of the dilemma had missed out the vital element of Parliament versus the Crown. In the back of Sir Edwin's mind, the two could never be reconciled. They were as separate as oil and water.

He thought about chivalry, how the concept had been handed down the generations from Eleanor of Aquitaine. He had to hang on to the Cavalier code of honour. This is what had made England great. It was this he was fighting for. This is why he had sacrificed his sons.

Sir Edwin did not go. He went back to his study and sought solace in his books, while his family enjoyed an uneasy respite from their fears.

Two days later Lizzie and her mother were in the linen room darning the sheets and coverlets. Ruth had approved, giving them the advice her own mother had told her: 'When the big things go wrong, keep the small details in perfect order. When the time comes for action, you'll be ready and prepared.'

It was a fine morning and life had assumed an uneasy state of calm since Sir Edwin had decided to remain at the manor for the time being, and half-heartedly agreed to a change of loyalty. Lizzie knew he was shattered by what he had had to do. But she felt a ray of hope when she discovered him deep in his books. He was embarking on a long translation from Greek of an obscure work of Plato.

'It feels good to be back among my friends, Lizzie,' he told her, patting the red embossed leather of one of his prized volumes.

But the morning was too good to be inside. Lizzie decided to pay a visit to the village. There were errands she must see to and what better time than when the sun was so warm and inviting. She set off at a brisk pace and was approaching the centre of the village by the well which served most of the residents, when the peace was abruptly shattered by a commotion of soldiers clattering noisily on to the village green, scattering geese, ducks and people alike.

Their rough clothes and loud voices spelled danger. The green had emptied and doors could be heard slamming shut and bolts sliding.

Lizzie hesitated a moment, seeing one of the men had a youth held by the hair. But a strong pair of hands took her by the shoulder and dragged her into a cottage door. She watched, trembling, from the window through the blackthorn slats. The boy was whimpering and seemed to be pleading. Abruptly and with rowdy encouragement from the ragged mob of men, the leader jumped from his horse and drew his sword with a flourish. With a cry of delight from his men, he sliced down the side of the boy's head. The boy let out an agonizing scream, and one of his ears fell on the ground.

Lizzie stifled a cry and felt the bile raising in her throat. She watched in horror as the sword was raised again to slice off the other ear.

Mary was still quietly sewing when she was disturbed. Suddenly there was a commotion. Loud voices came from the kitchen and a long moan which became a scream and then several more shrieks. Mary dropped her sewing and ran.

As she approached the kitchen, the noise became louder. The door was open. Jacob, the lad who ran errands to and from the village, stood in the middle of the room covered in blood. It was pouring from around his head like a bright red fountain.

His family had worked at the manor for generations, and his mother Nan ran the dairy. She was on her knees at his feet trying to tear up her apron to staunch the flow. Her screams had become low, terrible, racking sobs. Ruth, Sam and the other servants stood, white-faced, staring at Jacob.

For a moment Mary couldn't quite take it in. There was so much blood, Jacob looked as if he had been painted red. It had soaked his white shirt and leather jerkin and saturated the coarse wool of his dark grey breeches.

His mouth hung open, his eyes staring as if he could

not comprehend what had happened to him.

Lizzie was there looking deathly white.

'Bring him to the pantry, Ruth,' Mary ordered. 'And Nan, get the sheets I was darning in the linen room. We must bandage the wounds before they fester.'

'They stuffed his ears in his mouth, and tied his hands behind his back . . . he choked on his own flesh,' his mother wailed frantically.

'Come, Jacob,' Mary said gently, taking his blood-soaked hand.

She led him to the pantry and set Sam to boiling water, and getting brandy for the boy. It was hard to stop the bleeding, so Mary folded the torn linen that a few moments ago had seen her careful darning and made two pads and bound them tightly to his head. She sent Ruth to the herb room for something to deaden the pain, and set the boy to rest, on a couch in the parlour. Only when the boy was asleep, heavily dosed with belladonna, did she set to find out what had happened.

Sir Edwin had been alerted by Sam. Sam rushed him to the kitchen with a jumble of words, none of which Sir Edwin could fully understand. All he knew was that something dreadful had happened to one of the young manservants. He thought it was young Jacob, for whom he had a particular fondness. His father had been one of Sir Edwin's most trusted bailiffs. Jacob's father had been killed falling from his horse, and Sir Edwin had taken the boy under his wing, teaching him his letters.

When Sir Edwin reached the parlour, everyone spoke at once. He could see Mary was preoccupied with attending to the boy. Ruth was placing a warming pan of coals at his feet for he was 'drained of blood from the shock' and would 'like as not die from it if he could not be warmed back into the land of the living', Ruth continued, 'I always knew he would get into trouble when I helped bring him into this world seventeen years ago, in a violent thunderstorm which had set the chickens to eating their own eggs and soured the milk in the pantry. He was trouble then and he is trouble now,' she said darkly.

The white bandage on his head was already seeping blood and it was a few moments before Sir Edwin realized the nature of his injuries.

He asked Nan, who had become a little calmer, to explain what had happened, but she was still incoherent. Sam stepped forward.

'If it please, your worship,' he said nervously. 'I will tell you how it is. Our Jacob has been handing out such words as would have been treason before the capture of our King. And this very morning he was out in the village before it was barely light and nailing them on the board by the stocks on the green, where he had a habit of putting such things. Our men usually pull them down before folk could see them. But the shame of it was that his sweetheart had been with him at the time on her way to the dairy. Out of the blue come these soldiers and, with a great deal of roughness, they took the girl and molested her in the thicket by the green. Our Jacob did all his strength could to save her, but they were too much for him. Then one of them shows the paper to the leader. And then they see red and before he knows it, young Jacob is shorn of the two good ears God gave him.'

'By God, Lizzie,' bellowed Sir Edwin. 'Is that enough for you? You've dealt with the devil, these Roundheads are not fit to eat with my dogs. Go to the village, man, and round up all the men you can find. We'll have these animals, even if we have to die in the doing of it.'

There was silence in the room and then Sam stepped forward again.

'Pardon me, sir,' he said robustly. 'But it was not the Roundhead men, it was the King's men that did this thing. They say they were out for blood, because the General Cromwell's men have taken our neighbour, Squire Molyneux. His wife is fled and the house is burned and more terrible to tell. So, begging your Lordship's pardon, there's many that ask why the manor at Hatherton was left untouched. Like the story of the Passover, they say. But with your Lordship's pardon, the word is the Parliamentary soldiers are better than the rag-tag-and-bobtail that call themselves the King's men, that would deprive an innocent young girl of her maidenhead.'

Later that day Lizzie told to her mother how Nan had gone to the girl's family and said that Jacob, even in his suffering, would take the girl as his bride at once, if she would have him. For everyone knew the village would be watching her stomach and whispering. It was said that rape was God's revenge for licentious thoughts. If she were with child, the sooner it could claim a father the better.

When the house was calmer, Mary and Lizzie took some elderflower wine to Sir Edwin. They needed to talk to him. The awful events of the morning had focused their minds. A time for decisions had come. As they approached Sir Edwin's study, they could see he was busy at his desk. On hearing their footsteps on the creaky wooden floor, he called them to come in.

'Wife, daughter,' Sir Edwin said resolutely. 'I've written to His Majesty. Now that I see what the noble King's army have become – just butchers and rapists – I can see that this has got to stop. The King will not negotiate for peace and continues to conspire, for I gather he's broken his word to Parliament even though they gave him the things he asked for and reunited him with his children. It seems he's been secretly raising an army of French barbarians to fight his own subjects on England's soil . . . I shall have none of it. I shall send a copy of my letter to Parliament so that none may accuse me of duplicity. I thank you, daughter, for seeing what I should have seen before with my own eyes. I only wish my sons could be brought home to us. We must pray for them, and for the King to be guided by the hand of God, to whom he forgets he's answerable.'

Lizzie and her mother both went quietly to Sir Edwin and laid their hands reassuringly on his shoulders. He looked like a broken man. All they could do was to let him know how much they respected the way he had tried to fight for what he believed in.

Nine

A month later Lizzie was in the pantry supervising the silver and plate cleaning with ashes of wheat and alum when she heard a commotion in the hall. She threw down her soft woollen cloth and instructed Sam to come with her. Jacob, who now lived with his wife Jenny in the lodge cottage and who had been set to keep a constant watch on the gates, stood at the open door, breathing heavily, his eyes wide with alarm, the straps from the leather hood he wore to conceal his injuries flying in a sharp April breeze.

'Parliamentary soldiers are on the road making for the manor,' he rasped, fear gripping him as he remembered past visits.

Lizzie's stomach lurched. 'Thank you, Jacob,' she said quickly, trying not to let her voice betray her emotions. 'You have done well, now we must all act fast. We must hide the valuables, the silver we've been cleaning, it must be moved at once to the space behind the wall in the cellar. And Sam must take the strong-box from which Father pays the wages and the accounts. It must be moved into the vault in the family chapel. I will see to her Ladyship's jewellery.' Again she thanked Jacob for his diligence.

'Go back to your lodge and show no alarm and look after your Jenny,' said Lizzie, thinking their trust had been well served. Jacob had become the family's devoted servant, since the celebration of his marriage to Jenny, his sweetheart, and they awaited the arrival of their baby.

'I hope we are right to trust that boy,' said Ruth disapprovingly. 'It was lucky for young Jenny that he had been more than bundling with her in the hay loft beside the dairy long before the wretched soldiers had their wicked way . . . Jacob is no better than he ought to be. Waiting until the devil stepped in before he made an honest woman of the poor girl.'

'Stop your clucking, Ruth, this is no time to talk of such things. Jacob is our friend and we must all trust each other,' Lizzie retorted, putting her arms round Ruth's shoulders. 'Now we must get about our business,' she said firmly, taking off her apron.

Lizzie ran to the top of the house and threw open the tower window to get a view across the park to the winding road from the village. Peering through the spy glass, she focused on the bobbing grey mass of men and horses. There were about a dozen of them, far fewer than on the last occasion. As the group became clearer, she could see that the leader was dressed differently to the others. With a gasp she saw it was Captain Mildmay.

Lizzie ran to warn her father and mother and ordered that refreshments be laid out in the great hall. This time the manor would be prepared, and both her parents would be waiting formally to receive Captain Mildmay with dignity and authority.

'Sir Edwin, my Lady, allow me to present myself, Anthony Mildmay, at your service,' said the captain, bowing as Ruth showed him into the parlour.

He looked about the room, and as his eyes found her his expression changed to the sardonic smile she remembered, and a gaze which seemed to pry beneath her gown and apron. She coloured a little and looked down as she gave him a modest curtsey.

'Elizabeth, I'm glad to find you here,' the captain said briskly. 'In truth I've come to meet your father, but it's his daughter who occasions the visit. Sir Edwin, I have but little time to this errand, but may I crave your attention?'

The two men exchanged formalities and the captain accepted the offer of ale and cakes. As was the custom in the house, Lizzie waited until her father invited her to sit. Her mother, seated a little apart, continued with her sewing.

The captain came quickly to the point.

Lizzie could not take her eyes from him: he exuded power and authority, and something else which set her heart pounding. Was it fear, or was it something equally compelling?

'Sir Edwin,' said the captain, 'as you know, the King is now the prisoner of Parliament and resides at Hampton Court, but his children, that is to say with the exception of his eldest son now fled to France, are a matter of great concern. It is not the desire of Parliament to do anything other than is in their interests, and they are presently under the guardianship of their Graces, the Earl and Countess of Northumberland.'

'I am, of course, interested. But how is that a concern of ours?' Sir Edwin asked.

'The present earl is a man of vision and circumspection,' Captain Mildmay replied. 'He's taken up the Parliamentary cause in an attempt to bring about a compromise between the King and Parliament. A task, I fancy, which will be of little success, since the King can see no further than his divine right over his subjects.'

He continued, as he could see the three were eager to know in what way they were to be involved in the affairs of the earl and his charges.

'There are three of the King's children in our care: the young Henry Duke of Gloucester who is but six years old, his older brother James and his sister the Princess Elizabeth who is thirteen. The girl is sickly, and it is said she has the bone-bending disease so often seen in the children of the aristocracy. But for all that, she is a clever child and has a sweet temperament, and the little boy likewise. The elder boy has a will of his own and has, like as not, inherited the worst of both his parents in their intransigence. But it is the two younger children who miss their parents. The King for all his faults is a loving father.'

'It's a sorry tale and one which is repeated throughout the country in these troubled times. But the royal family are far removed from our lives here. Why are you telling us this?' Sir Edwin asked.

'What I come to ask is of you, Lady Elizabeth,' said the captain, fixing her with a steady look. 'You have proved your loyalty to Parliament, and I am inviting you to come to the household of the earl and countess and give these children the benefit of your gentle and wise council and daily care. The princess is sadly in need of a young friend and companion. I fear there is much more to bear, for the King is soon to give General Cromwell little choice but to take a step which will bring a stain on our nation for years to come.'

Lizzie's mother put down her sewing and Lizzie rose from her chair as the captain continued calmly. They both knew this was not an invitation, it was a command. He told them the children were soon to be conveyed to Syon House on the Thames at Chiswick, the magnificent home of the earl and countess. The plague had reappeared in London and the confined atmosphere of the Palace of Whitehall was no longer considered safe for the royal children. He went on to describe the household which would accompany the children, and the duties which would be expected of Lizzie. The more the captain elaborated, the more panic stricken she became. The idea of mixing with the royal family on such an intimate basis was

73

something almost beyond her imagination. On the one hand, it was an honour beyond anything she could have contemplated in her wildest dreams. But on the other, would she know how to conduct herself? Would she be treated as a lowly country girl? She wouldn't know how to speak to them. Her gowns would be laughed at. She would be beset with danger, and alone, without the familiar comforting support of her parents, from whom she had never been separated.

She saw her parents exchange glances. They betrayed no concern, more a sort of surprised delight.

Sir Edwin thought about the troubles that had overtaken the family and realized they had changed the accepted roles between father and daughter. Previously a decision of this kind would have been in the gift of the father, and Lizzie's views would hardly have featured at all. Girls were to be married off as soon as a reasonable settlement could be made, the money given to the father-in-law, who would undertake to look after the daughter-in-law in the event of his son's death with a 'jointure' or pension. One of the effects of the war was to erode the fortunes of families, and the 'jointure' would as often as not be unavailable. He felt sickened as he thought how what money he had put by was now long gone. He knew of many young women were left destitute for one reason or another.

To Lizzie's relief and the captain's evident surprise, he asked to be given time to talk to his wife, before the matter was discussed any further.

'My dear,' Sir Edwin said bluntly when he and his wife were alone. 'So many young men of her class and group have been killed the likelihood of a good marriage is fast receding. The offer from Captain Mildmay comes as manna from heaven. I've nothing left to offer for her jointure, and I cannot think she will find a husband among our neighbours so that we might keep the estates together as we have always done . . . No, Mary, this is an offer we cannot refuse, I am quite firm on the matter,' Sir Edwin attested.

'But, Edwin, we must ask Lizzie. There's something about this which puzzles me,' Mary pleaded, thinking this was so unlike Edwin. She feared already that Lizzie's fate was decided and she did not like Captain Mildmay, she did not think he was a man to be trusted. She was puzzled by the way he avoided her gaze, as if he believed she would see into his soul.

'Nonsense,' Sir Edwin said emphatically. 'Lizzie will have a chance to widen her horizons. She'll gain experience which would render her a valuable retainer for an aristocratic family if she were never to marry, as seems more and more likely.'

'I know you're right in some ways, Edwin, but this is so unexpected. There must be hundreds of young women who are grander and more able to do this than Lizzie,' Mary replied.

'All this is beside the point, my dear. Let's be grateful for this unexpected turn of events. Lizzie can't spend the rest of her life at the manor.'

'Why not? After all, it's her home,' Mary said.

'I can understand that you haven't allowed yourself to think about the future in these uncertain times but the time has come when we must,' said Sir Edwin. 'Let's pray that one of our sons will be spared, and will marry, and take on the manor, or what's left of it. And what then? At least,' he went on, 'it hasn't been sequestered as others have.'

'Thanks to our change of allegiance,' Mary pointed out sharply. 'You should put away that blue kerchief and hide the bows on your stockings,' she added, referring to the old telltale Cavalier signs.

Her words were not lost on her husband, as his sudden change of loyalties still pricked uneasily with his conscience.

'Yes, I suppose Lizzie would be a burden to a new wife,' Mary conceded reluctantly.

'Added to which,' said Sir Edwin, 'the likelihood of both of us surviving more than a few years after the children are grown up is slim and we won't always be here to offer them protection in this new terrible world.'

He realized as he spoke that he had grown to love his daughter in a way most untypical of the time, he would miss her sorely, but a chance like this would not come again.

When Lizzie came back to the room, he could see she was flushed and confused.

'Are you all right?' he asked, observing the furrow on her brow. 'Your mother and I have been talking this over. It's a wonderful opportunity, and although your mother has her doubts, on this occasion I do not agree with her.'

'Dear Edwin, let Lizzie speak for herself. We don't know

75

this man Mildmay. Things may not be so simple as they seem. Tell us, Lizzie, how do you feel about this?' Mary asked, gesturing to Lizzie to sit down.

Lizzie stared at the floor, aware that she had been lead into a trap of her own making, her path had been decided the moment she met the worldly challenges that Captain Mildmay brought with him. There was something about Captain Mildmay which she found increasingly unnerving. She didn't know how she would put these things to her father, but put them she must.

'My dear daughter,' Sir Edwin responded ambivalently, 'these are a young girl's fancies. I saw nothing in his demeanour which conveyed anything of the kind. This offer will open up a new world to you.'

Sir Edwin continued in similar vein and it was obvious to Lizzie that argument was futile. In any case, although her head told her to be cautious, her heart raced towards the excitement of what life had brought to her when she least expected it. She could not forget the turn of Captain Mildmay's mouth when he first saw her, and the compelling message in his eyes. But for all that, Lizzie knew in a deep animal way that she would need all her wits about her. The captain was probably not the knight in shining armour her father believed him to be.

A few days later the matter was settled, and Lizzie set about packing her boxes and saying her goodbyes. Her gowns were shabby and unfashionable, but her mother did her best to reassure her.

'Why concern yourself, daughter? The lavish ways of the court are no longer the order. I'm told even the grandest ladies are now in their puritan gowns.' Even as her mother said the words, Lizzie knew the truth would probably be very different.

Mary gave Lizzie some money she had put by to commission a new gown when she arrived at her new home and a little more besides, for a good pair of boots and a shawl.

Despite her growing sense of anticipation, Lizzie's heart sank at the prospect of not seeing her family for many months. These were uncertain times. Travelling was difficult and dangerous. The hundred or so miles between Kent and Syon were a long journey, maybe several days by coach. She would have to treasure every last moment of the life she loved, for she knew in her heart it would soon be gone. She would no longer be a simple squire's daughter, but what exactly would she be? She did not know, but she would make the very best of it, whatever it was.

PART TWO

Syon House 1647

Ten

The old Roman road from Kent to London was in bad repair and full of potholes, and the constant swaying of the coach made Lizzie feel sick. They struggled through driving rain and soon the wheels were stuck in thick gluttonous mud.

'Everyone out,' said the driver, when the straining horses failed to move it. Along with the other occupants, a middle-aged couple going to see their daughter in London, Lizzie alighted to find the mud up to the steps. 'Let me give you a hand,' said the driver, lifting her lightly on to a grassy verge. 'Come on, lad, down with the bags. We won't move this lot in a hurry,' he called to his companion. Sacks were placed under the wheels and Lizzie and the other passengers waited miserably in the rain until finally, with a crack of the driver's whip on the exhausted animals' sodden flanks, and with an almighty lurch, the vehicle was free.

As soon as the bags were secured they were off at a brisk trot, but nothing seemed to have escaped the quagmire. The hem of Lizzie's best gown was ringed with mud and most of the bags were filthy. Inside the coach it was increasingly cold and draughty as one of the leather flaps above the door had come off in the commotion. A drop in temperature whipped the rain into hailstones which drove like bullets and found their way inside despite the coachman's makeshift repairs.

The first night they stopped at a wayside inn, where the chamber pots had not been emptied. Lizzie failed to get any sleep on account of the fleas which hopped merrily about in the soiled bed she had to share with another female traveller, who, to Lizzie's astonishment, informed her she had a nice slice of meat tucked into her corsets to deflect the bugs. Far into the night she listened to the sound of bawdy songs coming through the thin layer of wood between her and the ale house below as she thought with trepidation about the adventure awaiting her.

When they arrived in London early the following evening Captain Mildmay had arranged for a coach to take her the rest of the way to Syon. She was welcomed by a steward, who introduced her to the housekeeper, who showed her to her room where all she could think of was sleep. She sank into clean sweet-smelling sheets with a sigh of relief.

She met the countess the following morning in the Long Gallery. Unaccustomed to such grandiose surroundings, Lizzie plucked nervously at her gown. She had done her best to brush it down, but she knew she must look unkempt and tired. As she rose from a deep curtsey, the countess held out a welcoming hand. She was exquisitely dressed in a grey satin gown with lace trimmings and a velvet morning cap.

At once she put Lizzie at her ease although she remained seated at an ornate desk covered with papers.

Lizzie did not accept the offer of a chair but preferred to remain standing as she would have done in her own mother's parlour. It was not the custom for a young woman to sit in the presence of an older person of such high rank. However, to her surprise, the countess insisted and finally Lizzie did as she was asked. She tried to avoid staring at the countess, for she was the most elegant person she had ever seen. She had skin like marble and long delicate fingers covered in rings, as many as two or three on each finger. Lizzie was intrigued by her painted lips and her pale powdered skin. She thought of her own rough hands and tried to hide them in the folds of her skirt. She knew her nose was red and shiny, and feared she might sneeze. She had definitely caught a cold on the uncomfortable journey.

'Now, Elizabeth, I must tell you what is expected of you here,' the countess said in a gentle, beautifully modulated voice. 'You have come at a sad time, my dear, and I fear you will be much pressed by the task you have in front of you.'

She waited expectantly. It was obvious she wanted Lizzie to make some comment.

'I shall do my best, your Ladyship,' she stammered nervously.

'But I know little of the ways in London. I have never left Kent in my life before.'

'No matter, my dear,' the countess said reassuringly. 'Captain Mildmay says you have experience with your younger sisters and are indeed well versed in all matters domestic.'

'That's true. You see, my mother has been very ill, and as my brothers were away and I was the eldest living at home, a lot fell to my shoulders,' Lizzie replied.

'Well, I hope your mother can manage without you,' the countess said.

'Oh yes, she is recovered now . . . And—'

The countess stopped her in mid-sentence, holding up a delicate hand and waving a small lace handkerchief. 'More to the point, you are well educated,' she declared. 'In fact remarkably so, and this is important.'

Lizzie nodded and the countess continued. 'As you know, my dear, we are responsible for three of the King's children. The elder brother, James, does not concern you for he has a separate establishment. The youngest, the Princess Elizabeth, and Henry the Duke of Gloucester, will be in your care. They have been terribly disturbed by the last few months of their lives. The King's court was not a suitable place for young children. You might well ask how their mother chose to abandon them while she tried to raise an army abroad to butcher her husband's subjects . . .' The countess's voice shook with emotion, and Lizzie felt stupid and ill informed. She was sorry she didn't know more of the exact circumstances which had put the children in such an awful situation.

The countess liked the girl. She knew enough about human nature to make a good assessment of character. She decided Lizzie was just what the younger children needed but she would not elaborate on what she considered to be the disgraceful behaviour of the children's mother. The girl would hear enough gossip to make up her own mind.

'Enough of that,' she continued briskly. 'We do not want to dwell on this sad state of affairs. The earl and I wish to give the children as normal a life as possible in these tragic circumstances. But I must warn you, my dear, that worse is to come. They will find life hard to bear as they are exceedingly attached to their father.'

Lizzie caught the innuendo, a shadow crossed her face, and the countess saw she had understood. She invited Lizzie to ask as many questions as she liked before she met the children.

'But first,' she said, 'you're to meet Mrs Briott who is the children's servant. She is in charge of all domestic matters. She's been with the children throughout all their troubles. She'll tell you all you need to know.'

The countess rang a small silver bell on her writing table and a manservant, elaborately dressed in a blue uniform, entered the room and bowed. The countess asked for Mrs Briott to be sent for and then returned to her work at the desk, telling Lizzie to be seated at the opposite end of the room.

Lizzie sat on a brocade chair at the side of the long room. There was a row of these chairs of a design and type she had never seen before, with delicate legs and rounded upholstered backs. Lizzie felt small and insignificant in such grandeur, and wished she had worn her high-heeled boots for the occasion. As the minutes ticked on the countess seemed to have forgotten she was there, and she began to take it all in.

Behind the row of chairs was a panelled wall on which hung many portraits in a style which took her breath away. The intricate detail and vibrant colours brought the sitters to life as if they might step out into the room at any moment.

The wainskirtings, doors and windows were intricately carved and gilded. There were more of the gilt leather and damask hangings similar to the ones Lizzie had seen on the grand staircase. Two huge coal burning fireplaces warmed the room, the surrounds intricately carved and inlaid with marble. Beside them were highly decorated face screens on slender pedestal legs.

To Lizzie the vastness and perfection of her surroundings were more sumptuous than she had expected. Even the smooth wooden floor seemed like highly polished glass, as it reflected the dazzling morning sun slightly tinged from the bright green of the parkland outside.

The windows were set low enough for Lizzie to get a good view over the park with sweeping swards of grass such as she had never seen, since most Tudor houses had constricting terraces and steps.

The countess broke the silence. 'I see you're looking at the gardens, my dear. They are of great interest. A hundred years ago the owner, the great botanist Dr Turner, Physician to the Lord Protector the Duke of Somerset, laid out the first botanical garden here. The ninth earl redesigned the gardens from his prison in the Tower of London, where he languished for seventeen years for his part in the Gunpowder Plot.'

She had put down her pen and, spreading some sand from a china shaker, she blew on the wet ink and placed it in her blotter when the sudden arrival of Judith Briott put Lizzie in more familiar territory. She was a woman comfortable with her middle age yet still attractive. She had a wholesome round face and dressed simply, her hair plainly wound under a flattering white lace cap. She inspired trust and confidence.

After a cursory introduction, Mrs Briott led the way to the children's quarters. 'I am married to the son of the King's silversmith,' she replied to Lizzie's polite enquiries. 'A Frenchman who came over with the Queen,' she added proudly.

'So he knows the King well,' said Lizzie.

'He gained the King's friendship and trust,' said Mrs Briott proudly. 'And that is why I have care of the children. It is a great honour, but I have had to undertake to give up my husband's Catholic faith as part of the conditions imposed upon me by Parliament, if I am to retain my position with the children,' Mrs Briott replied ruefully.

'I am sorry,' said Lizzie slowly. 'We all suffer from divided loyalties.'

'Let us not talk of such things,' said Mrs Briott quickly. 'There are more practical matters to be discussed.'

She apologized to Lizzie about the neglected state of the children's affairs. It was, she said, as a result of the many changes Parliament made in the appointment of their retinue. Servants never stayed long, and those who would be loyal were constantly under the threat of dismissal for some triviality which offended General Cromwell or his mouthpiece Captain Mildmay.

'There are three different establishments – one for each child,' she informed Lizzie. 'But now the idea is to combine the princess's and the duke's. Parliament is less than forthcoming in reimbursing the earl for the great expenditure involved. Some servants have gone without pay and are beginning to get restless,' she added.

Lizzie detected a wariness, as if the older woman did not yet know exactly where Lizzie's loyalties lay. Mrs Briott told her of the heightened security for the two children after an attempted escape by their brother James, and warned Lizzie that she would be watched.

'The poor children, it must be awful to be separated from the people you love. I already miss my own family,' said Lizzie.

'Then, my dear, you will understand that all the children's prayers are that they be reunited with their brother and sister in Holland and that the Queen will join them there, although it would grieve them to leave their father whom they love very much,' said Mrs Briott, placing a reassuring hand lightly on Lizzie's sleeve.

'And why is this not possible?' Lizzie asked. 'Surely the children are no threat to Parliament since the eldest son has already fled?'

'Parliament thinks they're useful pawns,' Mrs Briott said disgustedly. 'But they should have learned the King is an obstinate man, and Parliament plays cat and mouse with the King's heart. He loves his children and when he is able to see them they must be a great comfort to him, but he knows they would be better off with the rest of the family and out of danger ... nothing will change his resolve,' she added. 'He will see it all through to the bitter end, whatever that may be.'

'The Queen must be desperate,' Lizzie probed carefully. 'It seems unbearable for a mother not to be with her family.'

Mrs Briott thought for a moment. 'Don't believe the things you may have been told. She's been sorely tried,' she said slowly. 'She loved her children dearly. But I fear she was too meddlesome in affairs of state. When she fled, she took the crown jewels ... thinking she would raise an army and return to save the King and the children ... but all the returning she ever did was to cost her dear, for she gave birth to another child in Exeter.'

'Yes, I think I remember that. Where's the child now?' Lizzie asked.

'She had to leave it there,' Mrs Briott shrugged. 'But they say, after all this time, the poor mite has arrived in France, smuggled there by her faithful Scottish governess. And they all live off the French King's charity.'

'But what about all the money for the jewels?' Lizzie enquired.

'Oh, all the jewel money went to naught . . . She was tricked and deceived, but no more than she had deceived others, I dare say. Desperate circumstances breed desperate remedies,' said Mrs Briott, shaking her head.

'It's terrible,' said Lizzie angrily. 'When I think of my own parents, I can hardly believe it. My mother would never have abandoned us.'

'We mustn't judge her, my dear. It's difficult to imagine what goes through the minds of royalty. One thing I've learned is they're not like other people. In some ways, she *is* a loving mother. She wept for days when God took her little daughter Anne some eight years ago. And some say nothing went well for the family after that,' she signed. 'I've seen happier times. Before the troubles, you couldn't have imagined a more devoted family. I cry bitter tears at night when I think of how they've all been scattered to the four winds. I love those children as my own.'

Lizzie could see that Mrs Briott was devoted to the children and had cleverly maintained a healthy impartiality in the affairs of Parliament versus Crown in order to retain her position. She never asked Lizzie any leading questions but she had no need to. Lizzie's credentials had been carefully vetted and Captain Mildmay had satisfied Parliament as to her suitability.

Soon they moved on to practical matters. Lizzie found out how to address her new charges, and what the daily routine would be.

'The young prince likes to play bowls,' Mrs Briott told Lizzie proudly. 'And he excels at archery and tennis.'

'And have they been able to continue their studies despite all the upheavals?' asked Lizzie.

'Oh, yes,' replied Mrs Briott decidedly. 'The children have

a regular routine of tutors and instructions. The little princess is fluent in the philosophers and Latin and Greek and has a knowledge of theology.'

'She sounds extremely clever,' said Lizzie.

'She is,' Mrs Briott laughed. 'Her knowledge exceeds that of the house clergyman who takes prayers in the family chapel three times daily. Her first instructress was the celebrated Mrs Bathushua Makins who taught her to study the Bible in its original Hebrew. When she was but five years of age she was reputed to have said, "I'd rather be a beggar than not go to heaven." She's a girl wise beyond her years,' Mrs Briott explained. 'In her short life she's never had the luxury of childhood. If you can help her through the tragedy – which will surely come – you'll have done well, my dear. We shall work together.'

As if she were immensely tired, she sighed again, then put a hand on Lizzie's and gave it a little squeeze. Lizzie noticed a tear hastily brushed from her kindly face, and her heart warmed to Judith Briott. She was glad the royal children had such a true friend, because she was rapidly becoming aware that this was the before the storm.

'I'll do everything I can,' Lizzie reassured her.

The girl was small for her age with very white, almost translucent skin and pale honey hair which sprang in pretty ringlets from her lace cap. Her dark eyes drooped slightly at the corners and her cheeks were curiously full, contrasting with the slightness of her build and giving her a somewhat disdainful expression, which Lizzie was soon to find belied her true nature. She held the hand of her little brother who, although seven years her junior, was already up to her shoulder. The boy stood back, clearly indicating his sister's dominant role. The sibling likeness struck Lizzie at once, not so much in their features, but in the frank and intelligent brightness of their faces. Lizzie curtsied to the little princess, who extended a pale limp hand, which Lizzie took delicately in her own. The child smiled at her, and her face immediately lightened. A little spaniel frisked at her feet. It had a blue bow on a collar covered in silver bells which tinkled merrily as it moved.

'This is Minette named after our youngest sister whom we have never seen,' the princess said, leaning down to pat the little dog. 'My father His Majesty has a little spaniel very much like her, called Rogue, because he is so naughty. I would like Minette to have puppies, and she is unofficially betrothed to Rogue . . . Do you like dogs?'

'Why, yes, I do,' Lizzie replied. 'But we don't have any small dogs in my family. My favourite animals are horses. I have a mare called Snowdrop. She was born when the first flowers were in bloom on a very cold March night.'

'That is good, then we have a lot in common . . . We already have something else in common,' the princess said brightly. 'We have the same given name.'

Lizzie noticed that she spoke with the faintest trace of a continental accent, a reminder, she supposed, of her mother's origins, as she was the sister of the King of France, and it was said had never lost her strong foreign accent.

'Your Highness, with your permission, I should like to be called Lizzie, or even Lizzie Anne, as I am at home,' said Lizzie.

'Well, that is good,' the young duke piped. 'I, for my part, would be called Harry, for I understand you are to be our companion in all things, and therefore I would have you as a friend, and I shall call you Lizzie. It is lucky I call my sister Beth, so we shall not get muddled.'

The boy looked over her shoulder and she heard footsteps. She turned, tripping as she did so. A hand came, steadying her arm. She raised her eyes and found them fixed in the bright gaze of a young man of about twenty. Her heart gave a lurch; she could not look away, for he had the brightest blue eyes she had ever seen. He was handsome in a courtly way, unlike the country squires' sons she had danced with on feast days. He wore doublet and breeches of dark blue and his fair hair shone with vigour. The morning sun had come round to the south-east window of the room and caught him in an orb of light.

In Lizzie's heart there was a silence, as if time had stood still for just one moment. It was one of those rare occasions of complete and absolute inexplicable happiness: she would remember it in the dark days that were to follow. Because of the way he looked and the way he looked at her, it was the first time in her life she had ever felt beautiful.

When she thought about it later that day, she couldn't work out what his eyes had said. It was a reflection of her, a new beautiful independent Lizzie.

'May I present our tutor, Sir Richard Lovell, a kinsman of the countess,' Beth said. 'You will see a good deal of him, for he is our dearest friend. He teaches us everything except music. But no matter, for I do not care for it much, and have no talent for the keyboard.'

'But you, my Lady.' The young man turned to Lizzie. 'Do you have skills in that direction? Her Grace tells me so, and we all want to hear you play. The earl and countess have a fine instrument in the music room, built in the newest style,' Richard said.

'I play the harp, and the dulcima,' said Lizzie eagerly. 'But I gather there's a fine harpsichord here which has the same principal of hitting the strings with sticks.'

'And what do you like to play?' Richard asked.

'My father and brother Philip are very taken with the madrigals of Mr Dowland, and we used to sing them in our family chapel . . . But such things are now banned in the local parish church. They are now a sin against God,' Lizzie replied.

'You see, Richard. Even beautiful music cannot be given to God as a tribute,' Beth said, lifting the little dog and kissing it on the nose. 'I think,' she continued, 'God will tire of the dismal offerings from the so-called Puritans. I for one will look forward to some musical instruction from you, Lizzie, for in this I am very deficient. I have spent so much time at my books, which my father His Majesty says accounts for my headaches.'

Young Harry had been looking eagerly at the park through the tall casement windows during this conversation. The spring gales had left a scattering of blossom and leaves and some of them blustered against the glass.

'It is not that,' Harry said firmly. 'It is because you do not venture out into the open air enough. Sir Richard, I would like to go with you into the park this morning.'

'A fine idea, let's all go,' Richard agreed enthusiastically, looking directly at Lizzie.

'That is settled then,' Harry said. 'I am very excited,' he continued. 'The earl has fitted a new archery board for us and I would like to show you, Lizzie . . . That and my falcons. For it will surely rain again. And we must take this opportunity while the weather is so good.' He looked at his sister with concern and Lizzie saw the smile which passed between them, and thought to herself how touching his consideration for his sister was. He was so young and yet he took it upon himself to be the guardian of her welfare.

He turned to Lizzie. 'And soon His Majesty my father will come and visit us from Hampton Court. He has promised to bring me a new bow.' Harry flushed with excitement.

'Oh, that will be a happy time,' Lizzie said encouragingly.

'It should be, but it is always spoilt by all the guards and spies and Papa's sad face,' Beth interrupted.

'Yes, whatever they say,' Harry added, 'he is treated as a prisoner. Our every word is recorded and repeated.'

'Oh dear. But I expect you find a secret way of talking? I know my sisters and I have a special language,' said Lizzie.

'Oh yes. You're right,' Harry cried. 'My sister and I have a lot of fun with it, especially with Captain Mildmay. We tricked him beautifully the other day when my elder brother James nearly escaped.'

'I hoped he would be made the fool by it and stripped of his rank,' Beth said. 'He does not deserve the rank of a gentleman, since he would twirl with the wind like the turn-coat he is.'

Lizzie's mind raced. She was going to see the King with her own eyes, but what the children said about the captain showed him to be a dangerous man, something she had instinctively felt, but had not been able to admit to herself. She did not hear Beth scold her brother and caution him for his unwise words or see the expression in Richard Lovell's eyes as the captain's name was mentioned. And she did not see the shadowy figure which moved the curtains in the corner of the room, or hear the creak of the boards on the stair as they set off to find their outdoor clothes for a trip into the park. She was too much aware of the presence of Richard Lovell.

Eleven

A week later saw a great improvement in the weather. Lizzie delighted as the ornamental gardens in the park burst into life. Tulips of every variety opened their faces to the spring sunshine. How Lizzie wished her mother could have seen them. Some were striped and flecked with astonishing combinations of colours, with feathery petals, that looked like the finest silks.

She was beginning to feel more at ease with her surroundings, and one morning while the children were at their lessons she decided to take the princess's little dog Minette for a turn in the gardens. Approaching one of the long walks, she could make out the tall figure of a young man silhouetted against the strong morning sunlight. Her heart gave a lurch when she realized it was Richard Lovell. He did not see her at first as he was engrossed in reading a letter. Lizzie considered turning back in case he should feel her presence might be contrived, but it was too late. He saw her and quickly hastened his step towards her.

'This is an unexpected pleasure,' he said, smiling broadly and removing his small feathered hat and sweeping her a bow.

'Isn't it a beautiful morning? I thought I would give Minette a little walk,' said Lizzie.

'Would you do me the honour of letting me accompany you both?' asked Richard with a broad mile.

'Why yes,' Lizzie agreed, trying not to reveal her enthusiasm. 'And perhaps you could tell me something about the gardens. At home our gardens are so much more closed in, I love all this grass. I have never seen it cut like this before, it looks like velvet.'

'And you will never see the men who tend it for they get at it with the cutting machines the moment the sun begins to rise,' Richard explained.

'Where do they all the plants come from?' asked Lizzie. 'There are so many.'

'Well, that is a story in itself,' said Richard. 'The Duke of Buckingham, the Royal favourite, travelled the world collecting rare plants for the King and many of them ended up here as gifts to the earl.'

'I read in one of my father's pamphlets that the duke was murdered for the price of some of his tulip bulbs as each bulb was worth many thousands of pounds . . . Is it true?' asked Lizzie excitedly.

'In a way I suppose,' replied Richard. 'But there were a lot of reasons why he could have been killed. He made many enemies. And he was extravagant. For example, on one visit to the French court he contrived to have pearls sown lightly to his garments in order that they could scatter about him as he walked.'

'Well, I for one would not have hesitated to pick them up,' Lizzie laughed.

They walked on in silence for a moment, Lizzie glowing with happiness. As they turned into a long rose-walk bordered with low box hedges, the sun behind them, she saw their shadows precede them and the movement of his arm towards hers as they came to some steps. She felt his touch as he took her elbow and she glanced up at him to thank him. For a second their eyes met and their gaze held before she felt she must look away.

'Minette,' she called hastily, turning to look for the little dog.

'Sir Richard, I must go inside now, for I have things to do with the children's clothes which have been much neglected.'

'The next time we meet I will tell you about the house. It is known as the White House, because of the distinctive white stone which was brought from Dunstable. The old house was not so beautiful as this. It was the earl's father who put in the casement windows and the battlements and leaded the roof,' Richard called as she turned from him to walk up the steps. She had the delightful feeling that he wished to detain her, and was on the point of staying a while, for the stories of the house were a pleasant excuse for remaining in his company, when she saw the figure of a man watching them intently from one of the windows near the countess's apartments.

Richard's eyes followed her gaze and he too saw the figure, it did not move but stayed still and purposeful as if delivering some sort of warning message.

'I must go, but I will see you later today for we are to play bowls with the children,' Richard said pointedly, his head turning challengingly towards the window. He bowed abruptly and was gone.

As Lizzie returned to the children's quarters, determined to concentrate on the tasks before her, she mused on the fact that, despite the luxury of the house with its lavish furnishings, life here was in many ways less agreeable than in her own home. There, at least, attention was given to hygiene. Her father had installed latrines which fed into the moat from where the effluent was carried away into the river, but at Syon no such convenience was apparent. On her first day she saw one of the countess's waiting-women relieving herself in a fireplace. She had covered her nose with her handkerchief and averted her gaze, but very soon realized that in a household where fleets of servants performed the intimate tasks for their masters there was nothing unusual in this.

She had been appalled by the state of the royal children's clothes and undergarments when she arrived and as she sorted through the young princess's chemises now, she thought how Ruth would have tut-tutted at such things.

She discovered that Beth had started her monthly visitors and no clean white cloths had been used. Her underskirts were stained and foul. Lizzie summoned the laundry maid and told her to take all the children's linen for boiling in lye. 'We have none, begging your pardon,' the girl replied pertly. Lizzie demanded to be escorted to the laundry to see for herself. She found plenty, but it had not been used for her charges' clothes. She boxed the girl's ears for her laziness and reminded her to return them sprinkled with lavender from the herbery.

Lizzie also found meal times a forbidding affair. Apart from breakfast which the children had served in their quarters, meals were eaten in a dining room with the family and retainers. The earl's family and the royal children sat at a high table set on a dais with a long table looking towards it. They had a substantial meal at midday, off porcelain plates, with silver forks and spoons and delicate Venetian glass, some of it poised on brass feet, in a contrast to the manor where each person had their own bowl and silver-mounted drinking horn and knife to spear the meat. Lizzie watched carefully to see how these new things were used and looked around for the customary cloth to wipe her hands and clean her teeth. She soon realized that in these circles ablutions of this kind were carried out, if at all, in the privacy of the chamber.

The royal children had little brushes for cleaning their teeth which they dipped in salt. Lizzie acquired one for herself from the house store, a room replenished by travelling salesmen. Mrs Briott had insisted she take a brush when she admired the children's.

Lizzie was beginning to see that her new life had brought many challenges and she would need her wits about her to decide what was good and what was bad, but one thing was sure and she thought about it as she dropped off to sleep later that night: she must proceed with caution with Richard Lovell lest her heart began to cloud her judgement. Her guard must be up.

The next day the young children were unusually excited. Their father would arrive by boat from Hampton Court and alight at the landing stage by the house, but that morning the princess awoke with a pain in her side. Lizzie went early to the kitchen and instructed the under-cook responsible for the children's food in the art of tansy, made with eggs and breadcrumbs and cream and berries. She took it to Beth herself.

'Oh, thank you, Lizzie, I hope I feel better later on because I want to look my best for father or I know he will worry about me,' said Beth gratefully.

Lizzie was concerned: the child looked paler than ever, her long hair hanging loosely from her night cap and blue circles under her eyes.

'Your Highness,' said Lizzie, 'you must not go out in the cold to meet His Majesty. Stay awhile in your warm bed that you may look better for your father and not cause him worry.

When the sun has burned the mist off the river, the air will be warmer, and this sharp breeze will have stopped.'

The child's big eyes followed her about the room as she prepared the elaborate clothes for the day. Today she was to wear a grey satin gown with a small train hung from the shoulders. The skirt was caught up at the side to show a Brussels lace petticoat and two pairs of stockings edged with ribbon. There was a lace pinafore which Lizzie thought very pretty, but, as to the gown, the neck was cut away in a style which she considered more suitable for a grown lady of fashion.

'I have found a little lace scarf which might serve to keep you warm in the draughty corridors,' said Lizzie.

'Oh, how pretty,' said Beth, holding the lace up to the light.

'Well, your hands certainly won't get cold,' Lizzie joked. 'Mrs Briott says you are to wear three pairs of gauntlet gloves on top of each other to keep them white and soft.'

'I'm always cold, Lizzie,' said Beth plaintively.

'There are so many corridors here and one room leads into another, but at least there are more than a dozen men feeding the fires,' said Lizzie. 'I will bring you some of your books.'

Beth settled happily back on her pillows, saying a silent prayer of thanks for whoever it was who had sent her Lizzie.

'What is Henry to wear today?' Beth asked. 'You know how particular Father is about such matters and he likes to be proud of us.'

'You can rest assured there will never be a prouder father,' Lizzie replied quickly. 'Today Harry will wear a winter baize cloak edged with squirrel over an ash-coloured satin suit, with double hose stockings, silk garters, a taffeta ruff and his sword fastened with a green scarf.'

'Perfect,' said Beth, settling down happily with Minette beside her.

On the way to Henry's apartments Lizzie had to go to the linen room where she met the housekeeper, Mrs Bounty.

'And how are you finding it?' asked Mrs Bounty.

'The children are delightful, and I already love them,' said Lizzie. 'They are both so open and friendly.'

'Well, Lady Elizabeth, there is the true aristocracy for you. His Majesty is the same,' Mrs Bounty replied. 'You will see for yourself, he has no airs and graces. All his subjects are as one in the eyes of God and the King.'

'So how can the Puritans have a complaint about him?' Lizzie asked.

'There's many a Puritan who could learn a lesson from him. Them so high and mighty in their mad hats poking at heaven. They'll be turned away from there, when the day comes.'

Lizzie was alarmed by such careless talk in the Percy household.

'We must be careful what we say,' said Lizzie guardedly. 'Some people here make me feel uneasy, they don't all seem to have the children's interests at heart.'

Mrs Bounty laughed and put a friendly arm about Lizzie's shoulder.

'Girl, this is one place where you can speak your mind for no one can hear in this room. You've much to learn about what goes on in this house, and many others like it. But I'll tell you, they all have their snouts in the trough. It warms my heart that one such as you should have come to help those poor mites.'

'The princess looks very frail, but she's always smiling and courteous. I can't understand how anyone could fail to love her or little Harry.'

'Oh yes, there're some cruel people about. It breaks my heart to see how brave they are. I can't see a happy end to it all. But we must pray.'

'But surely there are many who are touched by their predicament?'

Mrs Bounty stopped and thought for a moment, biting her lip, as if there was something she would say which bothered her.

'You're a sensible girl, Lizzie,' she declared. 'I like you, and seeing as how you're the same age as my own daughter, whom God saw fit to take from me with the scarletina, I'll warn you of something, so you may best be prepared for it.'

'I'd be obliged to you, because I know very little about the ways of the people here,' Lizzie said.

'Beware of Captain Mildmay,' Mrs Bounty whispered. 'I'm told he brought you here. It's his responsibility to choose the royal servants to Parliament's satisfaction.'

Lizzie looked at her steadily. 'Please tell me,' She said. 'I'm nervous of him, but he's been very good to me . . . and my family. But there is something about him which . . .' she faltered in mid-sentence looking awkwardly at the floor.

'He's not to be trusted . . .' Mrs Bounty went on huskily. 'And his brother, Sir Henry, is a worse villain.'

Lizzie felt herself going pale. Mrs Bounty was an honest woman, she was sure of that, and as she spoke about Captain Mildmay, her face became suffused with anger. Lizzie was horrified. She felt sick to her stomach. There had been no mistake. She had found the captain compelling and intriguing, and, after all, he had come out of the blue and changed her life for ever. This change might have a price. She did not want Mrs Bounty to see how much she was affected by her cautionary remarks, so she continued the conversation as casually as she could.

'Is his brother a soldier as well?' she asked.

'No. He was Master of the King's jewel house,' Mrs Bounty replied. 'And there are many who'd like to know why he and his family suddenly live like royalty. Contrive not to be alone with the captain. That's all I'll say to you.'

'I'm bewildered by people,' Lizzie said, suddenly on the verge of tears. 'Everywhere I look there's conspiracy. How can a person ever trust anyone?'

'Well, you know you've a friend in Mrs Bounty, for it's those little ones I care for. And it's good to see the little princess being coddled as she should be, and by a young woman who's the sense she was born with – and no stranger to the kitchen and the laundry, with a knowledge of the still room, who can give the poor child the herbs and cures which may ease her sufferings a little. There's not many round here that'll get their hands dirty with a pestle and mortar.'

'I'll do my best. I think of my own sisters and how they're affected by what has happened. The King's children have been through so much, it's hard to imagine.'

'The captain has done us a service bringing you, though I doubt his motives,' Mrs Bounty went on as Lizzie gave an involuntary shiver. 'But the Lord moves in mysterious ways,' she said finally.

Later that morning Lizzie stood in an arched window looking

towards the river. Beth was standing on a stool to get a better view. Harry and his brother James had gone ahead to greet their father on the landing jetty.

Beth could hardly contain her joy. 'We have not seen Papa for over a month, but I have all his letters here in my purse. I am never parted from them,' she confided, just as the barge carrying the King rounded the bend in the river. 'There he is,' she cried.

Lizzie could just make out a group of people alighting from the barge. The group began to advance up the slope to the house.

As they drew closer she distinguished the King, young Harry walking beside him holding his hand, and the older boy James walked confidently in front of them. To her surprise, the King was much the smallest in the group, but his bearing was slow and majestic, and the magnificence of his clothes – red velvet breeches and satin jacket heavily ruffed at the neck, a blue silk sash and a kind of velvet cape trimmed with fur hanging curiously over one shoulder – marked him out. His hat was a magnificent concoction of feathers, some of which contrived to hang behind him, and he had long ringlets worn shorter on one side. The absence of a sword also singled him out from the rest. He used a kind of swaggering stick to walk with, which Lizzie had never seen before. About his feet a little black and white spaniel frisked, until he scooped it up in his arms and kissed it full on the nose just as the princess had done with Minette.

Lizzie was also fascinated by the thick waxed make-up and heavily rouged cheeks of some of the court ladies and gentlemen.

Downstairs in the stone-flagged entrance hall, the countess stood with her family and many people Lizzie had not seen before. There was a strong smell of gardenia from trees standing in china pots at the bottom of the staircase, but even these could not disguise the smell of so many people gathered together. Some had nosegays and pomanders hanging from ribbons.

She saw the King looking anxiously about, and then he caught sight of his daughter. His face broke into a large smile. Beth went running to him as the crowd parted to let her through.

She swept him a deep curtsey. The joy on his face made an indelible impression on Lizzie, and while she was thinking on it, she heard Beth calling her name, this time so loudly that it echoed about the room. Heads turned in her direction and she saw the countess signalling for her to approach. She felt herself colouring as she so often did, and with beating heart she walked, head down in respect, to meet the King.

Every notion she had developed about the mendacity of the King was dispelled at the moment when he looked at her and their eyes met. Here was no ogre but a kindly and gracious man, beloved of his children, and with a chivalrous concern for the welfare of someone as insignificant as Elizabeth Anne Jones.

'How grateful we are to you for leaving your family to care for my beloved children,' the King said, looking her full in the eye. 'My son the Duke of Gloucester has already talked of you as if you are old friends. He tells me you play well and can read music. I look forward to seeing you again, my dear, when we will play the children's favourite game of indoor bowls in the Long Gallery.'

Lizzie thought she heard a mocking titter from the crowd at the King's natural and kind manner with a servant. And she was right. The King had heard it too, and a flicker of resigned pain crossed his features.

'The weather is not good enough for the princess to venture out of doors,' he continued, in such a friendly way as if it were her own father talking, that Lizzie forgot to be nervous at all. 'She feels the cold and the house is near the water, which is not good for her,' he continued.

Lizzie nodded and curtsied, smiling sweetly. She knew, if she spoke, her words would sound awkward and she would be scoffed at.

'Make sure the princess takes her medicine which has been sent from France by the Queen,' he went on.

'I have done so, Your Majesty,' she heard herself say in a high nervous voice.

'Good. It is prepared by King Louis' own apothecaries. His Majesty, her uncle, is concerned for his niece's health,' he explained loudly. The room became silent as he spoke to Lizzie. However much people abused the King in his absence, when he mentioned powerful relatives abroad, he certainly inspired attention. The royal approval still counted for something.

Lizzie's was delighted when the next moment on older boy, to whom she had not yet been introduced, swept her an elaborate bow and complimented her on her popularity with his younger brother. 'He does not usually like any of his servants,' he said lightly. 'But he thinks you are a great improvement on the last ones.' She noticed how bright blue the boy's eyes were and wondered why they differed so much from the younger children.

At noon, the great dining hall was set for a meal and she was placed down the table, with the other governesses and some of the family's waiting-women. Richard was seated further up the table and she watched him chatting with one of the guests, a young woman of fashion, clearly one of the Percy relatives. She felt a stab of envy as she saw the ease with which they laughed and talked. She remembered their walk together, the way he took her arm and the way his face lightened into a smile when he saw her, and she tried to stop her hopes running away with her. Realistically she knew he had moved in these circles for most of his life, he was part of this in a way she knew she never could be. She had been taught to look modestly downwards, not to drink too much ale or make loud conversation, or indeed laugh as this young woman was doing. Her thoughts and observations were rudely interrupted by a hand on her shoulder. Looking upwards, she found herself in the steely gaze of Captain Mildmay.

'Madam,' he said, 'it is good to see you so well settled, and I would speak with you tomorrow, before I leave with the King's party, for there is something I have to say to you.'

'Can you not say it now?' she asked bravely, relieved that her neighbours were not paying attention to the conversation, for it took little to set tongues wagging in this strange place.

'Pray, do me the honour of awaiting me in the Orchid House,' he said formally, ignoring her suggestion. 'Before the princess and the duke are up at about, say, seven.'

He did not wait for her answer. He swept her a bow and proceeded to his place at the high end of the table, but she felt his eyes upon her.

Twelve

Before dressing to meet the captain in the Orchid House, Lizzie washed her face and hands in scented rose water left in a ewer beside her bed. As she slipped into her chemise, Mrs Bounty's warning words, 'Don't be alone with him,' rang in her ears. However, the captain had been instrumental in her new life with the royal children. He was a rich and powerful man, he was obviously trusted by Parliament or he would not have charge of the royal children. How could he be the charlatan Mrs Bounty said he was? Surely he would protect her? After all, he was an officer and had a position to uphold. She had to admit she did find him compellingly attractive, she felt flattered and excited by the assignation, but in her bones she knew she was flirting with danger and must be careful. This was unknown territory for her. She had never been alone with a man in these circumstances before. Besides, since she had met Richard Lovell some new kind of romantic dream had begun to form in her mind, quite different from the initial feelings aroused in her when Captain Mildmay burst into her life. It did not have the frisson of danger and the heady sweetness of power, redolent with something dark and forbidden. Richard Lovell brought with him sunlight and reassurance; he fitted naturally into Lizzie's scheme of things.

She took the precaution of asking one of the housemaids, Margaret, with whom she had become friendly, to accompany her and remain at a discreet distance during the encounter.

A sweet citrus smell filled the gallery where she was to meet the captain with an almost cloying scent, as adjacent to the Orchid House was a small orangery, where the earl grew prized and unusual fruit, a fashion inspired by the King's favourite, the Duke of Buckingham, to impress the King of Spain.

'The place gives me the shivers,' Margaret hissed at Lizzie. 'The wicked Duke of Buckingham, who helped the earl make this place, was murdered, you know . . . and it's said his ghost comes here to haunt, and the fruit can make a young girl forget her modesty.' The girl's eyes widened alarmingly. 'I shall be right there, my Lady, with the poker.'

Lizzie thought of the dark deed which led to the duke's infamous demise and trembled slightly. She made her way down the stairs to the hall. The household was already busy, warmth and cooking smells wafted up the spiral stairs which led to the basement kitchens.

Margaret followed at a distance, well-trained in the art of being invisible in a household where privacy was well nigh impossible.

He was standing looking out at the park as she arrived. He heard the sweep of her gown on the stone floor and turned. She curtsied, and he came to her conveying an intimacy she did not return. He gestured towards an S-shaped seat designed for two, securing a closeness which put her on her guard.

'So how do you like the kissing-seat, my dear?' he asked, as he leaned back on his elbow, looking at her averted profile.

'I'm sure I do not have experience of such things, and with your permission, I would feel more comfortable seated where we can talk in a more businesslike manner,' Lizzie replied, with just enough haughtiness.

Upon the captain this had no effect whatever. He had stalked and secured his prey. A little resistance made the kill all the more exciting.

'Surely, my dear, you're aware of my interest in you. You are foolish enough to think it's only business, as you put it.' He pondered for a moment, a finger to his chin as if in thought, and then continued, edging closer, 'Although it's true. There is a matter I must discuss with you, and I will proceed without further ado.'

'Please. Wait while I move,' Lizzie said, making as if to rise from the seat.

But the captain moved quickly and with some force put a restraining hand on her arm and prevented her.

'Be so good as to remain where you are,' he said slowly. 'For it is the warmest spot in the place, and it sharpens the intoxicating fragrance of the orchids. They are so pure and virgin white, just waiting to be plucked, fresh with morning dew.' The meaning of his words was quite apparent to Lizzie. He held on to her arm, looked steadily into her eyes, his body exuding lust and desire.

She looked down, her heart beginning to pound as he continued: 'You see, it's near the earl's furnace, which heats this remarkable house where winter is turned to summer.'

'What has this got to do with what you need to say to me?' Lizzie gasped at last, the nearness of his body beginning to engulf her.

'It's a favourite meeting place for lovers, and my heart fills with warmth and desire, Lizzie, when I see your lovely young innocent face.'

'I didn't come here to talk of such things,' Lizzie said, barely able to conceal the tremor in her voice. 'Indeed, I should not have come at all . . .' She faltered. Her palms were damp and she pressed them into her knees to steady her shaking hands. 'You should reserve such matters for other ladies, who might be more receptive,' Lizzie went on bravely, wishing she could have tossed his attentions aside more lightly.

'Ah, but it is your face which shines out among the painted tawdries who call themselves ladies of fashion. Surely you must know how you have affected me, Lizzie?'

'Don't talk like that,' she cried.

'Why not, my beauty? The first moment I saw you coming down the staircase at your father's house, I knew you were destined for higher things.'

'I'm not your beauty. I'm not anyone's beauty,' she exclaimed spiritedly.

'Don't toy with me, madam. Why d'you think your family has been spared a Parliamentary sequestering? Why d'you think you find yourself in this place where many a young woman would dream of being?'

'I'm sorry, sir, if I've misunderstood the reason for my being here,' Lizzie said coldly.

'But it's your beauty, Lizzie, that has brought you here and saved your family,' the captain continued, unabashed. 'You must know it and it is a powerful weapon . . . so why not use it wisely?' he coaxed. 'And listen to what I have to say.' He put his arm about her shoulders and pulled her towards him. The movement took her completely by surprise.

Lizzie had never felt a man's lips upon hers, and when he pressed his upon her own, for a moment she closed her eyes with a feeling the world was spinning. His breath was all over her face. She felt her own body responding, as she fought against her natural desires with every sensible thought in her head. Her body tingled and then in a flash she imagined that instead of the captain's flushed, hard, demanding face that of Richard Lovell's was next to her own.

This was all wrong. No man should behave like this to a young woman for whom he should feel responsibility. He was insulting her by his behaviour, and she whom he had put in a position of great importance. Richard Lovell would never have abused her in this way, he would have been courtly and respectful.

She opened her eyes and heard Mrs Bounty's voice in the back of her head. Every fibre in her body rebelled against the nearness of the captain's body . . . the defilement of his mouth upon hers.

She heard a rustle amongst the leaves and knew Margaret was not far away. She stood up angrily and faced the captain.

'Sir, I must ask you to respect the frailty of my position. If you have brought me here away from the protection of my family to press some sort of illicit suit, you are to be disappointed.'

'Don't be a fool. You don't know what I can do for you.'

'I would not trade the simple life at Hatherton Manor for all the grandeur in the world. I would defile my home and family if I were to lose my good name.'

'I think you're mistaken. Your father liked me.'

'If you were an honourable man, you would have pressed your suit through my father. But you've misled him, as you've done me.'

'Well, madam, you've not lost your spark in the hot house of the aristocracy,' the captain sneered. 'For the moment at least . . . I won't speak of this again,' he said menacingly. 'I'll give you time to come to your senses, let you absorb some of the ways of the world in which you find yourself.'

'I'll never, never disgrace my family. All I have is my honour, sir. And you will never take that from me . . . Do you hear me?'

The captain ignored her remarks in a way which made his conduct all the more insulting and patronizing, as if she had no will of her own, and he had no doubt that she would ultimately succumb.

'Now I must come to the business I spoke of,' he said, for all the world as if the last few minutes had never happened.

'Pray do, sir,' Lizzie said formally, smoothing her skirt, and edging a little towards the doorway, 'for I must go to the princess with her breakfast and attend to her, as she is unwell.' Lizzie did not know how she could recover her composure after such an assault to her dignity and her status. But she had her job to do. She would try to rise above the captain's conduct. Maybe now she had rebuffed him, he would leave her alone. But one thing was certain, her feelings towards him had been irrevocably damaged. He was no longer her glamorous protector, with whom she could allow the faintest of flirtations. He was a dangerous man who wanted something from her, something which as she thought about it became more and more abhorrent.

The captain rose from the seat and his face clouded a little. His mouth was set and his eyes were cold and calculating. Although he was trying to conceal it, Lizzie knew he was seriously put out by her rebuff. She tried to control her breathing. She felt very afraid and wished she could run away. But she knew the captain had unfinished business and he would not let her go until he had said his piece.

'I will come to the point. You have an important position, besides your obvious charms, an asset which you will one day reconsider in the world you are now in. You have access to all the royal children's secrets.'

'Do not go on. I cannot believe what you are saying,' Lizzie gasped.

'Come down from your high horse, madam . . . you know the King is not to be trusted, and the children are cut from the same tree. We cannot have another escape. We know the King has his spies even here, and Parliament would have you keep a watchful eye and inform us of news which would be of interest. I must say you are quite exasperating.'

106

'Sir.' Lizzie rounded her voice, sending it to each corner of the room. 'I will answer only to my own conscience and so it will report to God. I will not spy on the two children, whom you have seen fit to place in the care of the earl and countess; and further . . . if my presence here is contingent on my doing the "devil's work", much as it would grieve me to leave the children and this place, when I have seen how much I can do for them, I shall.'

'And where will that get you?' he mocked.

'Perhaps the satisfaction of telling the world what kind of man you are . . . Yes, I will tell the earl and countess the reason.'

'Do you think they will think much of it?' he asked casually.

'I am sure from what I have seen of them, they are people of honour and would spit in the eye of anyone who played such dirty games with two vulnerable children. Goodness knows, they need friends they can trust to comfort them in their loneliness, separated from all their loved ones.'

'You are too dramatic, my dear,' the captain said coolly. 'They're well enough and should be quite happy here at Syon, with all the care lavished upon them.'

'That's wicked nonsense, sir,' Lizzie rounded. 'Why, the little princess tells me that she's asked to go to her sister Mary in the Hague where she may enjoy the company of her brothers and sisters and see her mother the Queen, but Parliament has refused.'

'Don't you think they are better near their father, who loves them, as you say?'

'No, sir. She knows full well that her father puts their welfare above his own, and would gladly lose the one thing which comforts him in his imprisonment. I now see the loving father he is, which confounds the reputation put about that he's a monster. Yet Parliament would keep these three innocent children as hostages, so that they may be traded like cattle, and you're no better than any of them.'

'Parliament is doing what is both expedient and right,' the captain interceded hastily.

'So much for all your high moral tone,' Lizzie cried. 'Sir, I've not seen the hand of God in this, but rather the fist of greed, for I dare say there're some who profit very nicely from the theft of the Royal possessions and the continued imprisonment of the King's children.'

'I don't think the Puritan ethic is one of greed, madam. And you should be more careful in what you say,' the captain said darkly.

'Not so, sir,' Lizzie returned angrily. 'I hear your so-called Puritans live like lords . . . off the lands . . . stolen . . . from families who've worked for generations to provide employment and shelter and food for their people, as indeed my own father has done.'

The captain made as if to speak and then gestured for her to go on, as if resigned to her outburst while not attaching any importance to it.

'I'll have none of it, sir,' Lizzie went on, ignoring his patronizing attitude. 'I believe there's nothing that matters other than the distinction between good and evil . . .' She hesitated a moment. 'And from the latter I will turn as I turn now, if you will be so good as to excuse me.'

And so saying, Lizzie swept the captain a curtsey and left the room, with the swishing of her skirts and the patter of Margaret's feet as she slipped from her corner behind the orange trees.

Lizzie heard the captain's voice as he called after her, and in it she detected not only mockery but hurt male pride. He would be vengeful, she knew that, and her heart fluttered with resolute fear. She had surprised herself with her own ferocity, but she had no regret, for she knew she could not approach her two young charges with honour, had she not spoken for them.

'You'll change, Lizzie,' he called after her. 'For no one's as incorruptible as you believe. Your words ring clearly in the security of this house . . . but they won't always do so. There's much more to come. You'll need a protector and I shall be there.'

Lizzie did not turn or acknowledge his words. She did not want to betray the emotion in her face. She kept her step and her resolve.

The captain watched her slim waist as she walked from the room, he thought she looked like a lily, pure and undefiled like her words. He was all the more thrilled with the challenge he felt to possess her purity. He contemplated the satisfaction he would experience, taking her into the garden of lust he had known with so many others. It made him giddy with anticipation.

He was, after all, a man who was not to be trifled with. He would have Elizabeth Anne Jones, and when he had vanquished her, he would be her master and she would dance to his tune, until he tired of her and passed her on to someone else.

And then, with a start, he realized that this young woman, a simple country squire's daughter, had stood up to his advances with a ferocity he had never seen in his other conquests. This made the prize all the more tantalizing. His heart thudded in his chest, whether from desire or anger he didn't know. But to the captain it was at any rate something new. For a moment he wondered if part of the challenge might not be to leave her as pure as she was. But then he remembered the way Richard Lovell had looked into her eyes and he thought not. Yes, he would have Elizabeth Jones.

Thirteen

Lizzie sat in the countess's pergola, sewing quietly while the children were on the bowling green. More than a month had passed since she had been alone with Richard Lovell but the contact was daily, mostly in the afternoons when the children played outside or when he joined her as she played and sang with Beth. Try as she might, however, she could not interpret his feelings and constantly asked herself if they were more than friendship. She was also plagued by feelings of homesickness which came in waves and overwhelmed her. Today they were particularly strong, as she smelled the fresh grass and a delicate scattering of blossom from the magnificent late climbing roses. They reminded her of her mother's garden. It was several weeks since she had had word of the family. She understood it was sometimes difficult: the roads had been impassable with unexpected heavy rains. As she resolved to ask the countess if she could have a week before the winter to go home to see her parents, she felt something brush her hair.

'You have petals in your hair. They suit you,' came a voice she recognized.

She looked up. It was Richard, looking down on her with an expression which made her feel at one with the joy of the warm day.

'Thank you,' Lizzie replied breathlessly, wishing her emotions were not always so plain for all to see. She knew she blushed whenever Richard was near her.

'Lizzie, may I sit here with you for a moment, for there is something I must say to you,' he asked.

'Of course. You look rather grave. I hope it is not bad news, nothing about Harry or Beth, I hope,' Lizzie said anxiously.

'No, it's a worry I have about you.'

'Me, why me? I'm in good spirits. I am looking forward to the move to Petworth, the children will benefit, even though they'll miss their father. They tell me they love the house. And I know the air will be better. There's talk of the plague again in London.'

'We are all looking forward to it, the duke's house in Sussex away from the damp of the river will be a pleasant change, and besides, Syon is filthy after a season's use. It will be so well cleaned when we return that you will not recognize it. They even restuff all the mattresses,' said Richard with a laugh. 'But I need to talk to you about something very delicate,' he added anxiously. 'There's been talk in the servants' quarters.'

'It's not like you to take notice of servants' tittle-tattle. Why should it concern me?' asked Lizzie.

'I'm glad that's how I am perceived,' said Richard. 'But, truthfully, I have to make it my business to hear all the gossip, for a reason which I may soon have to share with you. But on this occasion it was you, Lizzie, who was the subject.'

'I, Richard, how can that be?' Lizzie frowned. 'I'm nothing to them. Just another servant, however much I thought differently about my station before I came here.'

110

'You're wrong, Lizzie,' Richard said firmly. 'The improvement in the children's spirits and the princess's health have been noticed since you came. There are many among us who are more concerned for them than they would have known. For there are spies everywhere, as you know. Which is why I'm talking to you here, where no one can hear us.'

'Richard, I wish you would tell me what's troubling you so,' Lizzie rounded.

'It's about Captain Mildmay,' said Richard forcefully. 'And I am not going to mince my words.'

'Why? What's he got to do with me, sir?' Lizzie asked cautiously. 'It's true he suggested this position to my father, but I can assure you there's an end to it.'

'I'm relieved to hear it, Lizzie,' said Richard quietly. 'The story is,' he went on, 'he's been pursuing you and was seen making advances to you in the Orchid House. You've already earned the good opinion of people here. It's not seemly for a young woman to be alone with one such as the captain. There are things you in your innocence may not know.'

'Sir,' Lizzie exclaimed. 'I'm not the simpleton you think. Captain Mildmay can expect no friendship or anything else from me. And I'm surprised that your informants didn't tell you that.'

'But you were alone with him,' Richard insisted.

'I wasn't alone with the captain,' Lizzie rounded in high dudgeon. 'I was well aware of the danger he put me in by requesting an interview in such a way. I took one of the princess's servants, Margaret, to hide amongst the plants, and listen to the whole thing, and come to my assistance if needs be. I didn't like the captain's manner, but I'm also aware of the power he might wield and . . .' Lizzie faltered a moment. She looked at Richard and hoped she was not mistaken in her instinct, that she could at last trust someone. Her hands lay in her lap and she fiddled nervously with some petals from the roses.

'Lizzie, there's a lot about Captain Mildmay you should know,' said Richard slowly. 'For a start he's a married man, and I do not doubt that he's been paying you attentions which his state should prevent. But that has not stood in his way before, and he has in the past dishonoured a young serving woman. She fought for her honour and he overcame her. It's said that she died in childbed, alone and cast out by her family. And the captain would not own the wickedness of his deeds and denied them to his wife.'

As Lizzie digested what Richard was telling her, she thought she was going to be sick. She felt such a fool. It had never occurred to her that the captain was married. It made his advances all the more repellent to her. Perhaps, if she were really honest with herself, she would admit she had never had any doubt that he would have no compunction about dishonouring her . . . but to betray his wife as well.

'Oh, Richard, what am I to do?' replied Lizzie desperately. 'Nobody told me he was married. There has never been any mention of a Mrs Mildmay, not that it should make any difference to me,' she added hastily.

'No, Lizzie. He keeps his wife somewhere in the country. She never comes to Syon. Men of his type behave like this. It is not uncommon in court circles for a man to have a mistress and a wife. But then he's a man of some mystery. No one knows what his exact position is in the hierarchy.' He paused before he continued, because he could see Lizzie was very upset. She started to cry.

'All around us is evil,' she sobbed. 'I don't know what to think any more. Who will save me if he has the same plan for me? I'm all alone here with no one to turn to . . . it's exactly as I told Father it would be. No, it's worse because I've grown to care so for the children . . . and the King is not the monster he's been painted . . . the new order seems worse than anything *he* ever did. At least people had freedom. Now everyone's afraid. I must pack my boxes and leave at once.'

'Lizzie, I'll do all I can to protect you from this evil man,' said Richard gravely. 'I can well understand how difficult all this is for you, but you must not let this turn you away from the children. They need you, we need you.'

Lizzie's heart was pounding. She didn't quite know what to read into Richard's words. Why should he be taking so much trouble with her? But as she turned to face him, there could be no mistaking his feelings. He took one of her hands and raised it to his lips. She wished the garden were empty and that he could sweep her in his arms and that she could tell the sky and the trees about her feelings. It was as if the universe exploded into a million stars. She loved him more than she had thought she could love anything in the world, even more than she had loved Tom, her brother. Her lips trembled as she tried to think of something to say, but the words would not come. It seemed unreal and for a moment she wondered what she had done to deserve such simple reassuring happiness. But even now there was a certain poignancy which held her back.

Lizzie stood looking at him. She felt as if her whole life had been poised waiting for this moment. Soon he would kiss her as the captain had tried to do, but it would be, oh, so different. She would not fight him with every breath in her body. She would yield to his advances because she knew he was a man of honour and she could love him without fear. And yet he had chosen his words so carefully . . . the word friendship . . . She would have preferred another word. The moment had not come and she was right to be cautious: he was trying to tell her something, something she would not like.

'What is it?' Lizzie asked.

'I am betrothed to someone I do not love and can never love, Lady Jane Buckley. It was arranged by our families a long time ago. She has great wealth and comes from a powerful Parliamentary family. It breaks my heart, but I can only offer you the love of a brother, because anything more would defile the affection you must know that I feel for you.'

Lizzie stared at him aghast, and drew away. So many things raced through her mind. She knew he had feelings for her and that inescapably she returned them. They both knew it as lovers do: she had thought it needed no words. But now, it was a forbidden love at the very moment when she had found it. She could tell by the anguish on Richard's face that he was also in turmoil. She suddenly remembered seeing Richard at the banquet on the day of the King's arrival, the girl he had been talking to in such an easy way. She felt a fleeting comfort when she recalled her sharp angular face and sallow fashionable skin, and thought how Richard had complimented her on her fresh country complexion. His voice interrupted her thoughts.

'Lizzie, I will do all I can to protect and honour you . . .' Richard was in mid-sentence when Harry came running across the green.

'Lizzie, my sister has won for the first time ever,' he cried, glowing with happiness, for he worried constantly about his sister's health. 'It is because she feels so much better and all because of you, Lizzie,' he went on, rushing up and hugging her.

The princess followed him, wreathed in smiles, her skirts hooked up on two buttons that Lizzie had sewn on to the hem.

'Your invention made a world of difference, Lizzie, and no gloves, so I could hold the bowl properly.' The princess laughed. Lizzie looked at Beth and realized she was growing up fast. She seemed more confident in herself, and even though Lizzie felt emotionally drained, the children's happiness temporarily recovered her spirits. At least she had brought a little joy back into the children's lives. The little princess had dropped her formal mode of address and called her by her name.

She knew also that, despite all, Richard Lovell would always be her friend whatever life held for them both, of that at least she was sure.

'So, Prince Harry, you can take on your sister and now you can take me on as well. I will give you a run like your brother James does,' said Richard brightly, taking off his velvet coat and handing it to Lizzie to hold. He strode across the green with Harry. As they walked away, he turned and smiled at her.

As Beth sat down on the seat next to Lizzie and started chatting, Lizzie cradled the coat as she watched Richard's lithe figure on the bowling green. Suddenly it fell a little open, revealing the inner lining and pockets and something caught her eye. A piece of silk in deep blue, embroidered with a white Cavalier plume. She quickly covered it with her hand but not before Beth had noticed it.

'So Lizzie, now you know something about our tutor which could put his head on the block. I saw you together, and I know now that our secret is safe with you and we can be friends.'

'Your Highness,' Lizzie said. 'I've always been your friend and I've learned a great deal in the last few weeks. I've no secrets from you and will always be there to help you.'

'Oh, I thank God for sending you to us, dear Lizzie,' Beth said. 'But we must never speak of this in the house or anywhere except in the open. They would deprive us of both him and you, if they thought you were anything but an ordinary servant, and he just a tutor with no interest in affairs of state. So guard our secret well, Lizzie, for we may have things to ask you.'

The child's open face looked up at her, suddenly pale and anxious, and in a spontaneous gesture, Lizzie put her arms about her thin body and hugged her.

'I will do my humble best, you poor child, for I love my father as you do yours, and seeing you and the way you protect your little brother . . .' she said resolutely, feeling Beth's head against her cheek. She gently pushed the child away a little, so that she could look her in the eyes. 'I pledge you, on my honour,' Lizzie said reassuringly. 'I will do all I can to stay with you, however much I may have to dissemble in order to achieve this. I want you to know I do believe it is God's work that I have been brought here. I did not want it, but I obeyed my father and that obedience has brought me friendship when I least expected it.'

'Do you mean Richard?' Beth asked. 'It's a pity he is promised to Lady Jane. They do not love each other, you know,' she said disarmingly.

Lizzie was completely taken aback. She knew exactly what Beth was about to say to her, and she put her finger softly to the child's lips.

'Don't say any more, Your Highness. Let's talk of other things,' she said gently.

'I know you don't want me to say any more . . . but I want you to be happy, Lizzie, for I need you so . . . you see . . . it's not over yet. I can sense bad things are about to happen, worse than before. All I want is for my brother and me to be reunited with our family, and I know father's conscience will never permit him to bend to the demands of his enemies.' She began to cry. 'Although I dream of us all together with Mother and James and Charles and Mary and our little baby sister Minette . . . it will not happen.'

'You must keep faith,' said Lizzie encouragingly. 'We will

115

pray together in the chapel this very evening, you for your father and I for my brothers, Tom and Philip. We will ask God to care for them.'

Richard and Henry had finished their game of bowls. The boy hooted with pleasure and came running back.

'This time I won,' he cried. 'I beat Richard. I shall write and tell Father, and soon I will be able to take on my brother Charles when we go to the Hague.'

Fourteen

The move to Petworth did not, after all, bring the hoped for visit to Lizzie's parents. Shortly after their arrival at the house, where young Harry made the very best of the fine Sussex air, Beth was confined to her bed.

The child had been ailing for a few days when she complained of pain in her stomach. The local doctors were called, bleeding and rest were prescribed. 'Above all,' they cautioned, 'she must not venture outside into the sunlight.'

How Lizzie wished she could have the freedom to order the sick room as she had done during her mother's long illness.

After a week or two she realized all hope of going home must be abandoned, she could not leave the child. This was additionally hard as the strain of seeing Richard on a day-to-day basis was almost more than she could bear.

'Lizzie, what is the matter?' asked Mrs Briott one morning. 'The princess being so ill is bad enough. But you, girl, looking as if you were sickening for something, is not helping her. I'm not a fool. You are not yourself, and it is my business in the interests of the princess to know why . . . Are you ill?'

Lizzie realized the time had come when she must confide in Mrs Briott. She had grown to love the woman. She could not keep her secret any longer.

'I have a sickness of the heart,' she explained tentatively.

'The heart, my dear? I suppose you mean Sir Richard. I'm not blind you know, I thought as much.'

'Well, what am I to do? He is promised to another woman ... I love him so very much in spite of myself and I know he feels the same things for me ... but ...'

'But nothing, my dear. The matter is simple,' said Mrs Briott decidedly. 'You must put him out of your mind and for that he must be out of sight. I had already decided that Harry should go back to Syon Park. He misses his visits from his father and contact with his brother James and it is not good for him to be forever hovering about the sick room. Sir Richard will be told of this when I have spoken with her Ladyship.'

Lizzie looked dejectedly at Mrs Briott and, whilst agreeing with her good sense, she longed to try to explain how, even out of sight, Richard would still be there each minute of her day and in each moment of her dreams.

Mrs Briott saw the look in her eyes and softened.

'I, too, have been young, you know, Lizzie,' she said sympathetically. 'I know how you feel. You will recover, you have your life in front of you. The only cure for an old love is a new love. You must think of little Beth. She has not got a long life in front of her and it is my duty to see that she is protected from any more sadness.'

Lizzie suddenly felt ashamed. Mrs Briott was right, she must pull herself together. Perhaps she could go home for Christmas? If Richard went away things would be easier.

Mrs Briott patted her hand reassuringly.

October passed and by the end of the month Beth began to improve. Life had become increasingly monotonous at Petworth without the company of most of the household who had returned to Syon. At the end of November Captain Mildmay arrived.

Lizzie knew he would seek her out. It was a bitter November afternoon and Beth was sleeping. Lizzie waited in a large window looking out on to the park. The room was warm, a fire burned and the first candles had been lit. On a round table in the window stood a circle of greenery and berries she and Beth had made that morning ready to receive the first advent candle.

117

'I hope I find you well,' said Captain Mildmay, as he was shown to the room by one of the maids.

Deprived of Richard's presence for so long, Lizzie was even more aware of the captain's powerful presence as he stood confidently on the threshold.

'May I come in?' he enquired with surprising deference.

'Please do,' Lizzie answered politely, hoping he did not see how, against her better nature, she was almost pleased to see him.

He did not hesitate but came straight to her, as if sensing a change in her.

'My dear, I have some news for you,' he said seriously. 'Before I tell, you please come and sit with me, I don't think you will find this easy.'

She seemed to detect a genuine concern. For a moment she succumbed blindly to a need for the comforting maleness of his presence.

'Yes, come closer to the fire,' she answered, gesturing to a high-backed seat. He joined her and as they sat he took her hand. Lizzie did not withdraw it, something which did not escape the captain's notice.

'I'll come to the point,' he said, stroking her wrist and letting his fingers stray just slightly under her velvet cuff.

'The King has escaped from Hampton Court.'

Lizzie gasped and a smile lit up her face.

'No, my dear,' he continued. 'That's not the end of it. He fled to the Isle of Wight, thinking the Island would protect him. But this was not the case and he has been imprisoned at Carisbrooke Castle.'

Lizzie paled.

'There, my dear Lizzie, think of me as your friend,' he said soothingly. He put both his arms about her and drew her towards him. Her face was turned to him, her eyes closed. He slowly pressed his lips to hers. For some reason she would never quite understand, she allowed him to kiss her.

Her whole body cried out in loneliness and sadness. She could not stop herself although every bit of her mind told her to draw away from him.

It was Mrs Briott who saved her from the reality.

'Ah, Captain Mildmay,' she said calmly. 'I have heard the

news. I'm sure you have told Elizabeth Anne. May I ask you to now withdraw for we have the awful task of telling Her Royal Highness. If you will excuse us.'

She curtsied to him and gestured to the door.

'Lizzie, that will not do,' she said when he had left the room. 'I shall not mention this again. The captain is a dangerous man. I will not reprove you because I know how unhappy you are and how well you have disguised it for Beth's sake. But I will not stand by and see you ruined. Promise me you will never give in to that man.'

Lizzie felt the strong firm gaze from the older woman and prayed to God to forgive her for her weakness.

'I feel so ashamed,' she said faintly.

'Don't feel ashamed, Lizzie, you are only human. Remember, we must be very still and watchful, like animals when they sense danger. This is terrible news we have to tell our little Beth. Satan makes his best sport of challenging the good people in this world, and you, Lizzie, are a fine girl, I know that.'

That night Lizzie prayed harder than she had done for many years as she held little Beth. In her anguish she knew she had been tested.

Fifteen

It was a beautiful day when the coach drew up at the manor gates. The countess had insisted she did not go by public packhorse since the roads were dangerous with wandering bands of deserters and highwaymen. She had been allocated one of the many vehicles which were used to transport the family's retinue in their numerous migrations and it bore the earl's arms on each side. It had attracted a good deal of interest on the way. She asked the driver to wait for the gates to be opened by the lodge keeper.

'It will be a long wait, my Lady, for the lodge is empty, and no smoke comes from the chimney,' he remarked.

Lizzie saw Jacob come running down the drive, his leather helmet flying off, revealing his mutilated ears. She saw the coachman tactfully avert his gaze. She gave him a sovereign, taking her bag. She would alight here, as she wanted to savour the walk up the drive under the chestnut candles.

Jacob bowed and took her bag, barely able to conceal his delight at seeing her again.

Grass and cow parsley grew high either side of the track which in turn was unkempt with potholes and weeds.

'What's happened to the lodge keeper?' she asked. There was a pause while Jacob looked awkwardly at his boots.

'I may as well tell you, my Lady, you'll find things changed, and not for the better. His Lordship has to work with the men now, and your Lady mother must do her share in the wash house with your sisters. For there is hardly enough money to support the men who must work on the land to feed us, let alone for indoor servants and things are going from bad to worse.'

'This is all strange to me. Now I see why my family have not given me much news,' Lizzie said.

'But we're all happy in our way,' said Jacob hastily. 'We all do as we must. I've given up my political activities. I do whatever I can for Sir Edwin. I don't ask to be paid much. It's enough for Jenny and me that we've a roof over our heads and food for the baby.'

'Oh, Jacob, of course your baby. I'm so glad. Is it a boy or a girl?' asked Lizzie delightedly.

'A little girl just like my mother Nan, God save us,' Jacob said. 'And we're all in good health . . . but when you think of some poor souls not far from here. Sir Edwin with his kind heart would take them all in if he was given a chance, but we rebelled at that.' He stopped short as Lizzie gave him a penetrating look.

'What do you mean?' she asked sharply.

'Ah, I suppose you wouldn't know, my Lady, being away. But Squire Molyneux's, the house was burned to the ground by Parliamentary troops, and the land taken by Cromwell's men, and the tenants evicted. The squire is in prison in London.'

120

Lizzie crossed herself and bit her lip and gulped back her tears.

'Their homes are wrecked and they can't go back,' Jacob said. 'Sir Edwin let anyone who was related to people here come and live with their families on the manor, but he saw the sense in drawing the line. We can only just manage as it is.'

They continued up the drive in silence. Lizzie's mind raced as she put together the significance of the terrible news. The fact that Hatherton had been spared raised the spectre of Captain Mildmay and dulled the beautiful summery day.

There could be little doubt that he had put in a good word for them, even though many families had turned to Parliament for the sake of their lands, and in some cases to save their lives. It was not always enough to keep them from the same fate as those who were loyal to the King, a thing now punishable by death. Jacob broke the silence.

'My Lady, will you pardon me for offering an opinion,' he volunteered respectfully. 'It is one shared by us all at the manor,' he added hastily.

'Of course, Jacob,' she said. 'You must say what you please, but my heart is heavy when it should be joyful. I don't know what to think any more.'

'We all thank God, my Lady, that Sir Edwin saw fit to change his allegiance, and save our livelihoods,' Jacob went on falteringly. 'And no matter what he really feels; for they are all as bad as each other, and not one of them cares about the common man and his bread. But I know Sir Edwin does, you see, now I have a family, my Lady . . . All we want is peace and enough food to feed our families and a roof over our heads.'

'I'm sure, Jacob, as long as my father has breath in his body, he'll look after all of you as best he can,' Lizzie replied, patting Jacob's hand.

'I know it, my Lady. There has never been a better family than the Jones of Hatherton, and God is with them,' said Jacob emotionally.

Lizzie found her parents dramatically aged but Ruth hadn't changed, and her sisters looked well enough. The new baby

Emily was walking and Lizzie could not rest for cuddling her and marvelling at her brightness. Her sisters had grown inches and overwhelmed her with questions about her grand life with the royal children. Their faces fell in disappointment when Lizzie explained that her life was not one of grand parties and gatherings, but was rather of quiet domesticity such as they had at home. But they were impressed by the stories of all the servants who did the various jobs.

The house was in need of repairs, but flowers adorned the chest in the great hall and the copper and brass fenders shone brightly. The furniture was waxed and shining and there were roses in the urns on the forecourt as there had always been. She drew a deep breath of satisfaction to see that it took more than a civil war to bring the manor to its knees.

After the initial joy at being home again, she began to under-stand the reasons why her father was finding it increasingly difficult to keep the manor going. The rift with his sons had made him additionally miserable.

'With such bad blood between father and sons,' he confided to Lizzie on the first evening of her arrival, 'I can no longer see a future for Hatherton . . . my whole life has been devoted to protecting the family estates and now there is no certainty of anything. It seems as if your mother and I will have worked for nothing,' he went on sadly, with his head in his hands. Before she could comment, he got up and wound his special lantern clock of which he had always been very proud.

'I hope this wonderful thing will record some better times, Lizzie,' he said plaintively.

Lizzie saw how his hair had thinned and how calloused his hands were. He had been working on the estate instead of at his books, and she could imagine how he missed them.

'How's your translation of Galileo, Father?' she asked, hoping to turn the conversation to something more pleasing for him.

He shook his head wearily. 'I've not looked at it for many months,' he replied dejectedly.

She did her best to comfort him. She told him how she had met the King, how devoted she had become to the royal chil-dren, and how duplicitous the so-called Parliamentarians were.

'I must admit,' she said sadly, 'I fear there may be a complete abolition of the monarchy, and Parliament may fail to bring the country to a successful compromise with the King, because ultimately it's not their wish or desire.'

'Daughter, you're right,' said Sir Edwin. 'And you've changed from a young girl into a wise woman. But it grieves me you're having such a rude introduction to the world outside the manor. Life shouldn't be like this.'

'Don't worry, Father . . . I shall survive,' Lizzie assured him.

'I am sure of it, my dear . . . but, tell me, what of the King?' Sir Edwin asked in a low voice.

'The King has made a trap for himself and there doesn't seem to be a way out,' said Lizzie truthfully.

Sir Edwin had become very agitated.

'I am so ashamed of my conduct. I have betrayed him,' he bellowed dramatically.

Lizzie stopped him in his tracks. 'Father,' she declared, 'if I've learned anything in my time in the world of politics and intrigue which surrounds the people I now live with, it's not to wear your heart on your sleeve like some ignorant servant. You must learn to keep your opinions to yourself, because to lose all now will remove you from a position of power. One day the monarchy will be restored, and will need people like us. We must hang on to what we have, whatever it takes.'

Sir Edwin appeared to be deep in thought, considering what she had said, and then he clamped his fist to his head.

'Daughter, there's some news I've forgotten to tell you. Little Emily is to have a playmate.'

'Oh, no. Surely no, Father . . . remember poor Mother. She nearly died last time she . . .' Lizzie cried out in alarm, before she could stop herself. But her Father cut her short with a laugh.

'No, my dear, not that. Do you remember Sir Francis and Lady Hinton?' he asked.

'Why, yes, Father. But they left their home a long time ago to live in Scotland, didn't they?' Lizzie answered vaguely.

'Yes, they did,' said Sir Edwin. 'You're quite right. I don't suppose you could have been more than eight or so when you last saw them. Poor Francis, he's a fine man, no better on this earth I would say, and he has suffered a grievous loss. His dear wife passed away last month. She died giving birth to a son, but alas the child did not survive. He has two small daughters – it is very difficult for him. But as if that were not enough, he must leave his estates in Scotland. The situation has become intolerable for him, since his wife's family have always opposed the Presbyterians. He's coming back to Hinton with his children, and your mother is to have them here.'

Lizzie's first thought was 'more mouths to feed', but suddenly she recalled Harry and Beth without a mother, and to all intents and purposes a father, and her heart went out to Sir Francis Hinton's children.

'How good you and Mother are,' Lizzie said. 'When are they to arrive?' she asked, hoping it might be before she had to return to Petworth.

'I have word from Sir Francis that they left Scotland a few weeks ago. But it is a long and fraught journey. Your mother has the nursery ready.'

'How is Sir Francis's house? Who has been looking after it all this time?' she asked.

'Well, Sir Francis has at least been lucky in that respect, my dear,' Sir Edwin reassured her. 'For the house has escaped relatively unharmed, although the steward he has left in charge is a ruffian. Not a hand has been lifted for many a year to clean the cobwebs or chase away the mice, but Sir Francis, although not a political man, is now in sympathy with the Parliamentary cause. He is a clever man, my dear, and seeks to negotiate all things which might lead to a peaceful solution. I think he will be in London a great deal when he gets back to England and will not have time to set his house in order. He will need a new wife to do that for him,' said Sir Francis emphatically.

As she tried to get to sleep that night, Lizzie thought about Lady Hinton who must be so swiftly replaced, even though she was hardly cold in her grave. She had not taken much note of her parents' friends since she had been in the school room on the occasions they had visited. She had a vague recollection of comments on what a fine couple they made, and what a love match it was. They had been a loss to the neighbourhood, when they had left to go to Lady Hinton's family estates in Scotland. She also remembered that Sir Francis was an active participant in negotiations which had taken place across the border when the King had sought to strike a bargain with the Scots.

Eventually she fell asleep and dreamed she was a mother and had a score of daughters. Their faces were unclear. It was a troubling dream which left her puzzled and concerned.

When Lizzie awoke it was a perfect day and she made up her mind to get out on to the estate as soon as possible.

She rose early, looking forward to seeing Snowdrop and her new foal. She had thought of her so often and this was something she had anticipated with great joy, but she arrived at the stables to find them strangely silent. With horror she realized all the stalls were empty.

She ran to the paddock and that too was empty, except for a young foal and one of her father's oldest horses which had been put out to pasture for many years. She ran frantically to the stable cottage and found the groom at his breakfast.

When he saw her, a tear slowly trickled down his old cheek. He was lost for words. Then his wife emerged from the small back room which served as a kitchen and where often a young foal would be warmed on a cold winter night.

'My Lady,' she said, gulping back tears. 'They took the horses except for the foal, the daughter of your own lovely Snowdrop . . . it was the Parliamentary soldiers. They took all the animals in the area. Josiah cannot speak of it, for even though he is a grown man, he cries himself to sleep thinking of them and the fate that awaited them . . . His Lordship should have warned you . . .'

Lizzie wept openly and beat her fists against the door in her grief.

It was Mathilda and Beatrice who found her sobbing her heart out later in what would have been Snowdrop's stall.

'Oh, Lizzie dearest,' Mathilda cried. 'You slipped out of the house before we could stop you. We never meant you to find out about Snowdrop like that. We were going to tell you carefully. We are used to it all now so it doesn't hurt like it did . . .'

Mathilda hesitated, her eyes welling with tears. 'Life must go on, Lizzie. Mother is always telling us that. And we do have something really lovely to show you, which will cheer you up. Come, take my hand.' Lizzie looked at her sister Mathilda and for the first time could see the sort of woman she would grow into. She was reflective and clever. The horrors of the war had hastened her growing up and Lizzie realized, as she had not done so before, that Mathilda had had to step into her own shoes, when she had left to go to the royal children. She had the makings of a fine young woman and promised to be a beauty. How gently she held her elder sister's hand now, as she empathized with her pain. There was no doubt that Mathilda was wise beyond her years, and Lizzie's anger was assuaged by the thought of the comfort her sister must be to their parents, but there was also something other-worldly about her. Ruth had told her how devout Mathilda had become and that she had been secretly studying the Catholic faith. 'If her father found out, it would be the worse for her,' Ruth had said darkly.

The spaniel lay in a corner of one of the stalls on an old comforter. She was large for a spaniel, mostly gold with patches of white. She was suckling seven puppies, a mixture of black and gold and white. Mathilda and Beatrice reached down and removed their favourites from the gentle mother and held them close, kissing the tops of their soft routing heads.

Lizzie held one of the puppies to her face and closed her eyes as she inhaled the warm reassuring smell of puppy and summer and hay.

'You know how Father will never let us have dogs in the house,' she said pensively, 'because he says dogs are only for outside, and have to work like everyone else. The royal children and all their grand friends are different. Their dogs are like their babies. They sleep in their beds and they love them sometimes more than their own families.'

'Does the King have one for his friend?' Mathilda asked.

'Yes, he certainly does. It's a little spaniel. Not like these,' replied Lizzie with a smile. 'About half the size. They are called Cavalier spaniels. The King and his wife perfected the breed and all the ladies and gentlemen carry them about . . . sometimes in their sleeves. And they've bred them to have long silky ears like a Cavalier wig.'

'Oh, Lizzie, how I would like to meet the King,' Beatrice

cried. 'Is he handsome? Does he wear a crown on his head, and does the little princess look like an angel? Have you met a knight to make you into a grand lady, Lizzie?'

'No, dearest,' Lizzie replied tenderly as she ran a hand down Beatrice's long silky hair. 'The King does not wear a crown, but he looks very fine, for he is a kind man and he loves beautiful things. And, for all the shame of the predicament he finds himself in, he's still the King, and his bearing is royal and gracious and gentle. The King is the greatest of all Cavalier horsemen, you know, for he is small and athletic. He moves like a dancer.'

'But are you in danger, Lizzie? I cannot believe you would act as gaoler to the princess and her brother, without doing all you could to set them free, not fearing for yourself,' Mathilda exclaimed, bringing out a small kerchief and sobbing vigorously. As she did so, a crucifix, the like of which Lizzie had not seen before, more elaborate than usual, fell from her pocket. She picked it up and muttered something unintelligible, before hastily putting it away.

'Oh, what is to become of us?' Beatrice cried, bursting into tears. 'Will Tom and Philip come home safely? And will you have your head chopped off, like they are going to do to Squire Molyneux? Because you are good and true and loyal to the King's children?'

Before Lizzie could find the words to comfort her, there was a noise in the doorway. The sun still shone in brilliantly, silhouetting a figure.

Mathilda put her hand to her mouth in fright. Lizzie's heart gave a lurch. It was the figure of a slim man, booted and spurred. For a terrible moment she had thought it might be Captain Mildmay. But the figure was too tall and then, as he spoke, all her dreams turned into reality.

'No, young madam, nothing bad will become of your sister, for you see before you your sister's protector and devoted servant. May I introduce myself: Sir Richard Lovell, at your service.'

'Lizzie, I have so much to tell you,' said Richard, when they were alone at last. Lizzie had sent the girls back to the house to warn her parents of the arrival of their unexpected guest.

Despite the racing of her heart at the shock of seeing Richard again, here in her own home where she had never dared to imagine him, and where she had to admit he looked very much at ease, she was being as restrained as she could. But oh, how his hair shone in the bright light of the morning, how fresh and strong he looked, and how tenderly he looked at her. She wondered if he looked at Lady Jane in such a way. What did his betrothed think of him coming here? Perhaps she didn't know? Or worse? But knowing Richard that could not be . . . he would not deceive Lady Jane.

All these doubts were soon to be addressed.

'Lizzie, I couldn't wait to tell you something,' he blurted. 'In fact, two things, one good and one bad. Neither could wait. That is why I came without any announcement.' He gulped. 'Jane's family have broken off our betrothal.'

Lizzie thought she might faint. The implications were beyond her wildest dreams, and the fact that Richard had come straight away to tell her could only mean one thing.

Without any more words Richard gathered her in his arms and for the first time he kissed her.

Sir Edwin was working on the estate accounts when Mathilda rushed into his study with the news. 'Father, the most handsome young knight has come to see Lizzie. He's from the King, and he has a fine horse and velvet doublet and white lace collars, and the bluest eyes I've ever seen. When Lizzie saw him she nearly fainted with joy. He's put her on his horse and they're riding round the estate. If you go to our window in the tower, you can see them together. She sits in front of him and he has his arms about her, and when she turns to look up at him, I swear he would kiss her again and again. He's the finest gentleman I've ever seen . . .'

Sir Edwin was forced to stop her. He hastened up the winding stone steps to the tower to see for himself. The sight reassured him that his daughter was in no danger. An aura which bound the two of them was almost palpable, even from that distance.

At least an hour passed. He did not need Mathilda's sharp eyes to point out how flushed his daughter looked or the radiance in her eyes when at last she presented their guest.

Now he had a chance to inspect the visitor more closely. Mary arrived almost immediately and invited them to follow her to her parlour, where Ruth had laid some cakes and elderflower wine, chilled from the ice house.

As was the custom Lizzie sat at a stool near her mother's feet. After some ritual courtesies, Richard sat in a high-backed chair opposite her parents.

Richard did not speak of his feelings for Mary and Edwin's daughter at first, but he did not need to. The atmosphere in the room was charged with the delightful energy of their love.

Sir Edwin made some formal enquiries about Sir Richard's family. He told Richard that he had known of his father, and was sad to hear that he had left Lady Lovell a widow, a matter, he had, of course, concluded, when Lizzie had introduced him as Sir Richard.

Formalities out of the way, Richard came to the second reason for his visit. It was understood by all of them that he would speak to Sir Edwin about Lizzie when they were alone.

'I have some wonderful news. Prince James, the Duke of York, has escaped,' Richard announced triumphantly.

Lizzie gasped and clapped her hands with joy.

'Oh, Richard, this is wonderful,' she said breathlessly, overcome by so much good news. 'How did he manage it? Are the two children all right . . . why didn't he take them with him . . . ?'

Richard held up his hand to stop her.

'Wait a minute and I'll tell you everything,' he said firmly. 'It was the Princess Elizabeth who aided him. She is so clever and brave. They arranged a game of hide and seek in the gardens at St James's Palace. The boy hid in the garden, having got hold of a key to the gate . . . he waited and while the princess and her brother pretended to search for him high and low with some of the guards even joining in, the prince made his escape dressed as a laundry girl. Of course, the alarm was not raised until he had got far away because he was famous for the ingenuity of his hiding places . . . he is now happily with his mother in France. Of course, it was only possible to succeed on his own, the two children were his accomplices . . . but, one day, who knows, Lizzie?'

*   *   *

129

Richard had not known what to expect at the manor, since Lizzie had been characteristically modest about her background. Although she was obviously devoted to her family and had been well educated, he had not expected such a delightful house, or such cultured people as Sir Edwin and Lady Mary.

He looked at Sir Edwin seated behind his piles of manuscripts and surrounded by his astonishing collection of books and realized how much he missed his own father.

The smell of jasmine wafted through the open window behind Sir Edwin's head and the park was laden with green buds swelling on the trees. Richard looked about him with pleasure. Some family portraits, surprisingly modern and dimensional for a country gentleman's house, hung on the panelled walls, and tapestry rugs lay on the polished wood floors. A glass jug, obviously from Italy since such colours and texture were not available in England, stood full of late feathered tulips. He was pleasantly surprised by the charm and order evident in the house, despite the constraints that were so clearly the cause of the many fine lines on Sir Edwin's kind craggy face.

It was warm in the room and Richard took out his kerchief to wipe his brow.

'I'm sorry. Shall I pull the shutters for it's hot, such a beautiful day. God must be angered by the folly of men when he gives us paradise and we turn it into hell,' Sir Edwin remarked, making as if to rise from his chair behind his desk.

'No, my Lord, please. I dearly love the sun, and on such a fine morning I would rather not hide from it, but seek it out as your daughter is so oft to do.'

Richard slowly produced the blue silk square.

Sir Edwin's attention focused on a flash of colour and white Cavalier plumes embroidered clearly on the fabric and nodded his head. Slowly he leaned across the desk and patted Richard on the arm.

'Now we can speak freely,' said Sir Edwin seriously. 'For I see the white plume on your kerchief. I tell you I am very relieved, for these are dangerous times. I had to see for myself. You might have been a spy for the Roundheads for all I know. I expect Lizzie has told you how I have been wrestling with my conscience, but I have concluded that a compromise must sit with the Crown if it is to survive,' he said emphatically, 'though I do not think the King is of a mind to negotiate . . . But let us talk of Lizzie, while we have the chance. She is much more important at the moment.'

'You're right, sir,' said Richard. 'And chance has never treated me so well as when it led me to Lizzie. You must have missed her in the last few months.'

'Yes, more than you can imagine. Lady Mary has been miserable during her absence. We're thinking it's time for her to return to us.'

'My Lord, I've come to tell you that I share your love for your daughter, and to swear to look after her. I don't think she will think it right to return at the moment. She is greatly needed by the King's children, especially now. I will do everything to protect her.'

'And, sir, what form will this protection take?' Sir Edwin asked indignantly, for nothing had yet been said of a respectable offer of marriage.

Richard was well aware of the implication in Sir Edwin's question. 'My Lord, I love your daughter and I have come to pledge myself to her. With your permission, I would like to ask for her hand in marriage.'

'Hm,' Sir Edwin said.

'I must tell you everything,' Richard went on hastily. 'There can be no secrets between us. There was until lately an understanding arranged between families and I was betrothed to another.'

Sir Edwin leaned forward furiously. 'What d'you mean, young man? Explain yourself,' he boomed.

'No, sir, it's not what it sounds,' said Richard quickly. 'Her family have broken the tie. They've become radical Puritans and don't approve of my political allegiances. Truthfully, we were both relieved because she loves another, and besides I can offer her no great prospects of wealth such as she requires and expects. I may have nailed my flag to an uncertain cause, but I have kept my honour and will fulfil the expectations my father had of me.'

'Yes, young man,' Sir Edwin replied, shifting irritably in his chair, 'and I admire you the more for that, since we have all had to compromise our beliefs . . . It is easier, you know, to keep constant, if you don't have a family and retainers to think of . . . Conscience makes martyrs of us all in the end. Do you think Lizzie deserves such a high-minded husband?'

'She would take nothing less, my Lord,' said Richard. 'But it is you I ask first, to decide the matter. Should your answer be favourable, our betrothal will have to remain a secret for the moment for Lizzie's own safety.'

'This is an odd state of affairs and would surely put Lizzie in an invidious position. It precludes the chance of an alternative offer if she were to accept you,' Sir Edwin replied.

'I'm asking your opinion, sir,' Richard pressed.

'I'm a different cut from the old style,' said Sir Edwin. 'Lizzie should make up her own mind,' he went on. 'Although, she would, I know, as the good daughter she is, take her father's advice in this, as in all things. But there is something uncomfortable here.' Sir Edwin stopped for a moment and ran his hands through his hair in a gesture of bewilderment. 'I don't as yet fully understand you, there must be more you haven't told me.' He learned back in his chair and gave Richard a long appraising look.

'My Lord,' replied Richard, aware that Sir Edwin didn't quite trust him. 'I'm secretly working for the King. I may be discovered at any time, and my punishment would be swift and final. I would not wish to endanger Lizzie . . . a betrothal would implicate her at once. Besides I think you'll find that your daughter has pledged herself to a task which should be dear to your heart. She's in a unique position to achieve that end.'

'You speak in riddles. Pray, come out with it,' said Sir Edwin abruptly.

'My Lord, the final act in this terrible drama draws closer.' Richard saw that Sir Edwin was watching him closely. 'The King is adamant,' he continued doggedly. 'The children must be got to France to be with their mother. But since Prince James escaped, the security is much tighter. We're working on a plan, and Lizzie will be important.'

'This sounds a very dangerous plan for my daughter to be involved in,' Sir Edwin said in alarm.

'If she should be in any danger, she will be spirited away,'

Richard explained hastily. 'We've many outlets, not least a boat which is a familiar visitor to the cove not five miles from here. The hiding places in the sand dunes are perfect for our purposes and boats come in silently over the sands when the tide is up.'

'So, sir, you would have my Lizzie risk her neck for these two mites. And withall, if she's discovered, be taken to France to be a fugitive along with others, who'll like as not never return to the green land that is their own,' Sir Edwin retorted, barely concealing a mounting anger.

'If that were to happen, my Lord, she would not be alone,' Richard assured him. 'She would, on my word, be Lady Lovell. When the King is restored, which will be as soon as the nation has tired of this monstrous cancer of Cromwell and his men, she will be mistress of all I have to offer her.'

'And what precisely, sir, will that be?' Sir Edwin demanded.

'I hope the restoration of my family home and estates, when my mother is recompensed for all the devastations caused by the war on our family property,' said Richard.

'I see,' Sir Edwin said thoughtfully, looking long and hard at the young man, and to his relief finding his look returned unflinchingly. Sir Edwin decided he was a fine young man, both brave and true to his beliefs. In many ways he thought him not unlike Lizzie. Richard Lovell would be a good husband if life allowed it, though at the moment all life was fraught with risk. He knew his daughter would follow her instincts and that she had probably made her decision.

He patted the young man's hand, as if the matter were settled, and turned abruptly to the question of the King on the Isle of Wight.

'The King at Carisbrooke, a grim place by all accounts. You're right. This does not bode well for a quick resolution. You mark my words, the King will never sit on the throne of England again, except by the hand of his son who must raise an army. He will never be able to negotiate with the Scots on whom he pins his hopes. He has failed once, he will fail again. I see that the two children are cruel pawns in this, and it turns my stomach.'

There was a silence punctuated by the slow resolute ticking of the lantern clock on a wide stone shelf above the hearth.

Richard had a certain knowledge of clocks and had noticed it when he first entered the room.

Sir Edwin saw him looking at it 'One of the first in England,' he said proudly, glad to change the subject while he collected his thoughts. 'I found it before the war when trifles were commonplace.'

Richard nodded, thinking his future father-in-law a man of taste.

The silence continued while each considered the other, both momentarily overcome by the significance of their meeting and pleased to pause for a moment. Richard was the first to speak.

'Well, there is some encouraging news at least, my Lord,' he said. 'All the northern lords are raising and equipping an army. It is hoped the Scots will rally to the King and march south to join the Royalist army. One of your own sons is, I believe, engaged in this.'

'You must mean Tom,' said Sir Edwin, his brow wrinkled in concern. 'My other son, Philip, is in France with the King's family,' he went on. 'But I've not had word for many months. The usual channels are very quiet, which usually means some sort of activity.'

'If you'd allow me, my Lord,' said Richard, 'I could get word to him to let him know that your heart is still loyal to the King, for it would be a consolation.'

'You should know I cannot risk such a thing,' Sir Edwin replied emotionally. 'It's better to play the fool who doesn't know his mind . . . than risk the lives of so many who've been spared. And . . . the army being raised for the King . . . fills my heart with dread.'

For Richard the time had come when he must speak to Sir Edwin as an equal, for he knew he had more up-to-date information about the state of the King's supporters.

'I can't believe this,' he said quickly. 'After the battle at Naseby many lessons were learned and the Scots think of the King as their own. For don't forget, he's a Stewart and they're brave and fierce fighters.'

Sir Edwin wasn't convinced. He had seen so many of the fine brave Royalist plans end in disaster. He held little hope that the Scots had any such feelings of loyalty to Charles personally.

'Cromwell's New Model Army's a formidable fighting machine,' he said grimly. 'The best trained and fed this island's ever had. What chance do a rag-bag of ill-equipped men with a few pikes have against such a force? Besides it'll give ammunition to the Republicans who'll see it is a reason for something worse than imprisonment for the King. I've already heard it said that while he lives he's a thorn in the flesh of those who'd dispense with the monarchy and while he lives there will never be peace.'

Sir Edwin remembered when he had been young, he had shared the same optimism that shone like a beacon from the face of this youth who loved his daughter, and he nodded indulgently.

Richard felt encouraged and persevered.

'Whatever you say we can't lose hope,' he said confidently, 'and I pray God will be with us and prosper those who pledge allegiance so bravely.'

'Alas, the King will pay a heavy price for this,' Sir Edwin answered. 'He'll have to forswear his father's Protestant faith, for the Scots are vengeful in their hatred. A fear of the Catholicism kept alive by Queen Henrietta. Only the hell fire and damnation of the Calvinist Presbyterians will satisfy them. D'you think he could do this with a clear conscience?'

Richard thought for a moment. He knew he must tread carefully, things had gone well with Sir Edwin and he didn't want to fall foul of him over the complex issue of the King's predicament.

'My Lord, don't think me ill-mannered,' he said pointedly, 'but in these circumstances perhaps the matter of principle must be examined more carefully, and a solution expedient in the matter of preserving life must be looked at. Indeed you've been forced to do that very thing yourself.'

Sir Edwin's face darkened. Flashes of anger darted across his normally urbane features. But he recovered quickly. After all, he thought, there was more than a little truth in Richard's remarks.

'I'm well reproved, and you're right,' he conceded. 'And I don't regret the path I've taken my family down. Because, as you know, I'm in a position to be of great service to the King, more perhaps than before. This house is known as a safe haven for those who need to conceal themselves while escaping from the Parliamentary forces. You know of our priest hole of course. I keep it stocked and ready, and I hope, young man, you never have cause to use it.'

'My Lord, I hope it won't come to that, for I, like you, must continue my act as nothing more than a tutor. But I swear to you that if any harm should come to the King, I'll pledge my life to the return of the Prince Charles from the Hague to take the crown and restore the heritage which this sad monarch has so tragically lost. Not by any sin, save that of obstinacy. I think, even now, you may be right, and this will be his undoing.'

Somewhere in the house the bell could be heard, summoning the family to their midday meal. Sir Edwin wished to end the dialogue on a more personal note and the matter most dear to him at the moment was the future of his beloved daughter.

'Your loyalty to the monarchy commends you, sir,' he said formally. 'But at this moment it's Lizzie who's at the forefront of my concerns. What would you have me tell her? Her happiness is dear to my heart.'

'My Lord, it's for you, as her father, to decide whether or not I'm worthy of her,' said Richard humbly, 'but I can tell you, no other shall ever have my promise, and if she will wait for me, I will come to her as a true and loving husband.'

Sir Edwin considered for a moment, looking intently out of the long window on to the park. He rose slowly from his chair. He was tired and his body had begun to feel the strain of life's vicissitudes. Sir Edwin studied the tall young man who now stood slightly above him. There was something reassuring about him and his fierce noble loyalty and confident youth. He felt a chink of happiness such as he had not felt since the departure of his sons, and he answered in the slow deliberate voice he kept for important occasions.

'Go to her with my blessing. Lizzie's a clever young woman. She'll be your rock as you'll be hers. But it's for her to decide if your love is worth waiting for . . . I know how I hope she'll answer you.' And he added as an afterthought: 'I can only wish one thing for you both and that is the happiness I have found with her mother. I was indeed fortunate, for our families arranged it, and though I married her for expedience, if I were to do so now, it would be for love.'

The two men stood together and each hoped this was the first of many meetings in the stillness of the room in which the history of the family had been decided by men for generations past. But now it was a woman who would choose her own destiny. There was a gentle tap at the door. It was Lizzie.

Richard turned and their eyes met. Sir Edwin saw the joy on her face as Richard smiled at her encouragingly. He had no doubt that his daughter would make the right decision and he determined not to let his presentiments of what their future held spoil this happy moment.

Chapter Sixteen

They had all arrived at Petworth and Lizzie found the nearness of him was almost unbearable. Lizzie wanted to throw her arms about him, to feel the clean shaven skin on his face and to smell the velvet of his jacket which now hung slightly open, revealing his crisp white shirt. To save herself from betraying her feelings for all to see she looked down demurely at her sewing while savouring the ecstasy of the touch of his foot stealing stealthily up her calf. They sat in a window looking out on to the park, summer rain pattered gently on to the creeper outside the window and splashed on to the lily pads in the lake beyond the terrace.

Lizzie looked nervously at the children who sat quietly at their studies round a table in the far corner of the room, for she was at great pains to make sure they didn't realize the extent of her feelings for Richard. Even so she could tell by the sweet indulgent expression on Beth's face when she mentioned Richard's name that she knew that they were in love. But love affairs at court were commonplace and the child was used to the intrigue which lurked in the dark corners of closets and behind the thick curtains of the four-poster beds. As long as she knew they had not consummated their relationship and Lizzie remained chaste and pure, Lizzie knew none of them was in danger.

'Well, I have some news for you,' said Richard quietly. 'The children are to be taken to Carisbrooke to see their father. Mrs Briott is to accompany them with the earl and two of his servants.'

'I don't know what to think,' said Lizzie in alarm. 'It will be a terrible shock for them to see their father in such a place.' She laid down her sewing and looked anxiously at Richard.

'There is something else,' he whispered. 'I will meet you in the garden when you take Minette for her walk while the princess is resting, for she will not come out on such a damp day.' Richard's eyes creased into a tender smile as Lizzie nodded in agreement.

She saw him waiting for her at the end of the rose walk: when he saw her he shot into the maze of yew hedges where he waited for her to join him unobserved.

He pulled her into his arms as she rounded the corner. 'My dearest,' he said, breathing into her hair which, as usual, given little encouragement, had spilled from her cap. 'It won't always be like this, things are happening. Come sit on this bench,' he said reassuringly.

'We have an escape plan for when the children return from Carisbrooke, but we have to wait for the moon to wane, for darkness is essential.'

'Have you told the children yet?' Lizzie asked sharply.

'No,' said Richard. 'We cannot tell them until they get back from seeing their father for fear they might tell him and in a place like that there can be no secrets, as the King has found to his cost.'

'Presumably the plan is to spirit them away while they are supposed to be asleep. Who is to assist you?' asked Lizzie, knowing the answer.

'You, my dear brave Lizzie . . . if you will. Mrs Briott already approves the plan. There is a great fear of the plague,' Richard went on, 'and we will put it about that the children have succumbed and must be isolated in their rooms for fear of contagion.'

As Richard continued to outline the plan, Lizzie shuddered. It was fraught with danger and risk not, of course, to the children but to the people involved, for it was not like James's escape, where the only accomplices that could be found were Elizabeth and Harry. There were to be two coachmen and a loyal captain who was to smuggle the children on board his boat in a load of wool destined for France and of course herself and Mrs Briott, the children's close attendants. They were to be locked in a room when the birds had flown, claiming they had been overcome by the conspirators and powerless to prevent them.

'I am not afraid,' said Lizzie at last. 'Because this is the reason we are keeping our betrothal secret, that we may save the King's children and when they are safely with their mother we can be happy together in the knowledge that we have done our duty.'

Richard's heart missed a beat: there was one part of the plan he could not tell her. He would be going with the children and in so doing he would be identified as the main conspirator, the ultimate proof of Lizzie and Mrs Briott's innocence.

They took advantage of the time the children were away riding in the park. Richard on his own fine chestnut gelding and Lizzie on a white mare belonging to one of the Percy children. Sometimes on long summer evenings they made music together. Richard was a fine lutist, and they sat for many hours, Lizzie singing the words of songs quite new to her. Some of them were in French, a language in which Richard was perfect. Lizzie always took Margaret with her when she was to be alone with her lover and although the girl could not keep up with them on her small pony she was never very far behind. Lizzie had promised her father, and besides they both knew the danger of compromising her reputation, and raising the question of her suitability to care for the children.

Sometimes they talked about the life they would share when they became man and wife. Margaret would turn her head while Richard kissed Lizzie longingly and spoke of the sweet moments they would have in the marriage bed . . . Lizzie could hardly bear the frustration they endured. She wanted Richard to take her in his arms and to give herself to him completely.

The children returned deeply disturbed by seeing their father a prisoner in what Beth called 'that hateful place' and it was not long before events began to engulf them.

One damp summer's day came news of yet another of the King's failed escape plans. Richard told Lizzie and Mrs Briott about it when the children had retired to bed.

'It was bound to end in failure,' he said. 'The King has broken his word to Parliament not to escape once before,' he went on. 'Now he finds himself under strict guard. The castle is a gaunt place. I can't imagine how desperate he must feel.'

'But you can't blame him for trying to escape,' Lizzie stated.

'You are right he had nothing to lose,' Mrs Briott agreed.

'The King has continued to conspire with the Scots throughout the summer,' said Richard gloomily. 'All the while, Parliament has been still in the mood to find a compromise. When they realize the extent of what's been going on, it'll be a perfect excuse for the more radical Republicans to stop negotiations.'

'But the news isn't all bad,' said Mrs Briott. 'There've been Royalist uprisings in Wales, Essex and Kent, some near to your own home, Lizzie, as you've heard from your father.'

'I know, but they all came to nothing. Just more futile casualties,' Lizzie murmured disconsolately.

'The bad thing is, none of this will improve the children's situation. That is why I am going to tell the children of our plan for their escape tomorrow,' said Richard. 'We have to act now or it will be too late.'

They went to bed and Lizzie wondered how long it would be before they would be able to find comfort in the same bed as man and wife. When she awoke, as she often did, with fear and apprehension, she ached for the time when he would be there to reassure her. She often had nightmares about Captain Mildmay. He had not been seen for many months now, but she knew he would return. When the children were gone he would have no further use for her except for . . . She shivered with revulsion. She knew that before she could find happiness she would have to free herself of the debt the captain felt she owed him. She would return at once to the safety of Hatherton and Richard would come for her. When they married the captain would have to forget her.

'No,' the princess wept the following day. 'We cannot leave Father, he is the thing most dear to me in the world and we are all he has, so thank you, Sir Richard, and for your bravery.' She gulped and twisted her handkerchief in her small delicate hands. 'There is an end to it,' she said finally.

Richard bowed as he took his leave. He knew the visit to their father had changed everything and suspected the little princess had calculated that it would not be long before the reason for her remaining would no longer be there.

A week later the Scots army decided to march. Word came to Richard by way of a note written in ink which responded to heat, although at first glance it looked like a letter from a relative full of mundane domestic news.

They waited desperately for more information, and by August Richard had more disastrous news. The Scots had reached Preston, and Cromwell, having settled the uprising in Wales, was able to send the Scots hurrying home. He invaded the border himself, replacing the key figure of the Royalist Hamilton with anti-Royalist Argyll.

From then on Richard knew the die was cast. 'Clipping the royal wings is not enough, Lizzie . . .' he said to her solemnly. 'His enemies will clip more than his wings as your father predicted – and I did not believe him.'

He confirmed that, as Sir Edwin had feared, the Parliamentary commissioners no longer met with the King in the stuffy town hall in Newport on the Isle of Wight.

The bland autumn weather ended suddenly in November, and talk of appeasement faded.

The household returned to Syon and mist brought a cloying dampness which hung in swirls about the river. The days shortened and there was an air of concern in the house. Everyone felt it, but at least Lizzie was left more or less to her own devices. The royal children seemed yet again to have been forgotten. She thought of projects to occupy them as she

141

was painfully aware of how much they missed the regular visits from their father.

She missed her own family and she shared the children's sense of isolation and loneliness, but overriding all this, she had Richard to console her. As for Captain Mildmay, she still had not seen him for several months.

But news came just before Christmas that the King was being moved to Hurst Castle, a fortress prison on the mainland – from none other than Captain Mildmay. He appeared, suddenly, one morning, on the pretext of wishing her to be prepared for the children's reaction.

Lizzie was helping Beth to complete an embroidered cushion which was to be her present for her father. It was a likeness of Rogue sitting on a blue velvet cushion. They were just putting the finishing touches to the significant white plumes when the captain swept into the room unannounced.

Having not seen him for so many months, Lizzie was reminded of his all-engulfing presence. He still had the air of callous confidence. Minette barked protectively and came sniffing at his heels. With a deft flick of his boot he kicked her yelping into the shadows. He had not bothered to brush the snow from his cape, and as he swung it carelessly from his shoulders, melted droplets fell about the room, some of then on to the ink drawing for the sewing, causing the dog's face to run as if in tears.

He did not bow to Beth, but rather let his glance slide at once to Lizzie, whom he blatantly devoured with his eyes.

'What is your business here?' Beth asked coldly.

'I've come to speak to Lizzie,' he replied in a perfunctory way bordering on insolence.

'Do you wish me to withdraw, Lizzie?' Beth asked hesitantly, deliberately avoiding looking at Captain Mildmay.

'Perhaps it would be best, Your Highness,' Lizzie replied, not at all sure if it was the best thing or the correct etiquette, but she was sure the captain would have nothing good to say and she might be able to spare the princess some pain by filtering it first.

'Very well, but I will not leave you for long, Lizzie, for I cannot imagine what the captain needs to say to you. And I am sure it will not take long,' Beth said with a meaningful look. She knew all about the captain and disliked and feared him in equal measure. The thought of him alone with her beloved Lizzie was abhorrent to her. But at the same time she realized that it was in all their interests for Lizzie to maintain some sort of dialogue with the man, since it was within his power to send Lizzie, her best and dearest support, away.

When Beth left the room, the captain sat down and invited Lizzie to do the same. As she cautiously sat opposite him across the sewing table, the captain's expression changed to one she remembered from their first encounter, when he had come to Hatherton in the middle of the night. His face became serious and his voice lowered. He leaned towards Lizzie.

'I come to tell you, my dear, that the King is to be tried for treason. The children have not been told. When they are, they know enough of the way things are to realize what the punishment will be if he is to be found guilty.'

The enormity of what the captain had said needed no explanation. The unthinkable had become the probable. The King executed: such a thing could not happen. She thought wildly and illogically, as people do at times when things are more than they can deal with.

Her hands went to the King's present, the sewing still on the table. There could be no more poignant a symbol of the senseless waste of it all. So much sad agonizing love, so much wasted blood, so much wickedness and mendacity.

'And you, what have you done to stop this? Have you done anything to help the King? After all, once you were his friend,' she rounded on him, unable to contain herself.

'Lizzie, I admit I've changed my views and loyalties on occasions, but you misjudge me if you think this is an outcome I am happy with, or that I've come to these conclusions lightly.'

She looked at him long and hard, trying to get beyond the superficial mask he wore. She concluded that, for once, his words were sincere: even for him things had got out of control. Maybe, after all, his concerns for the children were genuine, and possibly he really did want her to be prepared for the task she would have in front of her – a task which filled her with a terrible, miserable feeling of hopeless despair for little Harry and Beth. He took his leave quickly with an uncharacteristic, hasty, embarrassment.

Lizzie could only have guessed at his feelings as he left her. Captain Mildmay was not a man who indulged in the luxury of guilt. He had not, in his own eyes, betrayed a friend. 'No, the King has behaved like a fool,' he muttered to himself as he made his way to the earl and countess's apartments.

They had been close once, he and the King, but he had lost patience with the man's inability to grasp the gravity of his situation. If he were going to run with the stag and hunt with the hounds, he should have perfected the game in the way Mildmay had done himself. . . But he never would listen, not to Mildmay anyway, only to his wife who knew nothing of the nuances which had created the King's own downfall . . . There was nothing anyone could do now. The captain prided himself on his choice of political bedfellows, and one day, in a different sense, Lizzie would be one of them.

Overall he felt quite pleased with himself as, with a spring in his step, he thought about the excellent wine he would be offered by the earl, of the deference with which he would be treated and above all by the clever way he had allowed Lizzie to lower her guard during the previous months as she thought he had forgotten about her. He knew about her friendship with the feckless Sir Richard Lovell, but it did not concern him. The callow youth was not in a position to marry her. It was a good way of keeping her on ice as it were. One day he would light a flame in her. Things would soon move inexorably to their final chapter in the King's futile battle against democracy. Anthony Mildmay would be more powerful than ever, and then she would think again.

Seventeen

'A sadder Christmas and new year cannot be imagined,' said Richard. 'I hope we never experience the like again.' He held Lizzie's hand as they tried to keep their spirits up, roasting chestnuts in front of Mrs Briott's merry fire. It was bitterly cold, snow covered the park and the river was frozen. She had done her best to keep the children's spirits up, but in her heart she knew they were about to experience a tragedy far more terrible than she could ever have imagined.

'Oh, Richard, I believe the earl will have the painful duty of telling the children of their father's fate before the day is over,' Lizzie wept. 'Her Ladyship has told me things have not gone well for the King. They will cut off his head before the week is out.' She looked at the date on Mrs Briott's candle, decorated with blood-red holly berries. It said January 27th 1649.

Richard took her in his arms and held her close, inhaling the fresh clean smell of starch from her simple cap. He wished they were a million miles away, married and living as his family had done in happier times: in the certain knowledge of what the day would hold. Lizzie would cultivate the herbs, for which she was now renowned at Syon. They would have children of their own, whom they would never leave.

It was as they sat together contemplating the flames that they both heard the princess's cry. It was a long piercing scream, such as might be heard from a trapped dying bird. It echoed down the long draughty galleried rooms with a sound which all who heard it knew they would never forget.

Later, as Lizzie held the little girl, she heard of terrors which so far the child had kept buried in her heart for fear of acknowledging them. She had consoled herself with the thought that nothing worse could happen than the things which already had. But this was worse. The force of evil which brought with it the disgrace of regicide had crept up stealthily before anyone fully understood. Here was the cruellest blow of all and it had its own unstoppable momentum.

'I shall die, Lizzie . . .' Beth said, when at last there were no more tears that could be shed from her frail body. Lizzie held her as close as she could. There were no words that could express the anguish which closed around her, suffocating any hope for the future, any rational restoration of common sense or Christian love.

The household was in turmoil. The countess feared the news

would kill Beth. Her pain and bewilderment were so terrible that all Lizzie could do was to be constantly beside her. She was inconsolable. Harry clung to Mrs Briott as if he would not be without her for a second. The only words he spoke were, 'We will never see Mamma again, and now they are going to murder Father.' Mrs Briott took him to his room and the countess's apothecary came to give him a potion to help him sleep. They all knew the next day was to be the hardest of his life.

Later Lizzie prayed quietly with Beth. The child would not sleep or take the same medicine as her brother. 'How can I sleep for the last few hours my dearest father has on earth,' she cried pathetically.

'You will . . . You will see your mother and brothers and sisters again,' Lizzie said, desperately trying to stifle her own horror. 'All this will pass and all we can do is pray for your dear father, and for God to give you the strength to comfort your little brother.'

'Oh, Lizzie . . . poor Harry,' Beth cried. 'He has never known what it is like to have a family. He was only two when our parents left us. Then our elder brothers became like heroes to him. He didn't fret when Charles went to Holland. But when James escaped, he changed, and he has got to know Papa in the last two years. Now he is to be cruelly deprived of him.'

'Beth, your little brother has always had your love. You have been like a little mother to him, and now he will need you more than he has ever done. I will help you,' Lizzie said gently.

'Promise me, Lizzie, you'll stay with us,' Beth pleaded. 'For tomorrow we must . . . oh, I cannot say the words, for my heart is splitting in two. I can feel it, Lizzie. It is swelling in my chest. It is going to break . . . If Father dies I want to go with him. I will hold his hand and guide him to our heavenly Father, because I know he will be afraid and his dear face will look so good and brave,' she went on as if the unstoppable torrent of words would in some way assuage the agony she felt. 'But his soul will be in torment at leaving so much that he loves . . . and what will become of Rogue? Oh, it is too much to bear . . . he will feel he has failed all of us . . .'

She collapsed her head in Lizzie's lap, her small shoulders heaving with sobs.

Lizzie held the princess tighter. She knew the child had at last come to the point of unburdening herself for the first time ever. Perhaps this was a good thing. She was letting down her guard. She was no longer the regal princess in waiting, but a small frail child bewildered by a grief so terrible that Lizzie knew she might never recover. At that moment she thought of the confused little boy now with Richard and Mrs Briott and she was determined the princess would survive.

'Dearest child,' she reassured her. 'I won't leave you and when you go to bid farewell to your father, I will be there. And let us ask for Rogue to be put in your care. He can live with Minette.' Lizzie had to utilize all her resources to keep from losing control. Tears poured down her face and her voice was thick with emotion. 'You must not think your father is weak,' she continued. 'He is a King and he will be brave. He's tired and he may be happy to leave this world and its wickedness.'

'But why, Lizzie, why?' asked Beth angrily. 'Goodness should have its reward and Father is good, It is the wicked who are flourishing. What is the point of being good? They will probably kill us as well.'

'No, my precious, you are safe,' said Lizzie. 'There are many people to protect you,' she continued, only half believing her own words. 'We must hold on to what we think is right as your father would wish. He will be proud of you both. My old nurse used to say when the wind blew in the trees round the park at night as the storms came from the sea, "The Angel Gabriel's hounds are hunting the evil spirits and keeping us safe". We'll pray that they'll come and lift your dear father gently to heaven and that we can try to live our lives as he would have wanted . . . for your brother Charles will come and avenge these people. He'll be a gracious and good King as his father's son, I swear it to you.'

Lizzie could hardly keep the anger from her voice and she understood the profundity of her words. She had meant to take the easy way and let the affairs of the world be settled by others who were prepared to die for a principle, and now she had, without knowing it, been drawn in by circumstances. Now she was fired with a passion which defied the value of her own small life. For the first time she understood what her brother Tom had been trying to tell her.

That night Cromwell received a blank piece of white paper from the King's eldest son Charles in Holland. It had his signature on the bottom, 'Charles Stuart', with word that he would agree to anything Cromwell wished to write on it, if it would save the life of his father. Cromwell declined to answer.

The following day a tragic retinue from Syon arrived at St James's Palace with the two youngest royal children. Mrs Briott and Lizzie were allowed to remain in a small anteroom while the children were ushered into the presence of their father.

The weeping figures of the two children walked into the room where their father stood dignified and formally dressed. He wished them to remember him with the countenance of a King.

Lizzie and Mrs Briott could see between the thick brocade curtains; their presence had been arranged in case the little princess became ill. Her health had been causing concern and, as Mrs Briott had said, spilling the King's blood would sicken the public, already uneasy about the alarm and unease of the imminent regicide: the blood of an innocent royal child would be the final straw in 'this dastardly act'. Richard, white and shaking, had told them that morning that the block had already been prepared outside the decaying palace at Whitehall. The King would walk through the once sumptuous rooms, the scene of so many happy family gatherings. He would pass under the ornate ceiling, painted by Rubens, to die a common criminal's death in the freezing January wind that blew easterly down the river. As Richard warned, the murder would be swift, before the full impact dawned on an ill-prepared nation who had never wanted the murder of their King.

It was not a King who stood at the end of the room, it was a father, a man who did not fully comprehend what had brought him to this end.

Although the blood of thousands had been spilled to fight his cause, he had not heeded the wind of change, and now, bewildered, he could focus on but one thing. He would spend some of his last precious moments on earth with two of his children. He had thought long on how best to ease their pain. His own was now of no importance. He had decided that if all the bitterness and destruction of the last terrible few years was to make any sense to Harry and Elizabeth, he must fire their young hearts with the ideals for which he had fought and lost.

He talked first to Elizabeth who clung to him, wracked with sobs, a sight so piteous that even the hard-faced soldiers at the door were seen to furtively wipe tears from their eyes. And then he took his son on his knee while the little princess knelt at his feet, his right hand clasped tightly in hers.

They heard the King's words, defiant and brave, and Lizzie could no longer contain herself. She cried on Mrs Briott's shoulder. Then the gruff voice of one of the officials announced the time had come for the children to leave. It fell upon the two women to drag Harry and Elizabeth away from the last vestiges of their family and vow to help them rebuild their shattered lives.

They were quietly at prayer the following morning, when their father asked for an extra shirt, so that he would not shiver in the freezing morning air, lest he be thought a coward. They did not hear the moan from the great crowd, gathered in silent disbelief, as the King's head was severed in one blow.

It was a noise so awesome that many heard it ring in their ears for years to come, and the stage was set for the long drama which would bring the King's son back to England to reclaim the throne. Before he died, Charles said, calmly and with the dignity which never left him, 'I go from a corruptible to an incorruptible crown.'

They did not see the shivering ball of fur which was the King's beloved spaniel Rogue as he was paraded by the Roundheads through the streets of London.

They had promised the little princess that she should have the dog, but they cared not for her broken heart, and would not even offer her that small consolation. It was this final act which gave birth to hatred in Elizabeth Jones's heart that winter day.

Lord Jermyn, the Queen's faithful servant who had followed

her to France, was sent to tell Queen Henrietta the terrible news. But he could not bring himself to utter the fateful words, and rather told her the crowd had risen up and saved the King. It was not until two days later that he found the courage to blurt out the truth. The Queen stood still as a statue, her grief so terrible that she was unable to speak for many hours. Somewhere in England two of her children wept. She heard their cries in the depth of her soul.

Eighteen

'I'm unable to continue my guardianship of the late King's children,' the Earl of Northumberland informed Richard in the April following their father's execution. The cost of maintaining the entourage was too much for him to bear, and he had tired of the long drawn-out arguments with Parliament on the matter.

He had persuaded his sister Lady Leicester to take on the children. In June that year they were to be moved to her home at Penshurst Place in Kent. For Harry and Beth, to say goodbye to the earl and countess who had been such kind and thoughtful guardians had been a blow. But that was a year ago and things had turned out better than anyone could have expected.

Late afternoon shadows cast long figures on the gardens of Penshurst Place. It was July and summer was at its height, the air full of warm promise from the heat of the day.

Blackbirds and thrushes were silent, waiting for the cool of the evening to begin their serenade. The only sound, the pat-pat of gentle water on lily pads, came from the fountains in the pool the other side of the hedge. The gardens were just coming into their prime, planted parterres, mossy green swards of grass, tumbling roses and brick paths.

The garden was all the creation of Lady Leicester who was

an inspired gardener, as she was in all other things. Since the children had been given into her care they had changed beyond recognition, and they, like the garden, bloomed and responded to the quiet comforting order of life at Penshurst.

Lizzie felt more at home in these surroundings. The beauty of the house nestling serenely in the rolling Kent countryside and the quiet domestic order was more reminiscent of her own upbringing, and infinitely more convivial than the grandeur of Syon.

Hide-and-seek continued to be one of Harry's favourite games in the unaccustomed freedom he and his sister had with the Leicester Percy family. Although Lady Leicester was instructed by Parliament to treat the children as commoners, she had her own way of according them both the respect their royal status deserved, but this did not preclude from them the carefree life they had for so long been denied. The children made firm friends with the Leicester's two youngest daughters, Elizabeth and Frances Percy. Unlike the atmosphere at Syon, the household at Penshurst was more intimate and informal. Meals were eaten together and although Lady Leicester still sat Beth and Harry at a separate table where they were served on bended knee, they felt at last that they had become part of a loving happy family.

Today the children and Lizzie ran through the gardens drinking in the fresh summer air as they had never done before. Beth discarded her shady wimple, gloves and voluminous underskirts in favour of a simple cotton gown that had been run up by the resident seamstress at Penshurst. She had a faint tan and rosy cheeks and the weakness in her bones had healed a little, so that she slept peacefully at night, and sometimes in the early afternoon after the family dinner at three o'clock.

Suddenly the game was disturbed by the clatter of hooves at the front of the house. Lizzie heard the rough voices of soldiers, reminiscent of other unexpected arrivals. Her heart missed a beat and, feeling sick to her stomach, she peered through the thick yew hedge, where she had a clear view of the carriage drive and front entrance. There were perhaps half a dozen outriders and a coach and four. One of the soldiers jumped from his horse and opened the door of the coach. A

151

man alighted quickly with the agility of a dancer, his sword clattering against the steps, the elaborate carved hilt catching the sun.

As he jumped swiftly down, ignoring the proffered arm of the soldier, she gasped. There was no mistaking the figure, even though she could only see the back view. It was Captain Mildmay. As if sensing her eyes upon him, he turned in her direction and she could see the familiar supercilious expression on his face. For one moment, for which she crossed herself and begged her God for forgiveness, she wished he might fall dead where he stood.

Lady Leicester appeared on the steps of the house and from her demeanour it was clear that her visitor was, although most unwelcome, very much expected.

There was the sound of light running footsteps on the garden path.

'Found you, Lizzie,' puffed Beth. 'I knew you were here, because Minette led me to you. She always knows where you are.'

She held on to Lizzie's hand affectionately and pressed her head to her chest. Lizzie briefly fondled the cap of straight silken hair which fell freely to the girl's shoulders. And then Beth saw the soldiers.

'Look, Lizzie,' she cried, peering through the hedge. 'Say you'll never leave Minette or me. I feel so safe when I'm with you.' Her eyes were tight closed, as if the reality of the world which had treated her so cruelly could be kept at bay for at least a few precious seconds. She had a habit of coming out with remarks like this. Lizzie always gave her reassurances, despite the fact that she often didn't believe them herself.

Minette jumped up excitedly, licking Lizzie's hand. Lizzie bent down to embrace Beth, not wishing her to see her anxious face.

'No, of course. I'll never leave you or Minette,' Lizzie replied resolutely.

'I mean it, Lizzie, even if I should die . . . which could only mean I would be reunited with dear Father.' Beth picked the dog up and it nuzzled her cheek. 'Who then,' she continued anxiously, 'would look out for Minette and see she was not torn asunder like poor Rogue?'

Lizzie noticed apprehensively that the child's eyes were fearful and all-seeing, as if she knew something of her future more terrible even than the things which had passed: the destruction of a way of life, to be replaced with a far more despotic order, which introduced into every aspect of life not the freedom which had been promised, but a purging of joy and laughter. Only the previous day Lizzie had been horrified to hear that a local village had been severely punished for having the traditional Maypole dance. At Penshurst there were to be no more hymns sung in the chapel or music-making in the hall.

As much as Lizzie had tried to put the past months in some sort of rational order, they had only served to destroy her confidence in the future. It was true that the protected life at Penshurst away from all the strife had restored a frisson of hope to the children, but now again she was aware that she had been lulled into a false sense of security, thinking that because the King had been dispensed with, the children might be forgotten.

The Leicesters were powerful, and surely they would protect them ... but there was something about the arrogant way Captain Mildmay had arrived, pushing his way into the house, and Lady Leicester's grim expression, which alerted Lizzie.

She knew she must be brave for the children's sake. She wished Richard was somewhere near.

'Your Highness, you're not going to die,' she replied. 'You have much to do and remember you are a Princess of England. One day your brother will return and be King, and you'll be reunited with your family here on earth.' She wished she believed her own words of reassurance.

Just then Harry came pushing through the hedge, careless of the prickly thorns from a climbing rose blocking his path. Lizzie heard the sharp snagging noise as thorns tore his breeches and shirt.

'Lizzie, have you seen? There are soldiers at the house and Mrs Briott has sent a steward into the gardens to find us,' Harry whispered, clutching hold of Lizzie's arm. She remained still as a rock between the children, supporting them like the iron swirls of the pergolas with their gargoyle tips which held up her Ladyship's roses.

153

'Oh, Lizzie, I am frightened,' Harry whispered fearfully. 'What can it mean? Perhaps they will not be able to find us?' He was still out of breath from running, his doublet and little bag of archery at sixes and sevens about his slim waist. Against his better nature, as he always tried to be the strong man of the group, he allowed Lizzie to put her arm about him. She could feel his heart like a trapped bird beating beneath her hand.

They stood together in an arc of solidarity, and as Lizzie held the two children, she steeled herself to fight the evil that had returned with the arrival of Mildmay.

The message came as she knew it would. She was to meet him in a small room off the solar, where Lady Leicester interviewed the house servants. Lizzie had heard Lady Leicester speaking to Mrs Briott, and heard the woman's laments. 'Whatever next. The poor lambs, how am I to tell them? Do these people have ice where they should have a heart, my Lady?' And then the door had shut and she could glean no more. She hustled the children into the great hall where they were to wait and she stood gazing dejectedly out at the beauty of the gardens. 'How Nemesis waits,' she said to herself. She should not have been so stupid as to think she could find her happy ending so easily, there were still battles to be fought.

'So, my little Lizzie, why so melancholy? Your countenance should be full of pleasure at our reunion.' Mildmay's voice had lost none of its mockery. Without turning, Lizzie gave a low curtsey, her head averted.

Before she could rise he was upon her, his arms about her, fumbling with her light summer skirt. He had it up above her knees and at the top of her legs before she could turn.

Holding her in his grip, her body against his, he whispered into her hair, his other hand slipping down her bodice, his fingers prodding and pinching her nipples.

'So will you come with your young prisoners, my little Lizzie? For if you do not, I may not be able to look to your family any longer.'

'I hoped you'd got more important things to think about, now the King is dead,' Lizzie gasped.

'You think I had forgotten you, my pretty piece?'

He smelled of male sweat, horses and leather. His breath was faintly tainted with wine. She felt repelled and violated.

Swinging round she tried to push him away. 'No sir,' she rounded. 'I could have hoped you had forgotten me if I had not known you better.'

'So you think you know me, do you?' he asked mockingly.

'Yes, I would guess that if you feel thwarted because you cannot get what you want, you persist by fair means or foul.'

'With me, the pleasures of love would not be foul, my dear . . .'

'You will not have what you want of me, if your conduct is a sign of it,' she cried as haughtily as she could, smoothing down her skirts. 'Enough, sir'. 'There are more important things to talk about. What do you mean? Go with the children, go where?'

He gave a derisive smirk, chucking her under the chin.

'Your virtue is a fine thing.'

'Yes, sir, that and my conscience. And you would do well to look to your own, if you have either,' she replied evenly, amazed by her own boldness.

'As to the latter, conscience makes martyrs of us all, as the late King found out. And as to the former, if you guard it too long, it may wither like the grapes on the vine.'

'Yes, but old wine is usually better, is it not?'

'Only when made from the best fruit plucked from the tree in its prime.'

'It is quite simple . . . I will stick to the things I believe, whatever you say or do . . . your desire for me is nothing to me . . . I will not trade my beliefs like some sort of currency.'

'How naïve you still are,' he answered laconically. 'Your beauty is your principal currency. You have no fortune, and your family does not improve itself.' He paused giving her along slow look. 'You . . . should think carefully, my dear, before you rebuff me.'

'I think your remarks smell of sour grapes, Captain,' she shot back spiritedly.

'Well, there are other matters for the moment . . . but I do not give up,' he said glibly.

'I don't flatter myself into thinking this is the reason for your visit. What can you want with the children? Why do you have to persecute them in this way?'

'Perhaps you should credit me with caring about their safety.'

'They are safe and not doing anybody any harm here at Penshurst with my Lady Leicester,' she said, her voice rising as she tried to disguise her apprehension.

'That may appear to be so, but let's not forget that the children are prisoners of Parliament. Lady Leicester has been warned, and our information does not please the Council. The whole situation is out of control.'

'They're only children and one of them is very frail.'

'It's not that simple. They are the King's children, and their brother is in the wings. My dear, one day he'll try to take back the Crown. Of that you can be sure, and then . . . those children will be of interest, won't they? Who knows what might happen with all the freedom they're enjoying? They might slip across the channel. We have the good of the Commonwealth to consider and they're a danger to it in the present circumstances.'

'Sir, do not preach to me about goodness. The children are in better hands than any they had before. Her Ladyship is a good and noble woman, beyond the corruption of the people you represent,' she continued bravely. 'And wicked as they are, I think they would not wish to misuse those children, or use a poor defenceless girl, as you want to do with me . . . and under the nose of your own wife, the mother of your children.'

'Well, have you quite finished?' he asked, smiling falsely.

Lizzie had struck him to the quick. Catherine, his wife, had not yet conceived and after five years of marriage. It was an affront to his manhood. There was something of the witch about Elizabeth Jones. How did she know his Achilles' heel? It made her all the more attractive. He felt wrong-footed and angry, but he would not let her see how her words had struck him.

'You are not so defenceless as you would have me believe, my dear . . . I think there's someone who's had a taste of the cherry you hide from me. Sir Richard's no stranger to my Lady's afternoon games, it seems.'

He had been saving this card, and now his eyes were cold

and calculating in the way Lizzie knew implied trouble, not only for her, but also, perhaps, for Richard. She said nothing while she collected her wits.

Of course there were spies everywhere, even at Penshurst. Her every move would have been watched. How could she have been so stupid? The royal children were a valuable commodity; each and every attendant would be continually watched.

'I dare say the new order would look less kindly on the matter of adultery than that of a chaste flirtation between two unmarried people, neither of whom are promised. Wouldn't you agree, sir?' Lizzie replied smartly.

Mildmay's face closed. He chose not to respond to this show of spirit but rather to get to the point of his visit.

'Well, my pretty one, the children are to be moved to Carisbrooke Castle in a few days.'

He waited, revelling in the effect this news would have upon Lizzie.

'How could such a thing be?' she asked desperately. 'Are you jesting?' she went on bravely. 'Why would anyone want to wrench the children away from the first bit of security they have known here with Lady Leicester and her happy family?'

Mildmay stared insolently at her for a moment. 'There are risks,' he shrugged.

'What possible risks could these two children be to the new order?' Lizzie demanded. 'This is cruel. Carisbrooke is a place that is hateful to them. It is the prison where they saw their father before his . . .' she hesitated. She was about to say 'murder' and then she bit her lip for such a remark could only damage her cause. 'The King's death,' she finished hesitantly.

'It is in everyone's best interests and after all they will still be well looked after,' he replied, looking pointedly at Lizzie.

Lizzie thought how Mildmay ratified the decision with less concern than if he were talking about a horse or a dog. To him the children were cards to be played as ruthlessly as the cards which ended in regicide and murder.

And so Lizzie agreed to go with them. What else could she do? She had given her word. Now they needed her more than ever. Later, when Lady Leicester spoke quietly to all the servants who were to accompany the children, a different explanation was forthcoming. 'The move is for the children's own protection,' she said ominously, 'because General Cromwell has become increasingly alarmed by the underground information he has received about plans to murder the two. The Roundhead maxim, "When you kill the lice, you must also kill the eggs", refers directly to Beth and Harry,' she told them as they gasped in disbelief. 'Cromwell has enough blood on his hands and the regicide has disturbed him. Although you may not believe it,' she went on, 'he is a man of conscience.'

Later she tried to calm the children. 'All is not quite what it seems,' she explained, deciding to try and lighten the atmosphere. 'Why, when your father his Majesty escaped from Hampton Court it was said that Cromwell danced with glee,' she went on brightly. 'He had hoped for the King to make his way to France and rid him of the inevitable choice between the King's life or Parliament which had not lain well with his conscience.'

'And would he feel the same if we were to escape?' asked Harry.

'It will not be long,' Lady Leicester assured them, not altogether believing it, 'before you are both reunited with your family.'

When the children had supposedly retired for the night, Lady Leicester talked to Lizzie and the loyal servants.

'The princess's health is a major concern,' she told them. 'I know how much better she has been since she came here and this is in a large part due to your devotion, Lizzie,' she said, looking at her appreciatively. 'But we all know what a move to such a place might mean. I for one feel the princess would deteriorate very quickly and all our good work would be undone. That is why I will be writing forthwith to Sir Theodore Mayherne, the King's old physician, now Cromwell's own, and greatly respected by the Council of State,' said Lady Leicester. 'It is my last feeble hope that, maybe, I can appeal to their sense of decency and they will think better of moving the child. Besides it would not look good for the Council to have the child's death on their hands.'

But Lizzie could tell from her eyes that Lady Leicester feared she would not win the battle for the children, whom she had come to love as her own.

It came as no surprise to her when she went to check on the princess and found her awake and feverish.

'I know Lady Leicester is trying to be kind and I pretended to believe what she said for Harry's sake . . . but if they make me go to that dreadful place where they kept poor Father, I will die,' the child sobbed quietly. And, as Lizzie felt her frail body in her arms, she did not doubt it. The children had been through so much already. This latest blow must be the final straw.

PART THREE

Carisbrooke Castle 1650

Nineteen

The journey was to take seven days. The royal party would consist of more than a dozen heavily laden wagons, besides the coaches for the children and their attendants. Mildmay, it seemed, was sequestering anything he could lay his hands on for the alleged comfort of his charges at Carisbrooke, which, having already been looted of the King's possessions, was now bereft of even the barest of domestic necessities. A wagonload of valuable hangings and furnishings had arrived at Penshurst from Mildmay's home in Middlesex where he had purchased a valuable collection of items 'for the children's comfort', and more still lay waiting in the coach house at Penshurst for his own use. All the royal possessions had been sold at ludicrously low prices, and most of them found their way into the private collections of leading Parliamentarians.

It was rumoured that in his position as Master of the Jewel House, Mildmay's elder brother Sir Henry had also assembled a priceless collection of royal gems, although the best of them had been taken by Queen Henrietta to trade for arms for her husband's campaign. Mrs Briott told Lizzie that a vast collection of the King's possessions, now the property of the Commonwealth, had been lodged at Greenwich Palace, currently inhabited by 'malignants and disaffected persons', and that Mildmay and his brother Sir Henry, also the Keeper at Greenwich Palace, the King's personal home, made good use of them for their own purposes. Mrs Mildmay had even been seen wearing the Queen's emerald necklace.

The five servants in attendance had been appointed by Mildmay and consisted of Richard, Lizzie, Judith Briott and John Barmiston, the gentleman usher, and John Clark, the groom of the chamber.

The princess deteriorated so much as the hour for the departure approached that Lizzie feared she might not survive the journey. She could not keep down her food, and the doctors were alarmed by a hard mass in the base of her stomach. It was feared she had developed a tumour.

In a last desperate attempt to stop them going, on July 31st Lady Leicester again sent a messenger to the Council, to Sir Theodore Mayherne, demanding a certificate to say the princess was fit to be moved. He would have to take responsibility for the decision which was made against her ladyship's advice and that of her own personal physician.

On August 1st 1650 at a meeting of the Council her pleas were overruled. No such certificate was produced.

Major-General Harrison, who was in charge of the travel arrangements, agreed with Lady Leicester, but reluctantly obeyed his orders. It was a sad contingent which left Penshurst on a bright morning in late August. Even the grooms could see the poor princess was too weak to sit up and had to lie across Lizzie's and Mrs Briott's knees. The extra allocation of six horses per coach for added comfort did little to prevent the bumping and rolling of the iron wheels on the ill-kept roads. General Harrison had been instructed to escort the party as far as the vessel set to carry them across the Solent.

During the voyage they would be the responsibility of Mildmay and the ship's crew. Mildmay was to travel in a separate coach with his wife and the party would be met at Yarmouth by the soldiers garrisoned on the island. The Governor of the Castle, Colonel Sydenham, would attend them at the castle, as would the Mayor of Newport, Moses Reed.

The ship, *The Pearl,* was an obsolete man-of-war, square-rigged and cumbersome. The space below decks had been converted from a gun emplacement to accommodate passengers and freight. Mrs Briott had been below to inspect and come up with a definitive opinion: 'Only fit for cockroaches and rats,' she explained pointedly, observing that Mrs Mildmay was making much of a descent into the space below decks where her servants had been transporting hampers of food and wine. Lizzie noticed the slapdash repair work on the side of

164

the ship where she had been holed in some naval conflict or other, and mentioned it to Richard.

'Never fear,' he reassured her. 'It's only a short distance to Yarmouth and the day's calm. The ship's lying high on the water, for she's designed for more than our small party. She would have had a hundred men and guns and provisions.'

'But where did they sleep?' Lizzie asked.

'They would have slung hammocks in the hold below the water line where no air ever penetrates,' Richard replied, 'and their bedding was stuffed with the waste from the tanners' yards, sometimes with the flesh still attached.'

The description caught Harry's attention. 'Didn't that make them ill?' he asked.

'Yes it did,' Richard replied. 'The sailors died like flies but it was of no importance. It paid a captain to lose his crew on the home straight, since the men's pay was only dished out on disembarkation. A good old epidemic of typhoid would relieve the captain of the sailors' money and the widows and children would never see a penny of it.'

Lizzie shuddered as she thought of the many poor souls who had breathed their last on *The Pearl*.

Just then Mildmay came swaggering up. He seemed to know some of the crew and the boatswain, a sullen-looking man with a heavily pock-marked face, spoke to him without introduction. They had a heated conversation and then Mildmay walked away. Richard clapped his fist to his head.

'Of course. Mildmay knows this ship well. He commanded it when it was a naval vessel,' he blurted. 'So he'll go below to some privileged corner, to which the King's children won't have access.'

'No matter, Sir Richard. We'll make a comfortable corner on deck, out of the wind, and I have some cold guinea fowl for us, and her Ladyship's peaches or what's left of them after the Mildmays helped themselves.'

The child sank down gratefully on to the assembled cushions and rugs and closed her eyes. She felt a kind of safety surrounded by her loyal servants, whose devotion had been underwritten by their willingness to come with them. Mrs Briott was more of a mother to her than her own and was wise enough to steer a clever path with both friend and foe.

165

Her homely competent command of domestic affairs left no room for argument. And Lizzie was more like a sister than a servant. When she and Richard were together the world took on a rosy glow in the light of their love for each other. It reminded the princess of the enchanted childhood she had had with her own parents, so deeply in love until their world had been torn apart, and her poor father had been so badly served by his advisers.

Beth fell into a quiet sleep with Minette in her lap, and her gentle sleeping smile spoke of hopeful dreams.

In fact she was not quite asleep, she was making plans. She would sell her necklace. It was safe in her velvet purse secured on a ribbon around her waist. Only Lady Leicester knew of its true value. It would raise enough money to help them get to her sister Mary in Holland. Harry would come with her, and they would all be a family again. Better still, her brother would be restored to the throne, and she would see that all her faithful friends were rewarded. Mildmay's villainy would not go unpunished. She had made a full account of it in her private papers. It was in a code known only to the family. The casual reader would think it the frivolous diary of a young girl. One day there would be retribution for those who thought to walk away from the misery they had inflicted.

She was nearly asleep when she heard Lizzie's voice.

'And I've the fresh bread from the baker, who kindly pressed it on us as we arrived here, and do you know he showed me his Cavalier feather,' Lizzie whispered, covering the girl's knees with a silk rug. 'And he said God would send us King Charles's son and save his precious children,' she confided.

'It is as I keep telling you, child,' Mrs Briott said firmly, 'there're many who'll help the children. When we get to the Island, we must find the sources to bring the poor lambs some comfort.'

'You're right, Mrs Briott,' Lizzie agreed. 'We're their family now, and we'll fight with our last breath to see they want for nothing. I've seen their noble courage and have never heard either of them utter a vile thing about the wicked people who decide their fate.'

She glanced towards Mildmay. He was now busy supervising the securing of his personal coach, which he had insisted on bringing with him to the Island. His horses protested violently, as the coachman tried to get them on board.

Mildmay viciously seized the man's whip and beat them until they screamed with pain and terror and eventually capitulated. One was a fine bay mare and her nostrils flared at the sight of the swaying ship's deck. She was foaming at the mouth and Richard pointedly went to her and calmed her, speaking quietly in her ear and offering her some sweetmeats from his pocket.

Mildmay had been watching him resentfully. 'Well, let's hope you have the same effect on the Island wenches, who prefer something more manly than poetry and a lump of sugar,' he taunted loudly.

'I think your jest is unfitting in the presence of ladies and young children,' replied Richard, coolly turning on his heel and walking towards Harry, who was now taking a lively interest in the business of preparing the sails ready for departure.

He thought how the boy was similar to his two brothers, Charles and James, reckless and brave, responding to any new adventure.

'What are you thinking?' Richard asked Lizzie, seeing her watching the boy.

'I was thinking that Harry is growing into young man. After all, his brother Charles was not more than a boy of twelve at the big battle, which one was it?' she asked.

'Edgehill,' Richard replied at once. 'He tried to take on the entire Parliamentary army single-handed and don't forget he was no more than nineteen when his father was murdered. He saw death on a massive scale. In a way Harry has been spared some of that.'

'And what will the children find if they get to Charles's court in Bruges?' asked Lizzie.

'That is a problem,' Richard admitted. 'Sometimes our King-in-waiting is so short of money that he cannot afford to get his washing done, but all that will change,' he added on a note of confidence.

'Harry is made of the same metal, and what his father and brother might lack in diplomacy he makes up for in full,' said Lizzie proudly, thinking about the letters he wrote to Parliament

167

pleading for himself and his sister. It had occurred to her that, had it not been for the undoubted goodness and charm of the two children, a far worse fate might have awaited them.

Perhaps, after all, she pondered, Cromwell was genuinely impressed by the King's children, and somewhere, after all, there was a God in his heaven. She had heard the Island was a beautiful place and that the people were friendly, and anyway, from the way Richard was talking, the children would not be there for long; in the meantime she hoped the castle would not be as grim as the children had claimed. Even if it was they were now perfectly placed to sail to France or Belgium . . . She had doubts, though, about a swift conclusion to the children's ordeal, since shortly before their departure from Penshurst the news had come that Charles was temporarily in Scotland, trying to raise support for his return to the English throne, a project which Richard dismissed as one doomed to failure.

Lizzie had never been on a boat of this size in her life and was sure it would topple over at the slightest puff of wind. Her feelings of fear and anxiety increased as she saw the surly way the crew of the boat addressed the royal party and their attendants.

Amidst shouting and confusion, orders were given to cast off and, with a great slap, the sails took the wind and the vessel gathered speed. Almost at once Beth complained of feeling ill, so Lizzie settled her on more cushions they had removed from the coach, and sat with her in the fresh air on deck. It was not long before Richard sought them out again and came to sit with them.

'Did you know, Your Highness, there's some good news?' he said encouragingly to Beth, firmly continuing to use her title, despite the instructions from the Council.

'Good news is a rarity, what can it be?' asked Beth.

'The Council have been considering sending you to your sister, the Princess of Orange, as is your dearest wish, and granting you a handsome annuity of a thousand pounds a year. So keep courage, for we are all of a mind that you are not at Carisbrooke for long.'

Beth was obviously cheered and sat up as the ship altered

course a fraction, and the strong August sun fell on her pale face.

'But what about Harry?' she asked urgently. 'Will we go together? I cannot leave him, and it is sure my feeble life is not of as much interest as my brother's.'

Richard removed his velvet cap and ran his fingers through his hair, trying to find the right words. He would never be seen without a hat in the presence of the children and when the sun was strong and he wanted to the feel of fresh air on his head, it would be tucked into his leather belt waiting to be doffed. He had noticed that, despite instructions given to General Harrison that no hats were to be raised to the royal children, there had been many on the route who tossed their hats. At one point the train had been stopped and orders given to the children to sit back in the coach so that they might not be seen.

He was concerned because he didn't know quite how the princess would receive the secret information he had on the plans for her young brother. Lizzie watched his face carefully.

His velvet waistcoat was open and the loose white shirt unfastened at the neck. The day was becoming hotter. She could see the skin of his chest and neck dappled with perspiration and the the cross his mother had given him when he was a boy, but as she looked at him she knew she must not let herself get carried away with thoughts of what might be.

'Your Highness, do not say anything of this to your brother,' Richard said seriously. 'There's a suggestion that he should go to your brother Charles in Scotland, as long as he doesn't conspire in any way against the new order.' He broke off as Beth's face clouded in horror.

'And he is to be handsomely provided for,' he added.

Beth looked puzzled. 'I do not understand. Surely Parliament would not let Henry go to Charles, who has forsaken his principles to join with the Covenantors in the hope of regaining his throne.'

'Your Highness, I dare say it's thought that your elder brother's confidence in the Covenantors has been misplaced. A more ill-suited alliance is hard to imagine. They make even the dour hellfire and damnation preaching of the Roundheads seem positively libertine. I think it won't be long before he's headed back to the Hague, and, God willing, will bring your brother with him so that you may be reunited.'

'I hope and pray so,' the princess replied. 'And I try to keep my brother's spirits up. You see how little he is disturbed by this move to the hateful Carisbrooke. I have assured him it is for his own protection, and that this a step nearer to freedom. For a boat can easily be prepared at Cowes.' Her voice trailed away and Lizzie could see she was feeling unwell. Mrs Briott appeared with the basket of carefully prepared food.

They had even polished the silver goblets and utensils and washed the damask napkins and ironed them with the innkeeper's wife's flat iron which had not been used for many a month. Mrs Briott had had to scrape the rust off it with a pumice stone.

Mrs Briott had a skill for turning even the most stressful occasions into harmonious affairs. Her kindly face crinkled in concentration as she fussed over the picnic, creating order in adversity. Lizzie noticed some of the sailors looking enviously at the party, who for all the world now looked like a happy family, without a care in the world.

'Do try to take some nourishment,' Lizzie coaxed the princess who looked increasingly pale and tired.

Eventually, after Harry had wolfed down more than his fair share of the food and Mrs Briott had tidied up the remnants and given Harry the left-over bread to throw to the gulls, Lizzie asked if anyone knew where the Mildmays were.

'Oh, below deck,' Mrs Briott replied. 'And mighty relieved they were when I told them the children would prefer to eat on deck with the food we'd brought for them. For they're filling themselves in a shameless way with fine wines and venison pie and peaches from her Ladyship's garden.' Mrs Briott's disapproval was gathering momentum by the second, and she would not be stopped. 'Which I saw,' she continued not too discreetly, 'Mrs Mildmay's servant stealing before we set off. A great basket of them . . . there's no end to the man's poisonous greed and dishonesty. The sooner the truth comes out, the better for a wager. This isn't the behaviour Parliament would want in an officer and his wife.'

Mrs Briott huffed on in her down-to-earth way, saying things that Richard would have liked to say himself but dared not.

His role was a more subtle one where cards must be played in secret.

He had been warned that Mildmay and his brother were a force to be reckoned with. Sooner or later the captain would hang himself with the interconnecting strands of his self-seeking mendacity. Meanwhile Richard would watch and wait and report. But despite his outward appearance of calm, he was a worried man. He feared for Beth – she looked so weak and vulnerable, dark shadows under her eyes, for all the rosy cheeks brought on by the fresh air.

She only picked at a little cold meat and sipped some fresh milk, and then lay back on the cushions, her pale hair falling from her cap. He wished they could do more for her. But the mention of the Mildmays below decks had raised the spectre he feared most, for he was well aware of the lascivious designs the captain had on Lizzie. He saw the way he tumbled the servants when his wife was not looking.

Mrs Briott had told him about the castle at Carisbrooke, for she had accompanied the children there when they had visited their father. The cramped conditions would be in Lizzie's favour at least. Richard felt reassured as he concluded that not much could happen there without everyone seeing. He understood the captain would live with his wife in one of the towers overlooking an enclosed courtyard, so his wings would be clipped insofar as Lizzie was concerned, so long as she was careful. Despite these reassurances, as he looked towards the shore of the Island, he felt a foreboding in his heart.

Later, when the wind had dropped in a late afternoon lull, the boat slowed down and progress was slow, Beth succumbed to the gentle swaying and dropped off to sleep.

Richard and Lizzie moved to the stern of the boat out of sight. She quickly moved into his arms. Their feelings of trepidation about the future did not need words. Richard held her gently and they watched the shoreline retreat into the distance, the beauty of the azure blue sea and the pellucid light on the water on such a perfect day seeming at odds with the darkness they felt they were approaching at Carisbrooke prison. Richard spoke, pushing Lizzie away, so that he could look longingly at her. They were all being swept along by events over which they had no control, but he believed with all his soul that man's integrity and survival must pivot on the belief that, with faith and determination, in the end, good would prevail; that order would supplant chaos; and that he must never cease to strive with all the means at his disposal, however obscure, to deliver the children safely to their freedom. They were the King's most precious legacy, and for all the King's misguided intransigence he had been a good man at heart.

'My dearest Lizzie,' he said, gripping her by her upper arms, so hard that she felt the warmth of his hands fire through her, and she would have melted into his arms and let him possess not just her heart, but every bit of her body and life.

'Whatever the future holds,' he said fervently, 'you are mine, Lizzie, to have and to protect, and even if the tempest of events may blow us apart for a time, I vow that I will come for you. I will find you even at the ends of the earth. Each day when the sun rises I will share it with you in my spirit, because I will know that you're under that same sun.'

She felt his love so powerfully that it was almost tangible. And she returned it with her whole soul. He stood so tall and handsome in the prow of the ship, his fine blue eyes and his fair hair falling to his collar. She loved him so much she wanted to share it with the world. She stood on her tiptoes and put her lips to his. She felt she would die of happiness, grateful even for those few brief minutes, as if her life had prepared her for this moment of understanding. For all the darkness of the months since she had left her family, Richard had been given to her: a ray of light in a dark and evil world. But underlying all this she felt her love for the King's children, and she felt her responsibility to them as profoundly as she felt her love for Richard.

Hers was no small part in these cataclysmic times which would echo for ever down the years, perhaps an extraordinary fate for an ordinary girl. But if, after all the sadness, she ended up with him, it would have been worth it. As they drew apart she could taste his mouth and savour his faint smell of maleness. Part of him was already hers.

'Oh, dearest Richard,' she said, resting her head on his

chest. 'How can you be so sure? I wish I could be as confident as you are.'

'Look, about you,' he insisted. 'Savour this wonderful day. Lock it in your mind. We will be together, if we have faith, and when we're old, I shall remember it – the smell of the sea in your hair, the light in your eyes, and the feel of your heart against mine beating as one.'

'Sir Richard, come and see. We're nearing the port,' came Harry's shrill voice. They broke away and Richard went to be with the boy for whom he felt a most tender love. He would reconcile his two loves however long it took.

Twenty

The short journey from Yarmouth to the castle had put Mildmay in a villainous mood. Although the population on the Island had been informed that there was to be no ceremony at the arrival of the children, now to be known as Master Harry and Miss Elizabeth Stuart, the route had been lined with curious onlookers, many of whom had tossed their hats into the air, and some of the women had curtsied low. Harry waved back from the window of the carriage and the captain sent a soldier to warn him once again to conceal himself, but the prince paid no attention. The men had noticed his spirited refusal to comply and the captain thought he detected a contagious mood of insubordination.

'Things will be different when I've complete control, you'll see, my dear,' the captain remarked to Mrs Mildmay as they sat in their coach for the journey to Carisbrooke and she wondered, not for the first time, if her husband would have been any different if she had been able to give him children. He was not the first man to switch loyalties as the country descended into near-anarchy, but in his case, when he betrayed the King, he had lost his honour and his sense of family. She knew, for all his posturing when he spoke to the Council about the children's welfare, he cared nothing for them. Of that, at least, she was sure, or he would not have suggested and supported a move to this awful place where they would have to make the best of it.

Her husband's philanderings were well known to her and she knew that power had corrupted him, but she, Catherine Mildmay, would go along with whatever her husband wished. She would feather her bed and hope to keep him in it, for there was still time. She might yet bear him a child. They would spend more time together now, away from the temptations in London.

She cast a surreptitious glance in his direction and, seeing his profile, although his lips were pursed in anger, she still felt an undeniable flutter of passion for him. He still had a power over her as he did over so many women. She must keep him at all costs, even at the expense of what she knew was right.

Recently she had heard people whispering in secret, 'What if the monarchy were restored? What then?' It had made her think . . . retribution for people like her husband? Anthony must not know of the hidden cache of funds she was accumulating . . . just in case she would go abroad. She would not mind being an émigrée, but she could not tolerate being poor. Her thoughts were abruptly interrupted.

'I do not care for the colour of your gown, madam,' Mildmay said suddenly. 'You must send for a dressmaker when we get to the castle. I intend to entertain the local gentry, and yes, to enjoy myself at last . . .'

Mrs Mildmay pondered for a moment thinking. It would be nice to spend some money on her wardrobe. She would become the leader of fashion on this silly Island where they were not used to people of quality. At last she would be important. People would bow to her every whim. She would be like royalty. She warmed more and more to the concept.

Interrupting her reverie, her husband continued, 'The last few years have been very difficult. This should be a good assignment. I intend to enjoy it for as long as possible.' He smiled, as if contemplating a life of tranquil indulgence.

Her stomach tightened a little because she knew he was

an animal who would not use his leisure soberly or wisely. On reflection, she doubted she featured profoundly in his calculations. She would be an ornament to his ambitions, a chattel to be discarded when it had fulfilled its purpose. As if to remind her of the reason for their being there, she heard the shrill voice of the prince from the coach behind them. It did not warm her heart, but rather hardened it for self-preservation.

The castle could be seen standing proud on a hill above the town. The last time the children had come it had been a grey day, the sky overcast. The sinister fortified building had loomed darkly over the town of Newport, the capital of the Island which sat comfortably in the plain below. Today, in the bright sunshine, it took on a less forbidding feel.

The party stopped abruptly at the bottom of a steep incline by the castle gates. Mildmay barked orders for the children to get out of the carriage which was too wide to get through. They would have to walk up to the castle itself. Richard explained that the baggage would be taken by mule to their quarters.

'The castle,' he explained to Harry, 'is so impregnable that even the water has to be drawn up from the well by mules, which are tethered and blindfolded while they walk round in endless circles.'

He did not tell the boy that this had been a grim prison, where prisoners had perished chained to the same wheel, now driven by the unfortunate mules. There were many things better left unsaid. They would discover them soon enough.

Despite Mildmay's instructions to afford the children as little deference as possible, following their arrival Colonel Sydenham was moved by an unforeseen sympathy for them, especially the princess, who was of the same age as his own daughter.

After a respectable interval during which he hoped they would have recovered a little from the shock of their new surroundings, he paid the children a visit.

The princess sat serenely in a large high-backed chair. She did not rise to greet him but held out her hand for him to take. This threw the colonel into some confusion and he found himself taking the proffered hand with what passed for a bow.

'I hope you have everything you need,' he said awkwardly.

'If I did not believe in God alone and his love and guidance for my family,' she said disarmingly, 'I would be very fearful in this place, but he is watching over us as he watched for my dear father who is now in heaven with our dear Lord and Saviour, whom,' she went on, 'will gladly receive me with more joy than I find here.'

The colonel could not bring himself to address the princess as Miss Elizabeth in the way he had been instructed, for her courageous and dignified bearing spoke of generations of royal breeding which he suddenly realized could not be eliminated quite so easily as he had been led to suppose. He replied without using her name.

'I will do my best to think of some things to occupy you and your brother,' he said, attempting to look cheerful and deliberately ignoring Beth's comments, which he found profoundly disturbing in so young a person.

'That would be nice for my brother, and I shall encourage him because it is my duty to look after him as I promised my father. He has already lost his best playfellow,' said Beth sadly.

'Oh?' replied the colonel enquiringly.

'Yes, our brother James,' she reminded him somewhat ingenuously, 'escaped to Holland dressed as a girl.'

'Yes of course,' replied the colonel, absentmindedly fiddling with a button on his cuff while he considered how best to respond to Beth's remark, so clearly meant as a spirited warning of things to come.

'I hope you will not attempt something like that while you are under my care,' he said eventually. 'I will look after your interests as if you were my own children and I am sure things will not be as bad as you think.'

'Well I hope you will not suffer the same fate as our own father,' replied Beth quickly. 'But since you are being so kind to us, Colonel, I wish you no discourtesy.' She went on politely, 'I should tell you that my brother Harry will never recover from the murder of our father and he has never known his mother because we have been the prisoners of Parliament since he was two, and there can be no useful purpose in keeping us here, away from our family.'

The colonel listened to her courteous account of her situation, delivered with a quiet charm, and felt distinctly uncomfortable. Her grace was in such stark contrast to Captain Mildmay and his ill-mannered wife, now installed in unseemly luxury in the tower.

Colonel Sydenham spent a sleepless night worrying about his little prisoners. Although the princess had spoken so confidently, any fool could see that the child was desperately ill, and the boy was a bright little fellow. The whole affair was beginning to make him uneasy. The assignment which had seemed so straightforward for a military man had assumed a quite different nature.

The colonel was under strict orders with regard to the children, and, mindful of the disapproval incurred by the previous governor Colonel Hammond, whom Parliament considered had been too lax with his arrangements for the King, he had resolved to do his job properly, but now?

Keeping his prisoners secure was one thing, but the soul of the little princess would not be secured by any earthly power. If it so minded to flee the Island prison, he would be implicated and he might be accused of negligence. The bodily health of the children was of prime concern. The public would blame Parliament for her death and lately there had been comments about the treatment of the young children. He resolved to summon two of the doctors on the Island, Bagnell and Treherne, at once.

On their arrival the colonel listened attentively to their concerns. 'The child is weak,' said Doctor Bagnell gravely. 'The tumour we were told about in her stomach has enlarged,' he went on. 'Moreover her state of mind is not conducive to a speedy recovery.'

'She spends a lot of time playing with her little dog and at her studies,' replied the colonel, 'and she seldom leaves her room,' he admitted.

'Is she getting proper care?' asked Doctor Treherne.

'Her attendants are doing all that is reasonably possible, of that at least I am sure,' said the colonel.

But he detected an atmosphere of apprehension, and the

doctors were so concerned that they announced that in future they would come several times a day.

The weather had suddenly turned unseasonably wet and cold, but on the Monday following the children's arrival, the day dawned fresh and bright, and Colonel Sydenham paid another visit to the children's apartments. It was early and he was impressed to find 'Master Stuart' already at his studies with Richard Lovell. Yet again he made his way up the narrow poky staircase which led to the children's apartments, and thought how they must contrast with the accommodation they had been used to. He had done his best to make the place comfortable, but the narrow stairs and small slit-like windows which had foiled the King's well-planned escape, and in which, despite his slight and agile frame, he had become firmly wedged, gave the place a feeling of claustrophobic gloom.

There was no disguising the fact that this was a prison and the surrounding fortifications and deep moat isolated the castle from the world outside. He was glad to leave the place at night and return to his family. The islanders said it was haunted by the souls of the many who had languished and died inside its confines. He did not doubt that the soul of the King would be there to watch for his children as the winter drew in and the wind from the sea rattled the ill-fitting shutters.

Mrs Briott was busy in what served as the parlour, mending some linen. She sang softly under her breath. A carefully arranged bunch of wild flowers stood in a pewter jug on an oak table beside her.

Her touch was evident in many things. As the colonel's gaze swept the room with a soldier's attention to detail, he saw there was a fire in the hearth, despite the season. The room was warm and friendly as it had not been before and the furniture had been polished and sparkled from dark corners. He wondered where Mrs Briott had managed to find the flowers in the castle confines, and how she had acquired wood at this time. He cleared his throat loudly to announce his arrival, and she carefully folded her work, her face betraying neither pleasure nor pain at his presence. She rose and curtsied, not the quick bob he would have expected, but deep and low, her eyes to the ground. Colonel Sydenham felt inexplicably embarrassed. He wondered in this new climate of egalitarianism if her elaborate behaviour was genuinely respectful, or perhaps tinged with a subtle kind of mockery.

'I come, Mrs Briott, to enquire after the health of . . .' He hesitated. 'Miss Elizabeth,' he continued awkwardly. Mrs Briott looked down at her feet, her disapproval palpable. She did not respond immediately, evidently giving her reply some careful thought.

The colonel had not yet considered the person of Mrs Briott, but as she raised her eyes and spoke he recognized she was a woman of some bearing and education, not the homespun housewife she would like to be thought.

'Sir, I thank you for your enquiry, but before I answer, I would beg your understanding on something which has caused the children's attendants great difficulty since our arrival here.'

'By all means. Do be seated,' he said politely. The woman struck him as both kind and intelligent, and they had a common purpose with regard to the welfare of the two children. He would need her co-operation.

She sat facing him and the morning sun shot a beam of light on the long oak table, curiously illuminating the embroidered royal crest on the pillow case she was repairing.

They both saw it. She raised it to show him more closely. She stared at him with her cool blue unflinching eyes.

'*This* proves my point exactly, sir. Am I to unpick this beautiful work, which I'm trying to repair, or do I leave it? It is a harmless thing, and of no consequence in the world outside.' She went on looking at him, waiting for an answer.

'I fail to see the connection,' came the reply.

'Well, sir,' Mrs Briott said quietly, 'the royal crest is part of this linen. It has always been. It is perhaps fifty years old, older than you or I. If you remove it, it's still a royal pillow case, just the same as before, only it will be damaged by the unpicking and it won't be quite the same, not recognizable in the way we've known it.'

'What exactly are you trying to say?' he asked impatiently.

'Well, Colonel Sydenham. To us the royal servants, the duke and the princess will be the same whatever we call them.'

179

'Well, couldn't you just . . .' he ventured.

'Sir, the King's children cannot be unpicked like a piece of linen. Nothing can change who they are, sir. So wouldn't it be best to leave things in case we upset them any more at this time . . .?'

Mrs Briott stopped short, dabbing her eyes with a handkerchief. The colonel cleared his throat loudly fearing the woman was about to get emotional.

'The angels are calling the little girl, our gentle princess. She will not be with you for long, sir . . . and we shall all be accountable both in this world and the next.' Mrs Briott challenged him with a look which spoke volumes. He shifted uneasily.

'Understand me,' he replied. 'Of course I would have had things otherwise. The children are innocent of any crime. I feel my responsibility for them keenly. The distinction between right and wrong has been lost in the moral turpitude in which men have drowned.'

'The legacy of the regicide, sir. That is what you mean?'

He thought for a moment, somewhat in sympathy with the woman's sound good sense. He knew he should reprove her vehemently, but truthfully he resented the fact that a soldier in his position should be playing gaoler to two innocent children, one of whom was an invalid.

He saw himself as Mrs Briott must see him perhaps . . . a man without courage of heart . . . but the fact was he was a man tired of the monstrous machine which had emerged from the war.

A New Model Army, built with the blood of the King and many of his own relatives, and now this. He did not want this post and the only way to be relieved of it was to remove its purpose. He would write to the Council at once. The children should be sent to their remaining family abroad.

But first he would extend a father's hand to the little girl, as he would do to his own daughter. He coughed uncomfortably and stood up.

'Mrs Briott, I am as concerned about the princess as you are,' he said pointedly, a trace of a smile on his stern face. 'The day is fair,' he went on. 'I should like to take the child into the fresh air. May I suggest a walk, to the bowling green,

180

and her brother might enjoy a game of bowls. Why, I might even challenge him myself.'

'Why, sir, that's a splendid idea. I will order Lizzie Jones to go at once and see if the princess feels well enough. I do agree both the children should take the air. The duke is a good lad and he will be overjoyed.' She bobbed him a curtsey and left the room excitedly.

The enthusiasm in the woman's voice pleased him. He had had enough of being the bearer of bad news. After all, he was not so much the children's gaoler as their protector. This conception restored his self-esteem. He felt better, more like the man of honour he tried to be in all things.

Colonel Sydenham's gesture of kindness did not have the result he intended. Shortly after Beth and Harry arrived at the bowling green, about five minutes' walk from the castle, the sky darkened. A sudden rainstorm soaked the party. Beth quickly developed a chill and despite a hurried return to her quarters and the warmth of her bed, her condition worsened.

The Island doctors did all they could and all the next day she lay in her bed looking pale. She refused a drink and Lizzie left her to get some rest. Her little dog Minette, from whom she was never separated, lay beside her on the covers, her nose pressed to her mistress's cheek in touching concern. Lizzie was convinced the creature sensed that her mistress might slip away, and decided to keep a careful watch. The dog whimpered quietly. Lizzie and Mrs Briott tried to move her gently away, but the princess became distressed and held on to the dog.

'She is the best friend I ever had,' she whispered faintly.

Mrs Briott touched Lizzie's hand briefly, they both had their own private thoughts.

It was September 8th and a bright autumn sunshine lightened the aspect of the castle now under the pall of the Beth's illness, and Colonel Sydenham decided to notify the council of the princess's condition. They at once instructed Doctor Colenden, a leading London physician, to repair to the Island.

Lizzie sat watching the child, the window of her chamber

181

was slightly open and birds could be heard cheeping on the castle keep. The only other sound was Beth's laboured breathing. She moved her pillows constantly in an attempt to ease her discomfort.

She began to sleep more of the time and when she quietly slipped into the merciful release of her secret world of dreams, her face became calm and serene. A gentle smile played on her lips and she softly mouthed words.

Lizzie leaned forward, listening intently. Was it her imagination? Did the child continually say 'Father'? Was it that which made her breathing slow to a peaceful rhythm?

'How is she?' Lizzie had not heard anyone come into the room. She was too engrossed in trying to decipher Beth's words. It was Mrs Briott, who placed a reassuring hand on Lizzie's shoulder. The gesture of sympathy was too much for Lizzie, and tears flowed silently down her cheeks. Beth opened her eyes and turned her head towards the women.

'Lizzie, Mrs Briott, come closer, I must tell you of the dream I have just had.'

Her voice was faint and her cheeks began to flush an unnatural red. Lizzie had often seen just such a look in the faces of the villagers when she had visited the sick and dying. An unexpected burst of life before they slipped into the next world.

'I saw Father and he is waiting for me. I cannot stay. And I must prepare myself for my journey.' She spoke so softly that they could hardly distinguish the words.

'Oh don't, dearest, you can't leave Harry,' Lizzie wept, no longer able to hide her grief.

'And what about Minette, who will care for her?' Beth asked faintly, stroking the dog's long silky ears which even in her sickness she had tenderly brushed that very morning.

'My dearest,' said Lizzie emotionally, 'you must not speak like that. Think of your family. How your mother must wish for your freedom. Please try to get well, and do not worry about Minette. I shall always care for her.'

Beth tried to sit up but fell back on her pillows, her pale hair spreading around her face in a bright circle, and as Lizzie looked at her childlike beauty, she thought what a tragic life the child had had and how good and sweet she had remained. She seemed untouched by the mendacity with which she had been surrounded.

The child suddenly regained some energy and called for her Bible. Lizzie gave it to her and bathed her fevered brow with rose water. Beth closed her eyes and seemed to be peaceful as Lizzie sat by the bed watching her but suddenly she stirred and reached for Lizzie's hand.

'My dear friend Lizzie,' she said, holding on to Lizzie's hand tightly as if she were drowning. 'You did not know me when I was happy,' she went on faintly, 'when Mother and Father were together and we were all one loving family . . .' She faltered, searching for the words. 'It was a taste of paradise, Lizzie, and then they took it away and I will never find it again on this earth. I hope God will give you that happiness one day, Lizzie,' she finished almost fiercely.

'Dearest child, you are so good, you will be the brightest angel in paradise,' whispered Lizzie hoarsely.

'Lizzie, I must say goodbye to Harry and make my will.' Her words were barely audible. 'I have my necklace of pearls and my diamond pin. Please will you send for Sir Richard so that he may write it down for me.'

Minette was licking her face as if to encourage her in the effort of speaking. Lizzie made as if to gently pull her away.

'Don't move her,' murmured Beth. 'She knows I am leaving. I will see Father's Rogue soon, Lizzie, for dogs have souls just as we do. How else could Minette have been my comfort as she has been?'

Lizzie went to summon Harry and fell into Mrs Briott's arms weeping.

'You must accept it, dear,' said Mrs Briott soothingly, 'it won't help her if you don't, and she has suffered so much already, who can blame her for wanting to go to a better world? Go and fetch Sir Richard at once and Harry. We cannot hide the truth from him any more.'

Richard led Harry into the room. The boy hesitated a little, hovering in the doorway. Richard had tried to prepare him, for he knew Beth had recognized that her own death was imminent.

The boy drew towards the bed, and Beth opened her eyes

183

and smiled. He rushed the final distance and fell weeping on the coverlet.

Lizzie heard heavy footsteps on the narrow winding staircase to the bedchamber.

'I'll not have any of them in this room, Lizzie,' Mrs Briott commanded. 'They are all stained with this child's blood, and I'll have no false tears to wash away their guilt. This is the time for those who love her to ease her path. Bar the door, girl, and let no one pass,' she thundered. The footsteps quickly retreated without protest.

Lizzie and Mrs Briott stood back as Beth gave her instructions to Richard. Harry lay beside her on the bed stroking her cheek. He had stopped weeping. He was experienced in the land of loss. When his father had been murdered, Elizabeth had said, 'Nothing worse could ever happen to him,' but for him this was worse than anything he could have dreamed of. He would be alone, terribly, unimaginably alone.

'What shall I do without you, dear sister?' he whispered. 'Who will assist me to find my family without you and your cleverness? I shall be forgotten.'

Lizzie and Mrs Briott came forward as Richard beckoned them.

Richard took the boy's hand across the bed and bent so close to Beth that he could feel her breath on his face.

'No, Harry, you're not alone,' he said resolutely. 'I'll never leave you until you're safely with your family, and your brother's restored to the throne. I give your sister my solemn word that though she may watch you from heaven, I will watch for you on earth.'

As Lizzie listened to the words, she knew that something greater than the love she and Richard felt for each other took precedence in his world. But as she saw him beside the children in their hour of such terrible need, she realized that anything else would make him a lesser man.

Later Beth fell into a peaceful sleep and Richard and Harry slipped quietly away so that Harry might get some air. The girl slept on and Mrs Briott went to prepare some weak tea with honey in case she woke with a thirst.

Lizzie sat by the window with Minette on her lap. The dog had been prised away from her mistress, so as not to disturb her, and although she lay still with Lizzie, her eyes never left her sleeping mistress. Suddenly, as Lizzie's attention wandered to the sight of Richard returning across the castle green holding Harry's hand, the dog sat up and ran whimpering to the bed.

Lizzie caught her breath and ran after her. Beth lay with her hand on her Bible, her finger pointing to the words 'Oh, come all ye that are heavy laden and I will give you rest.' She was at peace. She had passed safely into the loving arms of her father.

Twenty-One

The winter of 1652 came in to Carisbrooke Castle with a flourish. Two interminable years had passed since the death of the princess. Lizzie felt isolated from events in the outside world, not least the fact that the children's brother, Charles, had returned from exile and been crowned King at Scone in Scotland on New Year's Day in 1651. The event had brought with it a ray of hope for Harry.

Lizzie had managed to get home only once, and news from Hatherton provided welcome relief for Harry, who now felt he knew all Lizzie's family intimately. Tom had come out of hiding but as to the circumstances in which he had been able to do so Lizzie could only guess. Nonetheless, on her one visit home, he had been there: a different, less dogmatic Tom. He had formed a great friendship with Sir Francis Hinton, of whom Lizzie heard a great deal.

But for months and months now she had been refused permission to go home, and she did not have to look far to see the reason. Captain Mildmay had begun to notice her again. Up until now his attentions had been unashamedly occupied with a married lady in Newport whose husband had been coincidentally promoted in the island garrison. But it appeared the woman had become ill and the captain had time on his hands, and this he put to use implementing a host of petty economies and generally making his presence felt.

As Lizzie wrote home to her parents, life in the castle was difficult. Bitter winds now moaned about the castle towers and tore the few trees surrounding the bowling green from their roots. At least the rooms were warm due to their small size. Mrs Briott had hung the thick Penshurst tapestries in front of the doors, and the sad retinue did what they could to comfort Harry in his grief.

Harry, it was thought by all Royalist supporters, must go to his mother in France or to his brother Charles in Flanders. But it had soon become obvious to Lizzie that Mildmay would do everything in his power to keep the boy at Carisbrooke.

The clue came when Richard found Mildmay's servant removing one of the tapestry hangings. This was not the first item to go missing from the apartments, and it transpired that the captain was systematically making free with the royal possessions. Technically these were now regarded as the property of Parliament, but there had been the more scandalous issue of the princess's necklace and diamond pin: neither had been seen since shortly after the princess's death. Harry had been left the necklace in the will, and it was in the custody of the Earl of Leicester, who in turn had been left the diamond jewel. Repeated requests for the delivery of the necklace had so far been ignored. It being of sufficient value to set Harry up quite nicely should he get to France, Richard soon began to suspect that the captain had a hand in all this.

Letters to the Council of State negotiating the boy's release had met with a variety of responses, amounting to a confusing prevarication, which had gone on until the months had dragged on into years. Circumstances were no longer in Harry's favour.

'Hopes of a restoration for Charles have faded,' Richard announced one morning, following a secret communication received the previous day.

Mrs Briott crossed herself, Lizzie felt a thudding disappointment. How could they break the news to Harry, who had been so confident?

'Why, what has gone wrong?' asked Lizzie.

'It is simple,' replied Richard dejectedly. 'As I had feared, the Scots have betrayed him, it is history repeating itself, they did the same thing to his father.'

'Is he safe?' asked Lizzie anxiously.

'It was his final attempt at an invasion of England, but it ended in disaster at Worcester,' replied Richard.

'Yes, but Charles, where is he?' Lizzie persisted.

'The King is a survivor,' said Richard pointedly. 'He fled disguised as a woman and, at one point, sat in an oak tree while the New Model Army bayed for his blood below, and then he made his way to Brightholmstone where he boarded a ship and made for France.'

'Thank God,' said Mrs Briott.

'There is a rumour that he headed for the Isle of Wight, hoping to rescue Harry, but he was advised against it since it might have meant his own captivity,' said Richard. 'Now, unfortunately, he will be living the life of a displaced monarch, depending on the charity of his foreign relatives,' he added.

Later Richard broke the news to Harry. He was not surprised to find that the boy knew of the failed plot already. Latterly Harry had been allowed letters from his family and the atmosphere of security around him had become more relaxed.

'It may not be so bad,' Harry said with his usual optimism. 'My mother has improved her position in France considerably and all because of my sister Minette,' he went on proudly. 'Even though she is so young she has charmed the French court.'

'Of course,' Richard responded. 'One day, she will be a valuable bride in the tight incestuous market-place of Europe's royal marriages, and don't forget she is a Catholic, unlike your brother Charles, who has not endeared himself to the French royal family.'

'I am proud of my brother. Neither of us will ever forsake the protestant faith. I promised my father . . . It would be easy, would it not,' asked Harry, 'to sell one's soul as my brother might have been tempted to do, when he was encouraged to play court to King Louis' Catholic cousin, Princess Anne-Marie?'

Richard was pleased that Harry was so well informed, and realized that all the effort to keep the boy abreast of the world outside to which he would one day return had borne fruit. He knew the young Prince Harry was still regarded as a pawn in a world of fermenting loyalties. For the moment he was out of sight and out of mind until he might prove useful, but when he returned to his rightful place in the world he would be a force to be reckoned with.

But there was still the spectre of Mildmay and it was clear to all that he had everything to lose if their prisoner were to flee his not-so-gilded cage. Perhaps aware of an impending change in attitude to the young Prince Harry, he had begun to implement many petty restrictions as if to underline his continuing authority, and they had all begun to realize that few of the funds sent to support the household ever found their way to Harry. Lately there had been a reduction of candles and oil for the lamps, another of Mildmay's economies, which did not encompass his own domestic arrangements, where the lights blazed until well after dark as Mrs Mildmay entertained the local gentry in the tower.

For Colonel Sydenham's part, he overruled Mildmay and permitted Harry to continue to write to the Council, eloquently petitioning for his release, and to visit the Oglander family where he had a chance to be with boys of his own age. Colonel Oglander had already been imprisoned before the King came to the castle, had washed his hands of affairs of state. But he was a good man and was brave enough to invite Harry to his home and take responsibility for him. The visits to Nunwell, the Oglander home, meant a lot to Harry. He grasped any chance he could to maintain connections with a normal world. It helped him not to lose faith in his determination to be released.

Lizzie and Mrs Briott had slipped into a routine of sitting at table with Harry and Richard. This intimacy between servant and master met with a mixed reaction from Mildmay. On the one hand, Master Harry Stuart must live like any other lad of his age, with no deference to his birth, but, on the other, he did not conceal his resentment at the closeness which had evolved within the group. Much to his annoyance, ostensibly due to their straitened circumstances, Mrs Briott had insisted on abandoning the great hall where the food was always cold and privacy was impossible, and implementing a cosy eating

188

arrangement in a small upper room, where the food was kept warm on copper racks in front of a merry fire.

'So, Lizzie has discovered that the princess's beautiful coverlet has been warming the captain's wife while she sleeps,' Mrs Briott remarked as she handed round the portions of hare flavoured with chocolate, a present from the Oglanders.

'I hope,' she continued, 'she's haunted by the memory of her husband's villainy toward the fair child. It warmed her way to heaven but it might take Mrs Mildmay to hell . . . It's an abomination that it should be taken by her.' Mrs Briott's anger was visceral.

Richard shot Lizzie a glance. 'What is this, Lizzie? You were in the captain's private apartments?' His face was flushed in anger.

'Don't worry, Sir Richard,' Mrs Briott intervened hastily. 'Your Lizzie's no fool. You've been so busy with your letters to the Council that you haven't noticed the clever game she plays.' She noted the gratitude on Lizzie's face and continued unabashed, 'Making a friend of Mrs Mildmay's a wise move, the husband can't dally with his wife's confidante, and he's found other fish to fry. His eye no longer falls on your Lizzie, for which you should thank God.'

'I'm sorry, Lizzie,' Richard apologized, taking her hand across the table. 'It's just that he's cunning as a fox, and you shouldn't be off your guard. But I know you're clever, Lizzie, and I do not underestimate you. We both know his lady friend's unwell and the devil finds work for idle hands – and Mildmay's the very devil.'

'Yes, Sir Richard, Lizzie's been very clever,' Harry interjected, 'and she has a lot to tell you, because Mrs Mildmay is getting tired of the captain's bad ways. She tells Lizzie many useful things. When my brother the King returns, the Mildmay family and others will be punished on the testimony of people like Lizzie.'

Richard looked at her, sweet and calm in the light of the two remaining candles, and his spirits sank. He feared Mildmay must have asked himself why Lizzie remained in this God-forsaken place after the princess had died. Being the man he was, he would not have been satisfied with the fact that she had promised the princess on her deathbed not to desert Harry.

189

No, Mildmay would have drawn another conclusion. It probably suited him to let things ride.

'We are all together and no one can overhear us if we speak softly,' said Richard. 'Matters are at last moving to a swift conclusion. Shall I tell them?' he asked Harry.

'We have word from the Council,' came in Harry quickly, 'that a warrant for my release will soon be forthcoming and it has fallen to Richard to start preparing a boat at Cowes as soon as possible.'

There was a stunned silence from Lizzie and Mrs Briott. After so many months and years, that a conclusion should have come so suddenly on this winter evening seemed unbelievable and almost an anticlimax.

'Tomorrow I am going to ask Mildmay for the funds which have been allocated for that purpose,' said Richard.

Lizzie got up from the table spontaneously and went to Harry. She knelt in front of him and put her arms about his waist.

'Your Highness, God has heard all our prayers,' she said.

Later she and Richard contrived to be alone as Harry retired to his chamber to write to his family.

The night was cold and Richard threw more wood on the fire and pulled a pile of cushions to the floor and they lay together in the light of the flickering fire. He had saved some local wine which they shared.

'There is so much I have to say, dearest Lizzie,' he hesitated. Before he could continue Lizzie put a finger to his lips.

'Don't say it,' she said bravely, her heart inwardly breaking. 'I know I cannot go with you.'

'I did not know how to tell you,' said Richard ominously, 'but the stark truth is that Lord Jermyn, the Queen's adviser in France, has already let it be known that the financial situation which awaits the prince will be very difficult, especially as the Queen has been denied her pension by Parliament.'

'But that is outrageous, how can they do that?' Lizzie rounded angrily.

'Very easily I fear, because she has refused to be crowned a Protestant Queen, and consequently has no legitimate claim as the wife of the late King Charles.'

'I can see there would be no place for hangers-on at the French court, or with Charles,' said Lizzie quickly.

'It is not like that,' said Richard forcefully. 'I could not inflict such a precarious life on you, after all you have been through, but there is something else,' he said hesitantly.

'Well what is it?' she demanded. 'There can be nothing which can cause me so much misery as the realization that we may lose each other . . . I can't bear to think of life without you. We have been together for nearly four years.' Lizzie was determined not cry but her voice trembled nevertheless.

'It is bad news, my love. I received the news secreted in my tobacco – your father is going to be arrested.'

'Oh, may God help him,' she moaned, breaking away from him. 'I knew he was taking risks, it was only a matter of time until he was discovered,' she said desperately.

'You must keep this to yourself. If it was known that you had premature knowledge, we would all be implicated and it would make matters worse, but never fear, my love, there are powerful forces working for your father's defence.'

'Even if I could come with you to France I would not do so now, Richard. I must go to my family. My mother needs me now . . . fate is conspiring to drive us apart,' Lizzie cried.

'No, I will not let it be so, Lizzie,' said Richard, fumbling in his pocket. 'I have something for you.' Slowly he produced a ring whose twinkling stones picked up the light from the fire and darted beams like stars on the wall above them as Lizzie automatically let him set it upon her finger.

'We must marry before I go to France,' said Richard in a voice which trucked no argument, 'and then,' he went on, 'you will know I shall return for you and it will only be a matter of months. Will you be my wife?' he asked, taking both her hands and looking searchingly into her eyes.

'Oh yes, Richard, I will,' she answered. She decided in a flash to throw caution to the winds. Even if she were Richard's wife for but one day it would be better to have that one day than none at all, and in her mind her acceptance brought a kind of order into chaos.

'Harry and Mrs Briott will be our witnesses. I know of a priest we can trust. Let us marry the night before our departure,' said Richard as if the matter was settled.

The room was warm and the wine made them feel at ease with the world. He felt her breath against his hand, and as he'd done many times before, he undid her bodice and began to explore her body. She looked down demurely and then her glance caught the bright blue of his gaze and she let his hands stake their claim on her body eagerly and willingly.

As for Richard, for all these months he had restrained himself with superhuman effort, and often he felt she would have let him make love to her. Until now he loved her too much to take from her the one and only possession she might have to offer, but now she would be his wife she would not be dishonoured and he loved her too much not to consummate the long months of his growing desire.

She stirred in his arms and held the wine to his lips and they drank together. She stood up and her gown slipped down. They sank on to the cushions.

He could not stop himself. His beautiful innocent Lizzie was a passionate woman. This time there was no resistance, only unimaginable joy, which he told her bound them for ever.

Twenty-Two

They were to sail secretly out of Cowes on February 12th. It was late afternoon on the eleventh. Lizzie was alone in the royal apartments. Mrs Briott had accompanied Richard and Henry to Cowes, where final preparations were being made to put the boat in readiness for the journey.

It was bitterly cold. And worse, Mildmay had attempted one last act of spite. He had sought to impound all the coverings and bolsters, indeed anything that was necessary to equip the boat for the boy's comfort. Not so much as a candle was to be taken.

Richard had had to go to Colonel Sydenham once again, and with some fury Sydenham had arrived at the castle and ordered two wagons to be loaded with all that Harry and Richard would need.

Lizzie was packing up the final remnants of the children's personal possessions. She had carefully kept the princess's things to be restored to her family, and they were to go on the boat with Harry. Queen Henrietta had sent word that she would like to have them. Her daughter's tender writings would be a window for her mother to look through, to get to know the young daughter she had loved and lost.

The little dog Minette followed Lizzie's every step. She knew something was in the air and did not want to be left behind. She had attached herself to Lizzie from the moment of Beth's death.

Lizzie could hardly contain her sadness at the thought of losing Harry and seeing Richard depart, and her excitement at the prospect of at long last having God's blessing on her union with Richard. She and Richard were to marry secretly that evening. Nobody – nobody on earth except for the two of them and the priest – knew of the plan as they had decided not to tell Harry or Mrs Briott. She was torn in two, on what should be the happiest day of her life. Nobody to dress her in a white gown and strew her path with flowers. Not one of her family there to celebrate the most momentous occasion in her life. And to be left the following day without her husband, with no reassurance that she would see him for years to come. As she had these thoughts she found the dead princess's small sewing bag. She opened it and unwrapped her beautifully worked half-finished tapestry, and fell to sobbing as if her heart would break. This was the first time she had been alone for almost two years, given the cramped quarters at the castle, and she could finally let all her emotions out. There was nobody there to hear her.

It was Minette who heard the footsteps on the narrow stairs. She barked furiously. Lizzie did not have time to turn before she felt the arms about her and smelled the wine-tainted breath on her cheeks.

His hand was over her mouth. She could not scream. His strength was immense. He turned her about, pushed her on to Harry's bed, and fell on top of her. She felt she would die. She could not breathe. His hands tore at the linen of her petticoats.

193

He parted her legs with his knee. She heard the fabric tearing, felt him going inside her, hurting her in the most terrible way she could have imagined. In later months, words would never describe the horror of it, the terror she felt. His tongue was in her mouth. She bit it and he drew back in pain. She tasted his blood on her lips. He hit her hard on the face. Her head went back silently like a broken bird.

She knew that in five minutes he had ruined her life, her chance of securing happiness. He had waited all this time and seized his moment just as she would be free of him. He had not spoken a word. With a violent shudder he finished with her and rose almost at once. She did not attempt to cover herself as he looked down at her. She lay dumbly convinced that nothing in her life could ever be good or clean again.

'So, my little bird. You liked it, didn't you?'

The sound of his voice jarred. It shattered the silence of what was now her battered life.

'Don't pretend you didn't tease me all these years,' he continued coarsely.

'You're like a bitch on heat and, as I thought,' he laughed, looking mockingly at her nakedness, 'the way was easy for me, because others had done the hard work before . . . You'll want more now you've tasted a real man.'

He stopped abruptly. There was something cool and frighteningly unexpected about her. She had not cried out as others had done before. He had invaded her body but that was all. This time he had not broken her will, but he would in the end.

She did not think she could speak, but somehow she found the words. Minette lay whimpering beside her on the bed. She felt the little dog's soft ears fall about her face like a curtain. She gently held them aside. She got up and covered herself with a sheet, not in haste or confusion, but with all the composure of a Queen putting on her robes for a state occasion.

'One day you'll confront the ruin of my life, and I swear that this place will remember your evil . . . and you won't forget . . . it will come back to haunt you. You haven't seen the last of this room where you took my future from me.' Lizzie closed her eyes. She knew in the darkness of her closed lids that he would remember what he had done to her. She would make sure with every bone in his body that he would wish he had never done this to her. This room would be his Calvary.

Twenty-Three

She would tell no one, not even Mrs Briott. How could she ruin this joyous day of Harry's release by disclosing what had happened? If she told Richard, he would seek the captain out. He might even kill try to him, but Mildmay was a superb swordsman and Richard was not a man of war. As Lizzie thought about it, she realized it was a form of revenge. They had outwitted Mildmay, and now he would probably be discredited with Parliament. He was dangerous, perhaps more dangerous than ever.

She could not marry Richard now. If she did, she would have to tell him the truth, or their marriage would be based on a lie. She would tell him the future was too uncertain. They would have to wait until he returned in glorious splendour. She would not have to be alone with Mildmay again. He would not show his face.

When Henry and Richard left she would return at once to her family.

The news from home was not good. Her mother was tired and there was no mention of her father, which worried her. She didn't know if he had been arrested, perhaps the powerful voices Richard had mentioned had been able to protect him? There had been no word from her brothers, although it was rumoured that Tom might have been offered an indemnity by Parliament. Philip was a different matter. There was a price on his head. He was regarded as a danger by Parliament: he was an agitator and a powerful one. Unless the King claimed his throne, she doubted she would ever see her brothers again.

She managed to compose herself before Richard's return, and then came the most difficult thing she had ever had to do in her life. How she longed to collapse into his strong arms, and tell him the truth. But she summoned up her last residue of strength and told him her decision calmly and with conviction.

They were alone in her apartment. It was evening and already dark owls hooted in the trees outside the castle keep. Everyone was in a frenzy of packing.

'It is all arranged. The priest will be ready for us in the parish church in Newport,' said Richard excitedly. 'There will be a coach at the gates in an hour.'

When Lizzie did not respond as he had imagined, he took her by the shoulders and peered into her eyes.

'My love, what is the matter? You look ill,' he asked fearfully.

She broke away from him and walked to the fireplace. As she looked into the comforting flames she tried to find the right words to convince him and not spoil this long awaited moment when he would deliver Harry to freedom and receive his accolade from Charles. Richard had a world across the ocean at his feet and she . . . what did she have now except some remnants of honour and integrity that she must now salvage at the expense of all her dreams?

'My dearest, there is something we must discuss,' she said quietly. 'I have been thinking long and hard and have decided that I cannot marry without telling my parents. It goes against everything I believe,' she faltered as she saw the stark horror on his face. 'There is something else,' she went on tentatively.

'Something else? What could be worse than what you have told me, and anyway your father knows of my intentions and approves them,' Richard cried in evident bewilderment.

'I cannot marry you when our future is so uncertain. After all you might never be able to come back to England and our love would have been turned into a prison which prevented you from finding happiness with anyone else.' She spoke with as much conviction as she could muster. 'My mind is made up, Richard, you cannot change it. I love you too much to bind you in this way, and when we marry it must be as I have always wanted that joyful day to be, with both our families and friends and the certainty that we can keep our vows in a peaceful, normal world,' she finished adamantly.

196

At first he was angry and bewildered, but then, seeing that her mind was made up, he said: 'I'll be back, Lizzie, and sooner than you think.' He held her for a long time, as if storing the contact to reassure him during their separation, but in her heart Lizzie feared the future would not be as he promised.

Now it was morning. They had not been together again.

With relief Richard noted the wind had come round in a north-westerly that would take them on a straight course to Flanders, where Harry's brother Charles would be waiting. Colonel Sydenham arrived while it was still dark to escort the party to Cowes. There were to be no spectators to bid the young prince farewell. As Mrs Briott had said sharply, 'The islanders have more or less forgotten about the young boy leaving to join the Queen.'

When they reached the quay, the first fingers of light were filtering through a purple sky. Lizzie and Richard had said their farewells the previous night, but he never took his eyes from her face as they travelled in the coach. She tried to look calm, but how she longed to throw herself into his arms, tell him the truth, follow him to the ends of the earth. But her sense of duty was as deep-rooted in her as was Richard's loyalty to the prince.

Her own feelings were as nothing compared with the turn of events which must surely be the first sign that England might be restored to some kind of order. She would wait, however long it took. Now it was Harry's turn to say goodbye.

It was icy cold and a flurry of snow covered the harbour. The sailors rubbed their hands up and down their arms to keep warm. Sir Richard Oglander and his wife had sent Henry a fur cape to keep out the chill on his journey. But no Island grandee dared come to see the prince off. Harry thanked the colonel, who spoke with courteous formality to the boy, but Lizzie thought she detected a slight tremble on his lip as he took Harry's hand, wished him God speed and gave him an almost imperceptible bow.

The prince embraced Mrs Briott. She could not hide her feelings which, as she assured him, were tears of joy. 'Long live the King,' she whispered.

When it came to Lizzie, he manfully tried to keep the tears

at bay, but seeing her own turning to ice on her cheek in the cold wind, he stood, shoulders shaking, as she encircled him in her arms.

'Thank you, Lizzie. We'll be back. You're the best friend I ever had, and you stayed with me after Beth died, when you could have gone home to your family. You have been like a sister to me, and when I come back with my brother you will be rewarded.'

'My best reward is to see you go free,' she answered.

'I know my brother will thank you for what you did for my dear sister. How I wish she could have been here with us.' His lip trembled a bit. He bit it firmly, and then he turned and scampered up the boarding plank.

Richard was waiting on the ship's deck. The sailors drew up the board and hauled up the sails. With a roar and a clatter the wind took the boat, and the ropes whipped through the pillars on the quayside.

The Pearl moved slowly out of the harbour. Lizzie couldn't watch as the figures on the deck became smaller. She walked slowly back to the coach, arm in arm with Mrs Briott.

PART FOUR

Hatherton Manor 1652

Twenty-Four

'Sir Edwin. There's someone about, outside the house . . . Please, sir. You said the last time you wouldn't help any more. It's too dangerous. We're being watched . . . You must send them away . . .' Ruth stood at the bedchamber door with a candle.

Sir Edwin eased himself out of bed with difficulty, hoping not to wake Mary.

'Go back to bed. You saw nothing.' It was an order, but Ruth had no intention of obeying it.

He quickly put on the clothes he always had ready and made his way downstairs. He knew Ruth was behind him somewhere, but he did not look round. He went to the door at the back of the house – a frequent rendezvous for the secret callers who came at night, depending on him for their escape.

Sliding the bolts aside, he felt the door come towards him. And knew at once it was a man's body-weight which pushed it. He stood back, drawing his sword. A figure fell into the passage. He could smell blood . . . a wound – he knew the smell of old. The man would be in a fever, no threat to him, probably semi-delirious.

The body slumped to the floor with a moan, as cold night air billowed into the house. Ruth was there. She pushed round Sir Edwin.

'Sir, it's master Philip,' she cried.

It hit him so fast, he felt his breath catch in his throat. Before he could shut the door, there was the sound of hooves somewhere in the drive.

'They are after me, Father,' Philip gasped.

'Have you a horse, boy?'

'It's hidden . . . in Jacob's cow stall.'

'Call Sam. We must get Philip to the priest hole. There's not a moment to lose,' Sir Edwin ordered.

They got him to the hiding place just as the banging started at the front doors. Ruth just had time to pour brandy down his throat and cover him in a blanket. Sam opened the doors and more than a dozen soldiers pushed past without ceremony.

'Our orders are to search this house. It is surrounded. If anyone attempts to leave, they may be shot,' the officer in charge said.

They were standing in the entrance and, out of the corner of his eye, Sir Edwin saw a trail of blood staining the floor at the bottom of the stairs. Ruth saw it too and slowly moved over it, spreading her skirt to obscure it.

Soon the soldiers were crashing through the house, their swords clattering against panelling – turning over beds and rummaging in the closets.

But they found nothing and as dawn came they lost their enthusiasm. Seizing the moment, Sir Edwin offered them food and ale and spoke to their commanding officer. He managed to convince the man that no visitor had come to the manor, but the steward had heard a horseman pass the manor on the London Road during the night.

Eventually, the men set off on the London Road, and Sir Edwin heaved a sigh of relief and blessed Ruth for the quality of her salt beef and Sam on the potency of the manor ale.

Philip had fallen into a fever and was not aware of the search going on, nor of the questions, nor the nursing which took place in the confines of the priest hole, nor of his mother's joy, nor of her tears when she knew he must go the moment he was fit. But he recovered quickly enough to travel, thanks to Ruth, who bound up the wound and fed him oxblood extract. Within hours, he would have to take his leave and follow the route that so many had taken from the safety of the manor.

'The boat will be ready tonight. The tide's low and the moon is but a sliver, so you'll be well concealed by darkness,' Sir Edwin explained to his son the following day. He knew the journey to France was fraught with danger.

Knowing they had but a few hours left before they would

be parted again, Philip explained what he was doing in England. 'I came from the King,' he said, 'to talk on his behalf with General Monck.'

It was the first time that Sir Edwin had heard Prince Charles being referred to as the King and it heartened him. Not much had been made of the crowning at Scone in Scotland the previous year. His son's easy use of the title gave him a semblance of hope, added to which the mention of General Monck was news indeed.

'My dear boy, this must be good news: Cromwell's general receiving communications from the King. What can this mean?' he asked incredulously.

'It came to nothing, Father, but the general is a fine man. And as you know, Francis Hinton is becoming a skilful negotiator. Things are happening. Sir Francis paved the way for a deputation. But I fear, although not a soul knew of my arrival, somehow I was betrayed. I was on the road to you under cover of darkness. Unfortunately I must have been followed. My assailant came to grief, I think I killed him.'

Philip had put them all at risk in coming to the manor, but it was understandable. He was wounded, he needed attention if he were to make good his escape. He must have longed to see his family. After all, he had been in France for several years. But Sir Edwin was quite clear on one thing. 'You can't see your sisters, for they're too young to be burdened with such a secret. If the family's questioned, they must know nothing.'

Philip knew his father was right about the younger ones, but his great disappointment was not to see Lizzie, whom he knew was made of stern stuff. He would miss her by a matter of hours, which was especially cruel, as he had timed his mission to coincide with Prince Henry's departure from the Isle of Wight.

If Sir Edwin had doubts about many things, not least the probable return of Lizzie's lover with the King, he had no doubts that Philip must leave as soon as darkness fell. To stay would be courting danger for them all.

With a sad heart Philip wrote Lizzie a letter which he gave to his father. It was heavily coded, for nothing could be left to chance. Amongst other things he wrote of Sir Richard Lovell.

He knew of her love for him. He had tried to arrange for her to come with Prince Harry, so that they could be together, but circumstances were dire at the little court across the sea: there were barely enough funds for the King to survive. The boy and his tutor would have to throw themselves on the charity of the French court, as his mother had done. There was no place for Lizzie there. But he knew how strong Richard's feelings were for his sister. 'I will be your messenger and protector, dear sister,' he ended his letter. 'You will be rewarded for the brave and courageous way you've been loyal to the King's brother and sister. Sir Richard Lovell could hope for no finer wife.'

The sands felt wet and cold under their bodies. They lay concealed in one of the dunes, and when the glimmer of twinkling light came into view in the distant sea, bobbing with the waves, Sir Edwin grabbed his son in his arms and all the pent-up quarrels and muddled allegiances were as nothing. They were father and son again, with only one hope: for Philip's safety and his eventual return to a country free of tyranny.

When Sir Edwin got back to the manor, the soldiers were waiting again.

Twenty-Five

S am was at the gates looking older and smaller, but his bright smile had lost none of its roguish edge. His joy at seeing Lizzie was unmistakable. She had not been allowed to go home from Carisbrooke for well over a year. As he opened the gates, the door of the gate-house cottage opened, and out came Jacob. He was followed by three young children, all with Jacob's unmistakable gypsy looks, and bright red noses from the winter cold. Lizzie jumped from the coach and, to Mrs Briott's surprise, embraced Sam and then Jacob.

Jacob told her that Jenny was waiting up at the house. Lizzie kissed each of the children and got back into the coach. Jacob had not the heart to tell her that her father had been arrested.

Mrs Briott was astounded as she caught her first sight of the manor. She knew Lizzie was an educated girl, but she didn't think the Jones's family home would be a feudal manor house of such beauty. Admittedly, it looked quite run-down, but the charm of the house, with its roundel of stone steps to an impressive oak door over which presided the family arms, was as nothing she had expected.

As the coach drew up, the door opened and a bonnie round-faced countrywoman of about her own age came running down the steps. She and Lizzie fell into each other's arms, and Mrs Briott assumed this must be Lizzie's mother.

'Ruth,' said Lizzie proudly, 'I want you to meet Mrs Briott, who's been my dearest friend for the last four years. Mrs Briott, this is Ruth, my nurse, who brought me into the world.'

Ruth shook Mrs Briott's hand warmly, and hurried them up the steps out of the cold, while Sam took their boxes down from the coach. It had started to snow again and the light was fading, so they were glad to be inside where, in the galleried hall, a large log fire spat and hissed its welcome.

Lizzie felt she had come home at last. The high-pitched squeals of girls' voices could be heard approaching and in tumbled a little girl with Sir Edwin's dark hair and bright blue eyes. Emily hovered, uncertain and shy at the sight of her grown-up sister, whom she hardly knew.

Mathilda and Adela were now grown women with their hair smartly wound under their caps at the nape of their necks. Beatrice held the hand of a small child whom she pushed forward. The little girl bobbed a curtsey and was introduced as Mariah Hinton. 'My sister Alice is too young to say hello, but I'm three,' she told Lizzie and Mrs Briott brightly.

Lizzie bent down and kissed the child, and Mrs Briott, who had heard about Sir Francis's children being given a home, set to admiring her long fair hair which hung in two thick braids from under her cap.

'Yes,' said Mariah. 'Emily uses my braids as reins when we play horses. You see, I always have to be the horse, which is silly really, as Emily's bigger than me. She should be the horse.'

Mrs Briott smiled happily as she saw the charming reunion. Mariah reminded her of the little princess, whom she had never ceased to miss. Seeing the row of little girls with their apple faces, she let her mind race, while she considered the fun she would have with them while she stayed at Hatherton.

Just as she was wondering where Lizzie's mother might be, she heard the swish of silk skirts on a stone floor. She saw a tall elegant woman of obvious nobility. The girls bobbed a curtsey and Emily ran excitedly to her.

'Mother,' she cried excitedly. 'My sister's so beautiful, as beautiful as the ladies at the court of France where the Queen lives . . . I read about them in Father's pamphlets . . . but they don't have plain dresses like her.'

She turned to Lizzie and asked. 'Do you have a dress like the Princess Minette? She's going to marry the King of France's brother.'

'No, but I do have a little dog who belonged to Minette's sister, the princess who died,' Lizzie replied, 'and she's called Minette, after her. You see, the princess never met her sister and wanted something to remind her, and here she is.'

As Minette peeped shyly from under Lizzie's skirts. Emily pounced on her, picking her up and covering her in kisses.

'That's enough, dear. Stand aside and let your sister greet her mother,' Ruth said, firmly taking the child's arm.

Lizzie swept her mother a low curtsey. Her mother would have none of it, and raised her up, pressing her to her shoulder, her head next to her daughter's, her eyes closed. Mrs Briott heard her whisper in her eldest daughter's ear, 'You're home now, my dear. Thank God for your safe return. There's something you don't know, but not in front of the children . . .'

Lizzie had been looking round frantically for her father and wondering why he hadn't appeared.

'It's Father, isn't it?' she blurted, knowing instinctively that something had happened to him.

'My dear, come with me to the parlour,' Mary replied, making it clear she would not be drawn until they were alone.

The news of her father's arrest was dire enough, but later Lizzie heard of Philip's visit and was given his letter. Her heart was heavy. She thought how cruel it was that fate had let her miss her dearest brother by a matter of hours. Now he was on his way to France, he could not come back. She took the letter and put it safely in her pocket. It would take time to decipher. She would read it alone. As she felt it in her hand, she almost felt the warmth of her brother's skin. It was only then she realized the connection.

Of course, her father must have been arrested because of Philip. He had harboured his son and helped him to escape. How could Philip have put his family at risk in such a way?

She said as much to her mother.

Mary defended her son vigorously. 'I won't have you talk like that, Lizzie. I wouldn't have forgiven him if he hadn't tried to see us, for who knows, my dear, we might never meet again on this earth. Besides, he'd been betrayed. He was wounded. Where else should he go? He knew we had the means to deliver him to safety . . . Your father's not young any more. Philip is young with his whole life ahead of him . . . and besides they won't hurt me or the children. Tom has gone into the Parliamentary army.'

Lizzie thought she must be dreaming: Tom a Parliamentary soldier. It was not possible.

'How could he?' she cried. 'England's now a republic and Cromwell the self-proclaimed Lord Protector. Tom will never be able to work within the system.'

She found all this impossible to understand, knowing Tom's commitment to the restoration of a monarchy.

'Lizzie, my dear,' said Mary. 'Tom's clever. He's worked out if you can't defeat the wind of change, then work with it and harness it in the right direction. After all, we have done as much ourselves,' she added pointedly. 'He's formed a close friendship with General Monck's family . . .' She hesitated awkwardly. 'I think there's a romance blooming between him and the general's niece.' Seeing Lizzie's expression, she stumbled over her words.

'Once, yes, we had to survive,' said Lizzie angrily.' But now after all we have seen we know how dreadful the alternatives are.'

'It's . . . the . . . only thing now, my dear, to work with the system,' Mary ventured, 'and Tom's not the only one who's come to that conclusion.'

'Oh, dearest Mother, how awful it is that we don't feel anything is worth fighting for any more,' cried Lizzie plaintively.

'I'm so tired by it all!' Mary answered flatly, and indeed Lizzie thought her mother did look ill. She had lost weight and her face was lined and drawn.

'Mother, we must not talk of these things any more,' said Lizzie, changing the subject. 'Let's be practical. What are we to do about Father?'

'We must discuss it with Sir Francis,' Mary answered carefully. 'He's been the mainstay of the family since you left, Lizzie. He's coming here today to explain everything to you, and he'll be bringing news of your father. He's been pleading his case to the authorities and he is very hopeful, he's a powerful man in his own quiet way.'

'And exactly who and what are these so-called authorities?' replied Lizzie furiously.

'You know full well, my dear, and negotiate with them we must. Sir Francis is respected and trusted and he has been a firm friend, and we in return have done what we can to help him with his young family after the loss of his beloved wife.'

Lizzie saw, as she talked to her mother, that life was indeed what each could do for the other, and that the awful events of the war had united many families in a common cause of survival. Remarks her mother had made implied that Tom had some ongoing vendetta with Philip. Could it be that Tom felt badly about the way he had changed sides? So much so that his younger brother made him feel ashamed?

This was another reminder of the long way she had been distanced from her own family and background for the last few years. England had been divided, families had lost touch with each other in a way which was unprecedented. Many would never see their loved ones again and had no notion, in many cases, of what might have happened to them. Nothing

208

was predictable any more, and loyalty and principle had been clouded in the issue of survival.

As it happened, a terrible storm prevented Sir Francis from arriving until the next day. Jacob had forecast a deterioration in the weather. He was never wrong and the slight warming in the air and the darkening heavy sky meant serious snowfalls. The roads would be impassable. There would be no supplies or movement of foodstuffs and fuel. Lizzie knew already, within hours of her arrival, that plans must be made. Logs must be moved from the farthest store to the barn by the kitchen, hens brought into the coops near the house, the salt beef and pork brought in from the stores in the kitchen barn. They would need potatoes and carrots stored in leaf mould for the duration of the winter. They must be brought up from the far cellars before they froze and were spoiled. She must make sure of a good supply of salt. It was good to be home.

Mrs Briott for her part knew she would be with Lizzie's family for a long time, maybe weeks. In truth she was delighted with the prospect, since her own family was still exiled in France. One day they would return, but not yet. For the moment she had taken Lizzie's family to her heart. She must be careful, she knew things which the family did not know, could not even guess at. They were too close to see them, and why should they? They would know soon enough, then she would be needed. She would be there to protect Lizzie, the only one who now knew her secret.

Twenty-Six

Ruth showed Sir Francis into the parlour where the women were sewing. The room was cosy, a fire burned briskly and Minette, who had taken to sitting on Mary's lap as she sewed, was snoring happily. The smell of winter greenery from a massive jug of holly and firs, dried rosemary and thyme perfumed the room; nuts lay on a copper tray in the hearth. The shutters were open but the sky was heavily laden with snow and a sluggish light struggled feebly through the leaded panes. At three o'clock, it felt as if night were about to return. People had scuttled to their homes and lit the candles. There would be little outside work until the weather broke. Sir Francis had not seen a soul during his journey, the landscape had been spookily devoid of any life.

Lizzie imagined how the scene of such domestic order must seem to the widower. It would be as reassuring to him as it was to her after all these years in the bleak and forbidding households of the royal prison.

Sir Francis was still in his stockinged feet and snow clung to his thick grey-black hair. Surprisingly, he was all but clean-shaven, save for a small apology for a beard, which drew attention to a charming cleft in his chin and curiously gave his face the semblance of permanent humour.

He made a graceful bow to Mrs Briott and Ruth and then turned his full attention to Lizzie. She felt him appraising her with no pretence, and he was clearly surprised by the woman who stood before him. When he had last seen her, she was no more than a skinny child, climbing trees in the manor orchard. Lizzie took his hand as he raised her from her curtsey. Even without his boots he stood at least a foot taller than her.

Of course she had never paid much attention to Sir Francis, her parents' friend. With the exception of Richard, the men she had met during her time with the royal children had been so different from the country squires with whom she had grown up. The men she knew from home would turn their hands to anything, deliver a lamb in the middle of the night, till a field, even in some cases shoe their own horse, and at the same time be fluent in Latin and quote from the great works of Horace. They were real people living real lives. She had missed men such as this, and here indeed was a reminder that the true English gentleman had survived after all.

Here stood before her a good man. His worth shone from

210

the kindness of his lion-coloured eyes, his wide smile and fine nose. His hand was roughened by work and his clothes were of a solid serviceable nature without deference to fashion.

'My dear Elizabeth, forgive me for stating the obvious. You have fulfilled your father's hopes in every way.' He paused and then put his finger to his forehead, in a way she would come to recognize as the precursor to well-planned action. 'And talking of your father, that's why I'm here,' he continued, with a slight bow as he indicated the chairs by the fire. 'If the weather permits, I shall go again to London tomorrow to plead with the Council of State. I suppose, my dear, that you do not know much of what has transpired here at Hatherton in your absence?' It was both a question and a statement.

'No sir, I do not. I think you had better tell me,' Lizzie said.

Sir Francis told Lizzie, as her mother listened quietly, twisting her fingers in her lap as she did when she was upset.

Sir Edwin had been a brave man, Sir Francis explained. 'He's been as confused in his loyalties as have many of his friends. But then your father saw the regime had become both corrupt and cruel, one system had been replaced with another far worse. Cromwell's vision of saintliness does not fit with what is actually happening.'

'So, what are you saying?' Lizzie asked impatiently.

'Shush, Lizzie. Let Sir Francis finish,' said Mary hastily, observing that her daughter had lost none of her impetuousness.

'In a nutshell, when Sir Edwin offered Hatherton as a refuge for Royalists he put his family at great risk,' Sir Francis went on, 'but he did it for the last time when Philip came. It was this final mission and that was his undoing.'

'Oh, but Sir Francis,' Mary interceded forcefully, 'we couldn't have done otherwise. We're so perfectly situated and our places of concealment still undiscovered and our loyal stewards got them to the beach. And God was with us,' replied Mary. 'We were not discovered until that night.' She stopped, faltering at the memory of the last time she had seen her son.

211

'Yes, I would have done the same, my dear lady,' said Sir Francis.

'At least Philip got away. It was his only chance. My husband had my full support. These people were our friends. We could have done no less.' Lizzie had seldom seen her mother so fired up.

'Well, this is my point,' Sir Francis said briskly. 'Philip's escape was the last exploit. He was your son. There's no reason to link it with others. In the circumstances, I can plead for clemency for Sir Edwin. As you know, Tom is at present with General Monck of the New Model Army. He's realized that in order to restore order and peace we must all work together. This will also be a point in the family's favour.'

'I know Tom has defected to Cromwell's army,' Lizzie affirmed, unable to conceal her rancour.

'My dear, he's convinced that a Restoration is the solution, and this can only be done with the co-operation of the army. I know this is a long way off, but there are movements afoot.'

Francis went on to assure them that Tom would be home soon, and, glancing at Mary, he asked if Lizzie was aware of Tom's intentions to marry a niece of General Moncks.

'So, Tom will be bringing a Parliamentarian officer's daughter as a bride to Hatherton. You were a little more imprecise about that, Mother,' said Lizzie apprehensively, aware now that this was not a vague romance. The impact of this news was colossal. The wife of the eldest son would have a position in the household far above Lizzie's or any of her sisters. She had, of course, known this would happen. Her father had always said that when he married Tom would have the manor house, and Sir Edwin would take the family to live in a small farmhouse on the estate. But these plans had been made when the country was at peace, and he had assumed his elder daughters would be settled in marriage.

'My dear, I didn't tell you exactly,' cried Mary defensively, 'for we haven't had time in the short while you've been restored to us,' she continued, looking increasingly agitated. She knew she should have told Lizzie. But the consequences of such a development were as difficult for her to grasp as they were for Lizzie.

It only seemed like yesterday that she had been the bride

at Hatherton, starting out on what she thought would be a long and joyous marriage. By now, in the normal course of events, she would have been dangling a quiver of grandchildren on her knee. But now it was as if an entire piece of the jigsaw of her life were missing.

She had not seen her sons grow from boys into men: they had been absent for so long, and her not knowing from one day to the next if she could expect the cart to come with the lifeless body of a man she did not recognize. They would tell her he died an honourable death, but she would curse their honour. And now her husband was in prison. But, in truth, she must thank God both her sons had survived, and now Tom would bring home the woman who would live life as she would have liked to live it for just a little longer, in her house, with her things and her garden, living her dreams.

'As for Tom's plans,' she struggled eventually, 'we've not met the young lady in question and our first concern is to get your father home. Then we can decide what's best.'

'Yes, quite so,' Sir Francis agreed, coughing awkwardly, seeing the air was charged with emotion.

'I was about to tell you that I think your father has an enemy with influence at the Council, for his arrest was most strange. There is definitely someone agitating behind the scenes. There were no proper charges, as I said. I know for a fact that what went on here has never been properly recorded, so it's a mystery, and I intend to get to the bottom of it.' He paused, using the time effectively to consider how best to make his next point.

'But I've told your mother,' he went on at last, 'Lizzie, there must be no more concealments here. It's too dangerous and your family must now sit quietly while all the frogs come out of the muddy water and all will fall into place.'

As Francis had been speaking, Lizzie had been wondering who could such an enemy be? Provided that her father's activities were not documented, they were now of little importance to Parliament, for most Royalists had either fled or were thought to have changed their colours. The pockets of resistance were like a sleeping tiger.

Her father was just a simple country squire of no interest to anybody, and he was not a man to pick quarrels. He was

213

loved by all his servants and had done many a favour in the village. He had always cared for his tenants. Then came a small nagging thought, which grew with a devastating clarity. Captain Mildmay loomed into the front of her consciousness. How often he had threatened to harm her family if she did not give him what he wanted. He had said she would never be free of him. Suddenly the full horror of what had happened came to her and panic and fear engulfed her. She felt the blood drain from her face. Her head began to tingle and then everything went black.

The voice was far away down a long tunnel. Her eyes were still closed, but she felt strong arms about her and a gentle male voice, the wholesome smell of leather and tobacco. 'Elizabeth, dear, don't try to sit up. Just stay still. You fainted.'

She felt peaceful and safe. She just wanted to sleep. She had never before given in to her terror of things to come, not ever, in all the time since she had left her home and her family, and for a moment in these strong arms her fears seemed far away again.

Twenty-Seven

'I must speak to you, Ruth,' Mrs Briott said to Ruth the following evening.

'Of course, come with me and we will find a private corner, whatever it is it must be important, I can tell by looking at you,' said Ruth knowingly, little suspecting what was to follow.

'There are terrible things I must tell you about poor Lizzie,' said Mrs Briott bluntly.

Ruth had sat down with her at once in the private corner of the pantry, where she kept two chairs next to the wall in the laundry, a warm and cosy corner because it backed on to the copper.

The story of what the villainous Captain Mildmay had done

to her own sweet Lizzie whom she looked on as her own child filled Ruth with dismay and then a diabolical anger.

She knew at once it was not anything for which Lizzie could be reproved. But just the same, it was what every God-fearing girl lived in fear of. All Ruth's native cunning came into play and already in her mind she was thinking of what best to do.

'Now you listen to me,' she said when she had Lizzie to herself. 'I've been watching you pale as a fish each morning and not touching your food.'

'It's nothing, I caught a slight chill that's all,' said Lizzie hastily.

'Don't think you can pull the wool over my eyes. God help us all. You are with child,' said Ruth, putting a firm hand on Lizzie's shoulder to silence any protest.

'I know, child, that Captain Mildmay violated you,' she went on, 'and that you've spared Sir Richard from the pain of this truth. The babe you carry inside you is the seed of that evil man. If we do not get rid of it, we're all lost and the family's good name is ruined. Then you'll have to go away to hide from all decent folk.'

'No, Ruth. It's not as simple as that. In a way, I wish it were,' Lizzie told her quietly. Mixed with her despair, she felt a sense of relief that at last she could talk about her desperate situation.

'You see, Ruth, I don't know who the father is,' Lizzie whispered, her voice low, as if to acknowledge the shame she felt even though the deed was not of her making. And though she was mindful of the fact that she had given herself freely to her love before they were married, it was not a thing she would care to tell the world or indeed anyone at all.

'The Lord have mercy on us,' shrieked Ruth.

'No. It's not like that,' cried Lizzie desperately. 'Richard and I were betrothed. We were going to be married the very night after the captain ...' She looked down, unable to find the right words. 'Overcame me,' was the nearest she could get to it.

Ruth had not listened properly. She didn't quite understand what Lizzie was trying to tell her.

'There are women in the village who can take the child out

215

before it gets bigger,' she continued hurriedly. 'You won't be the first, Lizzie. These are terrible times and many girls have been ruined, as you've been, and lived to tell the tale.'

'You weren't listening to me,' Lizzie answered slowly. 'I can't kill the child. It might be Richard's. All I'll ever have of his, and besides,' she sobbed, 'I'll never forget that witch Mistress Snell who butchered my dear mother. That's what it would be like. It would be a miracle if I survived. And, besides, it's another murder whichever way you look at it.'

Ruth was silent for a moment, while she tried to grasp what Lizzie had meant. For once in her life, she did not know what to say. She put her hand over Lizzie's, thinking quickly.

'Child, you must get word to Richard that you're with child,' she said quickly. 'You mustn't tell him about what's befallen you. It wasn't your fault, you're a casualty of war. He'll never know and you'll have other children when he comes back with the King.'

Ruth was quite carried away with her solution. To her it seemed so very simple. Such things had been done in the village for generations. All men behaved like beasts of the field when war took hold of them. There was no difference between any of them. What Richard did not know would never hurt him. The child would be half Lizzie and if God had not completely forgotten about rewarding the good, as Lizzie most certainly was, the child would be his.

Lizzie looked at Ruth calmly. Of course what Ruth had suggested had crossed her mind more than once. Richard would now be in France with Harry and Queen Henrietta. She could easily get word to him by using the system which smuggled letters. She knew him well enough to know he would find a way to marry her. She could go to France through the route used by her father's network. She knew the boats sailed at night from the cove below the estate when the wind was fair. It was a day and a night to the coast of France where Richard could be waiting for her.

A minute later though, Ruth could tell by Lizzie's face that she was about to dismiss her suggestion. But Ruth had a rule in her life: never make a decision today if you can make it tomorrow.

'Child, don't say another word. You must think of the consequences of your decision overnight. You've carried this burden on your own for too long. I'm here to advise you like a mother as I've always done,' Ruth reassured her. 'Tell no one, and tomorrow we'll talk, when you're refreshed, and reason will take hold of your high-minded sentiments.'

Twenty-Eight

Two weeks later morning broke bright and fair. Spring had come, or was it an interlude before the biting weather returned?

For all the family it was a day of brilliance. The sun danced on them as they waited in the late morning outside the door of the house. The first crocuses had pushed through the melting snow. Lizzie remembered the better days when her mother had acquired the rare bulbs which looked like baby onions and placed them in the ground. Many had secretly scorned her work at the time, but these miracle splashes of colour in yellow, white and purple had spread, and now a sward of them slashed either side of the drive like swirls of silk in the shooting grass.

Jacob had come earlier. He had word that Sir Francis was not far away with Sir Edwin. They would be home within the hour.

Lizzie had slept, but her dreams had been confusing and alarming. She had held a baby. It was hers, but she couldn't see its face. It had some kind of bonnet which she could not pull aside. She remembered the dream vividly as she stood with the family to welcome her father home.

Lizzie ran to her father with open arms – it had been well over a year since she'd seen him, and she was the first person Sir Edwin embraced on his return. Then she saw Sir Francis as he greeted his own children who now seemed so much part of her family. She had watched them play with little Emily and run up and down with Minette and then scamper off to the kitchen to be chucked under the chin by the kitchen maids and plied with sweetmeats by Ruth and Mrs Briott.

Later they all gathered for a celebration meal of roast peahen and quince jelly on a puree of root vegetables prepared with great ingenuity by Ruth and Mrs Briott. 'And to follow,' Ruth announced, 'we have Sir Edwin's favourite, iced syllabub of our finest bottled strawberries and curds, thanks to Samuel who cut the first ice from the ice house this very morning.'

During the meal Lizzie felt curiously isolated from the family celebrations, as if she carried a great burden that could not be shared. She watched Sir Francis's open and happy face, as he described the way he had negotiated Sir Edwin's release, and expressed his appreciation of her parents' kindness to his motherless children Any reservations she had about him were quickly banished.

'But for them,' he said, 'I would never have found the strength to recover from the grief at the death of my dear wife.'

Lizzie picked at the delicious food while Francis told of the dark forces which had led to Sir Edwin's arrest. As he told the tale, he looked frequently at Lizzie, observing how pale she looked.

'This Captain Mildmay, he seems to have taken an unusual interest in Sir Edwin's case,' said Sir Francis thoughtfully.

Lizzie said nothing as Mary came in vehemently, 'I never liked the man, but dear Edwin is so trusting, he could not see the true nature of the man who was in essence a Judas from the start.'

'But even so I cannot understand why Captain Mildmay is so vehemently determined to do harm to the Jones family?' Sir Francis pondered.

'Lizzie, you are the person who knows the man best. Did anything happen while you were with the royal children?' Mary asked.

Lizzie caught Ruth's eye. The older woman's mouth had tightened and she had begun to crash about with the serving platters. She shook her head at Lizzie, as if to warn her not to say too much whilst she tried to compose an answer to the questions. Judith Briott, who sat at the top of the table with

218

Mary in view of her father-in-law's position as the King's silversmith, swiftly came to the rescue.

'Sir Francis, we all worked to get Prince Harry released to his mother. The captain and his wife did not want to lose the goose that laid their golden egg. The man's a villain. He would sell his own mother for a piece of silver, and Lizzie stood up to him.' Mrs Briott hesitated, choosing her words carefully. 'Lizzie was a force to be reckoned with. He used her family as a threat to her. And you, Sir Edwin, paid the price for your daughter's integrity.'

'I thought as much,' Sir Francis said. 'But you've nothing more to fear from him, Elizabeth,' he continued kindly.

'We have much to thank you for, my dear neighbour,' Sir Edwin said heartily, lifting his ale mug.

'Come, Samuel. Fill all the mugs, for we must drink a toast to our friends and family, and thank God that we're at least here together.'

As Sam filled the mugs, Sir Edwin rose to his feet. He faltered slightly as he stood up. He was thin and his collar hung loosely about his neck. His eyes were haunted, as if in their depths he stored visions of dark things he could never forget. Lizzie knew that the joy at his homecoming would soon be spoiled.

'I drink to my eldest daughter, Elizabeth. She's a brave woman and we're proud of her.' As they rose from the table he went on. 'I tell you, my dearest child, we won't let you leave us again – unless it's to a happy life where you'll learn to laugh again as you used to.'

Lizzie smiled for him, but in her heart she died a thousand deaths. She was in a trap, from which there seemed no escape.

'I've something to say to you, Lizzie,' Sir Edwin said to Lizzie when they were alone at last. 'But I don't want you to answer in the way you would have done before you left us. My dear, you've earned the right to make your own decisions, as any man would do.'

It was evening and her father looked tired. He had been out on the estate on his old mare, one of the few who had escaped the requisition by the New Model Army. It had been a bitter afternoon again. Spring had made its appearance and not liked

219

what it saw. Sam had lit the fire in Sir Edwin's study and now Lizzie's father sat with his feet in a copper bowl of hot water and mustard. They talked in front of Sam as if he were a part of their own minds. Occasionally Sam would even give a little nod or a barely audible grunt of approval or disapproval. Without notice of class or position, he and others in the household like him knew their place in the scheme of things.

'I'm not the man I was, dear child. The last few weeks in that prison haven't helped me and I've a fever in the lungs. I know I am not long for this world.'

There was an angry grunt from Sam, as Lizzie fell to her knees with her head in her father's lap. He smelt of tobacco and wood smoke. It was comforting and reminded her of all she held most precious. How could he die? How could there be an empty chair where he had sat just when she had come home and things were getting back to normal? Tom would be home soon. There would be a wedding, maybe grandchildren: all the things her father, a good and simple man, had worked for. In all his life he had never done harm to a living soul, but at least he would not have to witness her disgrace.

Sir Edwin could feel her shoulders shaking. He gently raised her chin and looked steadily at her tear-stained eyes. He thought how sickly she looked. She had a secret worry. He knew her well enough to be certain of it. No matter, he would address the matter in the front of his mind. It might lead to an explanation.

'I won't prevaricate,' he said, in a matter-of-fact tone. 'Sir Francis has been to me and asked for your hand in marriage. He's a fine man. He may be some years your senior, but he would look after you, Lizzie, and make you happy. It would set my mind at rest to know you were settled before I go to meet my maker. I've not asked you what has happened between you and Sir Richard Lovell, but you've never mentioned his name once to your mother or me, and we've come to our own conclusions . . .' He stopped and sighed wearily. 'This isn't a perfect world, my dear. Life must move on.'

There was the noise of hissing from the corner of the room by the fire. Sam was boiling a kettle. He came noisily to them and filled the bowl at Sir Edwin's feet. Steam rose in swirls and caught Lizzie's cheeks. She looked up at Sam and his old blue eyes smiled in a kind of all-knowing understanding encouragement.

'Don't make a decision without careful thought, my dear,' her father said gently. 'There are many things you must consider. I know you loved your Richard. I also know he may never come back, and neither may Philip. I know we're a long way from a Restoration. It may be many years, by which time you'll be an old maid and past child-bearing age, and you would have such pretty little ones . . .' He sighed again, his lids were closing. Lizzie thought her heart would burst with love for him, her own dear constant father. How could she cause him pain when it was avoidable? 'I shall watch your children from a better place, my dear,' he said as he fell asleep.

Lizzie cried quietly. It was the mention of babies. If her father knew the truth about his first grandchild, it would be a blow crueller than any other. She could never tell him. As her mind raced, Sam tapped her on the shoulder.

'You must go, my Lady. I must put your father in his bed in a clean warm nightshirt before the chill gets further into his bones.'

As she left the room, Sam whispered to her, 'If you were my child, I could wish for nothing more, my Lady. Sir Francis is more of a friend than you know.'

Twenty-Nine

Several months had passed, but Richard had not been able to come to terms with Lizzie's strange behaviour on the Isle of Wight. It had been so unlike her. She had always been determined and resolute. Something had happened to make her change her mind about their marriage so suddenly and without proper explanation. He had sent letters to her through the usual channels but had received no reply. His mood alternated between a supposition that she had found someone else, or that she was too busy with her family to respond, and then, perhaps for some reason, his letters had not got to her.

But he had to put his unhappiness aside, a thing at which he was most adept, and something he had endeavoured to teach young Harry. It was a philosophy which had spelt survival for the boy, and now at the end of it, Harry would be reunited with his family and free to speak and do as he pleased.

When they arrived in Flanders, things had moved swiftly and the change in the young prince's circumstances was instantaneous. Charles, the future King, looking every inch the part, met them from the boat. Richard could not believe how he had changed. The boy he remembered was now elegant and poised and extremely tall, unlike his diminutive parents. He exuded grace and courtly charm. Even though he seldom smiled, his eyes mirrored his mood with frightening accuracy as Richard would soon discover. As he saw his younger brother his laconic expression changed into one of great joy. He marched swiftly towards them surrounded by a pack of yapping spaniels and embraced Harry, lifting him from his feet.

'My dear brother, how I have waited for this day,' he said, holding Harry to him. The rest of his words were lost, muffled in the velvet of Harry's cloak.

They spent a few days resting in the shabby makeshift court in exile Charles had established in Bruges, before he escorted them to France where the boy's mother, Queen Henrietta Maria, his young sister Minette, whom he had never met, and his other brother James were waiting. They travelled together in a coach belonging to one of Charles's benefactors, Charles almost submerged in a tangle of fur rugs from which peeped his beloved spaniels.

'I have some good news, the Queen and our brother cannot contain their excitement and are travelling from Paris to meet us halfway,' Charles had informed them as they set off. 'Our uncle the King gave them the use of the royal coach, so we will enter Paris in style as befits the King of England and his family,' Charles went on with obvious pleasure.

Richard would never forget the moment when they saw

King Louis' coach in the distance approaching at a speed far superior to their own, the postillion splendid in the French royal livery and four perfectly matched grey horses.

When the two parties met on the road beside a delightful woody copse snow was beginning to fall and a sharp February wind blew the flakes into swirling flurries which clung lightly to their clothes, giving a fairy-tale feeling which suited the mood. James and Harry were the first to alight in the bitter cold. Too eager to wait for the steps to be unfolded, they leaped on to the frozen road and fell on each other with howls of joy.

The Queen waited in the warmth of the coach and Richard only had a glimpse of her gloved hand at the window before Charles quickly intervened.

'Harry, there is someone in that coach who is waiting to see you,' he said pointedly.

Harry broke away from his brother and as a footman opened the door Richard saw the Queen's gloved hand presented for a formal greeting so different from the one they had received from Charles.

Charles insisted that Richard join them in the royal coach.

'Sir Richard, you have been all the family two of my children have had for so long it is an honour to ride with you,' the Queen said charmingly, with her slight continental accent, as she gestured to the seat opposite. Richard thanked her and at once thought of Lizzie, who had shared his role with the Queen's children. He felt a stark pang of regret that circumstances had prevented her from sharing the joy of this long awaited and hard won family reunion.

On the journey the Queen remained silent as the boys chatted excitedly. Harry fired questions at James, the friend and playmate he had missed so much.

'Were you all alone after Elizabeth died?' James asked and Richard noticed a flash of pain cross the Queen's serene face at the mention of her dead child. He could only imagine the turmoil she must be feeling.

'I had friends, a special friend called Lizzie, and Mrs Briott,' Harry answered, glancing at Richard.

'When I return to England as King all your friends will be rewarded,' said Charles.

'To speak of happier things,' said Harry hastily, as he saw his mother reach into her muff for a small lace handkerchief, 'where is our sister Minette? Why didn't she come with you?' he asked.

'She was not well, my dear,' the Queen replied.' Nothing to worry about, only a cold, but I made her stay in the warm. She is so excited to meet the brother she has never seen.'

'Minette is a great beauty,' said Charles. 'And I suspect it is her beauty and charm which has changed the attitude of our French cousins towards us. Would you not say, Mama?' said Charles, wryly arching the famous royal brow.

'It's true, Harry. Mama and Minette have been moved from their horrible cold house, where all we ate was soup and Mother only had one dress that was presentable, to an apartment in the palace,' said James.

'Yes, your sister has caught the eye of the royal marriage brokers,' said Charles laconically. 'After all, the young, graceful and beautiful sister of the future King of England will one day be a useful pawn.'

'Minette has been very upset, which is the real reason she didn't come to meet you,' said James.

'Oh yes, the Horton business,' said Charles.

'Mrs Horton was her governess,' James explained. 'She has been with our sister since she was two weeks old. You know she was born in Exeter and Mother had to flee and left her with Mrs Horton who smuggled her to France, and now that things have changed King Louis has sent her back to Scotland.'

Richard felt a keen discomfort as these things were discussed, sensing the pain they must cause the Queen, but mercifully he observed she had pulled her veil over her face and fallen asleep. But Richard continued to think gloomily about the fate of the loyal retainer Mrs Horton and wondered how long it would take for his own future to be at risk.

Seeing his mother was asleep, and as Charles had also closed his eyes, James leaned forward to speak quietly to Harry.

'Mother does not want Minette to marry at all,' he whispered. 'She says she has suffered enough herself. She wants

Minette to take the veil. She has even founded a religious order at St Cloud in order that she may join it as soon as she is old enough.'

At this, Charles awoke from what had appeared to be a deep sleep and bellowed at his brother, 'I won't have you mention such things. While there's breath in my body, none of my siblings will turn to the Church of Rome, and you, my good brother,' he warned Harry, 'you'll do well to remember the promise that was made to our poor father the night before he died.'

There was silence in the coach, and Richard saw James's lip tremble a little. He was obviously slightly in awe of his elder brother. But Harry came back with a swift rebuttal. 'There is no need, your Majesty,' he began formally, 'for you to remind us. I was the last of us to hear my father's wishes, and they are dearer to me than my own life.' A smile lightened Charles's troubled face, and the mood in the coach became lighter. James prattled on about life at the French court, where it seemed to Richard that everyone lived entirely for pleasure. He heard how the King's niece, La Grande Mademoiselle, had set her sights on Charles, and he noticed Charles's mouth twist in what seemed to be wry amusement.

Later Richard had a chance to speak to Charles about plans for Harry, while the boys took a stroll to get some air. The sun crept in watery shafts through the threatening sky, casting shadows from the tall bare poplars which lined the road as they neared the city.

Thinking of his own position, he asked, 'Why did Mrs Horton go back to Scotland?'

Charles was an observant man, and the point of the question was not lost on him. He assured Richard that Mrs Horton was no longer needed, as Minette was destined to remain in France, where she would make a prestigious marriage in the noble line.

'There's no room for camp followers here,' he had added bluntly, and Richard thought of Lizzie. How right he had been not to take her with them. 'But Harry,' Charles went on, 'is a different matter. One day he'll return to England with me. When I take back the Crown,' he went on thoughtfully, 'Harry will be third in line to the English throne.'

'I know, your Majesty. I was saying as much as we left the Isle of Wight.'

'I'm sure you were . . . You, of course, are therefore an indispensable part of the English court which we're building,' Charles replied earnestly. 'We know of certain things, matters which may have tempted you to remain in England . . .' He thought for a moment, nearly said something, then changed his mind. Instead, he said, 'You can't go back to England, now your activities on behalf of the Royalist cause are too well known. You would lose your head. We need that as well as your heart.'

Charles concluded, in the disarmingly subtle and charming way he had, 'We know of your courage and your sacrifice, Sir Richard. When the time comes, you'll not regret your loyalty.'

In the following weeks, still no message in answer to his own came from Lizzie. He sent word several times through a different but trusted route of tobacco traders. He knew Sir Edwin would be unfailing in his need for the essential requisite that even the war had not managed to disrupt. His deep unhappiness had been mercifully submerged in the hectic life at the court and his pride as Harry charmed his aloof French cousins with his skills and quick wit. He watched how Charles loved his brothers and younger sister, and if ever he wondered at the ease with which the family assimilated into the forbidding stylized French court he reminded himself of the blood they shared with their uncle Louis, but he marvelled that no one had been able to save the Queen's husband from his fate.

Richard thought how lucky the Queen had been to have such brilliant happy children at the end of all her sorrows. They were her credibility. She herself had aged beyond recognition and without them she was just a disillusioned woman who could not accept any responsibility for her own role in the fate of her husband, and the loss of the English Crown. She saw herself as an innocent victim. But there were many, of whom Richard was one, who saw her as the woman who had so misunderstood her husband's people and the events of the time that she had driven him towards the path to the scaffold.

Thirty

Another letter had come from Richard. Lizzie could hardly bear to read it. Sam handed it to her after Sir Edwin's tobacco supply had been delivered.

'For you, my Lady, from France,' he hissed conspiratorially. 'You had best go somewhere private to read it. The messenger is to return in two days for a reply,' he added soundly.

She read it in the stables, the place she had met Richard when he had arrived to tell her he was free to marry her. She wept as she scanned the words quickly. She would go over them at length, again and again.

He begged her for news. Why hadn't she sent word to him? Something had happened, the more he thought about it, the more he found her sudden change of heart inexplicable. She was his whole world. If it were not for the danger he would put her in, he would come back at once, by the same route that her brother Philip had taken, to confront her. But he was now heavily committed to the plan to restore Charles to the throne. In England he would be a wanted man. If only she would send him word, he would do everything he could to get her to France. He would manage somehow. She could teach English at King Charles's court in Bruges. Many people there, new friends loyal to the King, saw the importance of perfecting their English. When the King returned, they would come with him. Richard wanted her to be part of the great triumph the return would be. It was her right, even the King had mentioned it. He would speak to him, he would want to repay Lizzie for all she had done for his brother and little sister.

The letter was a desperate cry from the heart. Lizzie felt sick. Her emotions tore at her soul as she thought of the man she loved. But she felt another kind of sickness too, one she had seen with the kitchen girl when she had fallen pregnant: the awful, gut-wrenching spasms of it each morning, which left her pale and languid for half the day.

What must poor Richard be going through? He must feel so betrayed by her. But he could never be told the real reason for her behaviour: the fact that it was her love for him which prevented him from knowing the truth. She knew him well enough to know what he would do with that truth. He would blow caution to the winds. There was no knowing what the repercussions would be.

How could she go to join him, bearing what might be another man's child? She put the letter next to her heart and agonized about what she should do.

'There's something you should know, Sir Francis,' said Lizzie.

She had told Ruth the previous day she would not marry Sir Francis and trick him into acknowledging her child. Ruth had boiled with rage because as far as the family was concerned the matter appeared to be settled. He would love the baby as his own and it was better he did not know the truth. She was remorseless in her onslaught, urging Lizzie to think of her family. Sir Francis would not take her if he thought she carried another man's child.

But Lizzie was adamant: she could not deceive such a dear kind man, who had done so much for them. The truth would be out soon anyway. She could not conceal her pregnancy much longer. The fact was that the future was bleak and she could not think further than today.

'Well, dear Elizabeth, I am listening,' Sir Francis said, taking her hand in his. They were sitting opposite each other in two high-backed chairs in the parlour.

Lizzie looked at him, preparing to speak, and thought sadly that so much of life was a compromise.

She had realized that whatever woman married Francis would be lucky indeed. There was something so wholesome about his clean open features, his strong hands. Today he had on his Sunday suit, and he was quite handsome. He looked at her tenderly with an expression of eager anticipation.

Sir Edwin had told Francis that it was up to Lizzie to decide whether or not to accept his offer. She might consent – he simply didn't know. But he knew enough of her to know that she was her father's daughter and that, if she accepted him, he could love her with all his heart and soul.

'I am with child,' she said quietly. She didn't look at him but felt his grip loosen. He did not speak. The silence was broken by the striking of her mother's clock on the mantel.

He got up and faced the long casement window, the morning sun silhouetting his large shoulders and narrow hips. He leaned forward, subdued, as if he had been deflated by her news, and then he raised his shoulders in a deliberate way and turned around.

'May I know who the father is?' he asked calmly.

'I don't know,' she answered, colouring shamefully as she realized how awful it sounded.

'My dear, what can you mean?' he asked, his voice rising in shock for the first time.

'I will tell you all, Sir Francis. I had given my promise to Sir Richard Lovell. We were to be married on the day before he left with Harry for France. and we had loved each other as man and wife, just once.' She continued falteringly, 'And then Captain Mildmay, realizing that I should be gone the next day . . . he . . . he was so strong, I could not stop him . . . I would have killed him . . . if I had the strength . . . but . . .' She started to cry.

Francis took her in his arms. 'My dear,' he said after a while, 'I must go and think and ask for guidance.' He paused, looking sadly at the floor. 'What dark things men do in the name of war. But you are so good, Elizabeth. Many girls would have hidden the truth and accepted the life-line I offered you . . . I know your family are waiting to know your answer. Your father must know nothing of this. It would kill him . . . I don't want you to be asked by them at the moment, until we've had time to think. Will you come to my home for the next few hours and sit quietly? There are things you've told me which can't go unpunished.'

She nodded, for there was something so strong and certain about everything Francis said. As she looked at him, secure in the steady warmth of his gaze, she thought how she felt a kind of love growing for this man, different to her feelings for Richard which now seemed almost like a dream.

'And besides,' he added, gently touching her cheek. 'You've not told me if you would accept me. You too must look to the future, and what's best for you and your child.'

Hinton Manor was larger than Hatherton, and had not benefited from the innovations and improvements that Lizzie's parents had implemented in their own home. The entrance was dark and gloomy, and the sun rarely saw the inside of the house. The windows were small and all faced north.

Francis took Lizzie's arm as they went inside. A cold draught from a big empty fireplace on the far side of the hall brought a damp smell of sodden soot and ash. A dishevelled steward came slowly through a doorway, which obviously led to the kitchens, his livery was soiled and his hair hung dankly on his collar. He bowed to Sir Francis, his eye running over Lizzie with undisguised curiosity.

'Sir, I didn't know you were returning with a visitor, or I would have set the fires,' he stammered apologetically.

'Well, set to, man,' Francis barked. 'And not just in the hall, but also in her Ladyship's parlour, and summon the pantry boy, for I want ale and fresh bread and some of the salt pork, for Lady Elizabeth must be made comfortable.'

There was a breathless excitement in Francis's voice, and the steward caught the mood, his face brightened and he clumsily fastened the top button of his collar and hurried down the corridor, calling loudly for assistance.

Alerted by the commotion, two large hunting dogs bounded into the room, leaping up at Francis. He greeted them affectionately, allowing them to lick his face, talking to them as he might to another man.

Lizzie thought how lonely he must have been since his wife's death and with his children spending most of their time at Hatherton. The dogs had naturally been a great consolation to him.

Francis invited her to follow him up the stairs along a large creaking gallery and into what had obviously been his wife's apartments. The rooms were fusty and neglected, as if the air had not been disturbed for a long time. The shutters were closed and the only light came from a small high round window beside a fireplace. Mice scuttled under the floorboards as she pulled back the shutters and the fading afternoon light stole into the room. There was a large oak bed with a beautifully worked tester. As she brushed it with her hand it felt cold and damp. The furnishings were heavily shrouded in cloths. She pulled one aside to find an inlaid dressing table with an ornate carved mirror. She sat down and stared absentmindedly at her reflection.

She could hardly remember Francis's dead wife, but as she looked at herself she recalled a vague and distant memory of a tall elegant woman with a thick coil of dark hair in a jewelled net behind her head.

Lizzie closed her eyes for a moment and the impression became clearer, almost as if she were in the room with her. Lizzie felt her presence strongly.

Slowly Lizzie braided her hair and felt the grief of a mother who has been taken from her children and her husband and the life she loved. And she thought how life was a thing so transient that she must be grateful for having survived to this quiet evening.

Francis had not been able to think about what his life might hold since his wife had died. Thinking about happiness was a luxury he could not afford. After Charles had given up his attempt to reclaim the throne, life north of the border had been impossible.

The country had become a dour thankless place, under the hellfire and damnation of the Covenanters. Voices never rose in song to worship and give thanks to God. There were no plays or masques to lighten the dark winter, no presents on a child's saint's day, the cathedrals were shut.

Back in England the news was not all bad. The New Model Army was the finest fighting machine in the world, and the return of a powerful Parliament was beginning to bear fruit. Roads had been built; the country was on the move again; trade had returned, and a new and fairer system of justice had taken the place of the old feudal system, which to Francis had always seemed deeply flawed. He held the view that the return of an intelligent monarchy could only be achieved by working with the system rather than against it, and if a healthy fusion of King and Parliament could not be achieved, so be it.

And now, when he least expected it, hope for domestic happiness had presented itself in the form of his friend's daughter Elizabeth: someone he could love and cherish. He had been deeply in love with his wife. Her death had, he thought at the time, closed his heart with a searing finality. But now he was thirty-two years of age and love had flown into his life again the moment he had seen Lizzie in her parents' house.

At first he had not even considered the possibility of allowing his sudden unexpected emotions to be more than a pipe-dream, but as more of her story had unfolded, and he had come to know her better, a small seed had taken root and grown. He knew that if it were not for her condition, she would not be there now, in his house, and he would not be thinking how best to persuade her to become his wife.

Elizabeth was no ordinary woman. She had played her part on a large and complex stage. She was proud, brave and clever. Marriage to him would not be her only option and he must not let her think that he was foolish enough to underestimate her powers of survival. No, marriage to him would have to be a fine thing, worthy of the high standards she had set herself.

'Come, draw nearer to the fire,' Francis said gently, indicating a comfortable embroidered chair. The fire now burned merrily, thanks to the hasty reparations of the steward, but the heat had brought out the damp from the unused, unloved room, and a strong smell of must filled the air. Lizzie drew her shawl about her. He thought how slim and delicate she looked, and how her appearance belied the fiery determination of her nature. And then an image of her great with child flashed across his mind. Soon her pregnancy would begin to show. If she were to accept him they would have to marry quickly, for he would not want the start of their married life to be spoiled by gossip and speculation.

'What beautiful work, both here and in the bedchamber,' Lizzie said nervously. She was aware that Francis was about to continue the subject of marriage, and her feelings were in turmoil. One minute the idea came as the answer to all her problems, and then she remembered her love for Richard, and felt faint with misery at the idea of planning a life without him.

But reason intervened and realistically she knew that fate had dealt the cruel blow, and she could not plan a life with him.

'Did your wife sew them?' she continued vaguely.

'No, my mother did them, but my wife was a fine needle-woman. Sadly, we left all her work in Scotland. So much of what we all value has been lost. Which is why I want to ask for your hand again, Elizabeth. I want to rebuild a life. I'm aware that you can't have the depth of feeling for me that I have for you. But I offer you security and I can spare your family the sorrow of the truth . . .'

He leaned across from his chair, and took her hand gently in his. How cold it felt. He chafed it softly between his own, and was encouraged to continue as she did not pull away.

'These are uncertain times. This would give great joy to your father, and I would make you happy. I respect you and admire you, as well as loving you. For you are a most beautiful woman, whom any man would regard as a treasure. This house needs someone like you to give it back a soul. I would be a father to your child and love it as my own . . . but I do not do this out of pity, my dear, for it would be me who would be pitied if I could not gain the great prize of such a wife and mother to my poor children who already love you.'

He faltered for a moment, for he could see that she was crying silently, her head bent, tears pouring unchecked on to her velvet skirt. He did not know what else he could say, and so he did not speak. He could see her lips moving, as if she were formulating an answer, and he could feel his heart beating faster.

'You do me great honour, and you are a fine man,' she began falteringly, looking earnestly into his eyes. He looked down, unable to hide his disappointment, for her words were surely the beginning of her refusal. 'And I accept your offer, and will be a good wife to you and mother to your children.'

He let out a long satisfied breath. He felt a quiet confident happiness, a certainty he had not felt for many months. He put his hand in his pocket and brought out a small silk purse. Giving it to her he raised her hand to his lips and kissed it.

Inside was a ring made of a circle of diamonds and pearls.

'It belonged to my mother. It's for you, Lizzie.'

He took the ring and placed it on her finger. All the drama of the last years went through Lizzie's mind, her blind commitment to the King's children, the awfulness of the little princess's lonely death. The gaunt captivity at Carisbrooke, which could not dim her love for Richard, and over it all hovered the menacing figure of Anthony Mildmay.

It was he who had lost her her own true love and the chance of the life she and Richard had planned. As she looked into Sir Francis's strong kindly face, she felt that he was more than a match for the evil man who had left her with the lifelong uncertainty which now grew in her womb. But, surely, she thought, the moment when her love for Richard had been consummated with so much sweetness would have planted the seed for this life she carried within her, not the ferocious and wretched skirmish with Mildmay.

No, she would will the baby to be Richard's, and as for the child, Francis would be the keeper of the secret. Her son or daughter would love him as she knew she would herself, albeit in a different way from the way she loved Richard. Married to him she would finally be free of the man who had shaped her life since she had left her home and family for the unknown life which had brought her so much joy and pain. As if he read her thoughts, he asked her a question.

'I must ask you something which has been troubling me greatly, before we dispense with the troubles that have befallen you.'

'Of course,' Lizzie replied willingly. 'There must be no secrets between us.'

It was Mildmay which concerned him, although it was not the paternity of the child he would bring up as his own, but more the vengeful nature of the man, and how best to dispatch him once and for all.

'I have a list . . . a record made in Prince Henry's own careful hand,' Lizzie said hesitantly. 'It is a meticulous record of the man's mendacity and greed . . . but he does not know of its existence . . . I would not have dared to tell him . . . for he would stop at nothing, I'm sure, to get his hands on it.'

Francis looked concerned.

'What exactly do you mean?' he asked.

She explained to him as carefully as she could about the plundering of the royal assets which Mildmay and his odious wife had perpetrated. About the princess's trinkets and

234

jewellery, some of which she had seen on the person of Lady Mildmay. 'The hangings and furnishings,' she went on, 'gradually disappeared over the months until Prince Harry hardly had a covering under which to sleep.'

'The man is a blaggard,' Francis said.

'We noted each disappearance in detail and the times at which the Mildmay coach had trundled down the hill laden with spoils, later to be sold by the captain for the maintenance of his lifestyle on the Island and improvements to his family home on the mainland.'

As Francis listened to the tale, his face hardened in disgust. Lizzie looked so small and vulnerable, and yet she had had the wit and forethought to record the crimes against her charges. He believed in retribution, be it divine or earthly, and that one day Mildmay would be brought to book for his conduct. But to keep him in fear of discovery, that would indeed be the way to keep him from their lives until the time was right . . .

'Lizzie, my dear, there's something I must tell you about your father. It was of course Anthony Mildmay who brought about your father's imprisonment. He's a dangerous man, and still powerful . . . I managed to convince the Council of your father's position. He's not well and he poses no threat to Parliament, but I can see a pattern emerging. I'm quite sure Mildmay intended to wield his power over you by offering to be the instrument of your father's release, and indeed he would have been a powerful weapon against your virtue . . .'

'You need tell me nothing. I know how bad he is.'

'But he doesn't know of the weapon you have in your power to silence him completely. And I'll make it my business to inform him of its existence.'

'And why not do so now? I know, technically, the royal possessions had been sequestered by Parliament. Surely, they'd take a grave view of such conduct,' Lizzie said.

'No, my dear, this is not the time. As things are going, I'm beginning to see that one system's been replaced by another far more corrupt . . . The time will come when the King has returned. Then Mildmay will pay for his crimes in the proper manner.' Francis pondered for a moment. 'No, my dear,' he added as an afterthought, 'he won't know a moment's peace of mind, for he'll live and sleep in fear of exposure, and he'll not trouble you again, while I have breath in my body.'

As Lizzie looked at Francis's open honest face, he appeared to her as a safe craft in a storm-swept sea of treachery, and she saw in her mind's eye the spectre of the Mildmays sailing far into the distance, where in the end they would be called to account. She knew now that while Francis lived, she no longer had anything to fear. For the first time in her adult life, she could begin the business of living, of looking forward to what each day might bring.

But before she could do it, there was Richard. She decided to ask Francis what was the most honourable path to follow.

The question was no surprise to him.

'I've been thinking about this myself,' he replied steadily. 'I want you to know, my dear, that another man's loss is not something I crow about, although of course in this case it's my gain. Richard is young. You've known a great love for each other, as I did with my wife and I lost her. I thought I could never find happiness again, but look what happened. I found you.'

He paused and took her hand gently.

'You must send him a letter. Tell him of the difficult times your family is having. Tell him it's your father's wish that you should marry. Tell him about Tom's plans, that Hatherton is soon to be *his* home. Tell him you love your father too much to come to Bruges, and besides, your family does not wish you to go. They have suffered enough. Your mother is not well. It would break her heart if you were to go. The pain will heal, my dear. For all of us, pray to God.'

They married a month later. Tom came home for the wedding, bringing Anne Monck with him. They too were to be married in a few months, and his future bride lost no time in exploring the manor which was soon to be her home. Ruth did not take kindly to this and gave her a frosty reception, which only thawed when Francis took her on one side and asked her if she would come to Hinton and take over the running of the house. She would be there for the birth of the baby.

'What more important responsibility could you have?' he asked.

Mary was surprised by the speed with which Sir Francis had got her daughter with child so soon after the proposal, but there were many things about which it was better not to ask too closely in these times. Her daughter's happiness was enough for her.

The bridal couple were to go back to Hinton after the wedding and a transformation had been performed. The house already felt lived in and restored to some of its former charm. The wedding was a happy affair and a bride never had prettier bridesmaids. Her sisters and Francis's daughters held a chain of hellebores and rosemary and Lizzie wore her mother's wedding gown with an extra panel sewn in the front.

Mary wept unashamedly as the couple took their vows. She wept with happiness that Lizzie had found such a good man. She wept for the years lost in strife, for the absence of Philip, for the prospect of losing her dearest Edwin, for she knew that once the wedding was over, he would retire to his bed. She knew he wanted to die at Hatherton. He would not live to see another bride in the great bridal bed where he had loved her each night for most of her adult life. But in a strange odd way, she also thought of Richard Lovell. In her mother's heart, she knew in a perfect world that it was he who should be vowing eternal love to Lizzie.

There were things she could only guess at, but once or twice she had caught Lizzie's expression unawares. She had seen the ghostly wisps of poignant, bewildered regret. As the couple walked radiantly down the aisle past the family, she caught her daughter's eye just for a fleeting second and she knew it all.

She felt connected for an instant to a young man far away, and wondered if he would ever come back, and if he did, what then?

Philip heard the news in a letter from his mother, not only of the marriage to Sir Francis but also of Lizzie's pregnancy. He knew at once that all was not as it seemed. His mother urged him to seek Richard out to give him the information in person and he did so as soon as he could.

'My dearest Lizzie, is all well with her?' asked Richard.

'As well as can be expected,' Philip replied ambivalently.

'What do you mean by that?' Richard asked suspiciously. 'What has happened, something's wrong, isn't it?'

'Let us sit and have some wine,' said Philip, noticing a flagon and two glasses on the table in front of a merry fire. The room was warm and comfortable and morning sun came between heavy swagged curtains. Philip had been pleasantly surprised at the circumstances in which he found Richard and the royal party. Now he began falteringly, fearing the impact of what he was about to say.

'I shall not prevaricate,' he said nervously, fingering the brim of his wide brimmed hat. 'In short, Lizzie is wed.'

'What an earth do you mean?' cried Richard, his face going ashen white as he jumped to his feet.

'I know how hard this is for you,' said Philip gently, 'which is why I have come to tell you in person.'

'Who is the man?' Richard asked dully, going to the window and staring at the sky.

'Sir Francis Hinton, a friend of the family, a widower, a good man,' Philip answered in a matter-of-fact way.

'I do not understand. This is not like the Lizzie I know,' said Richard faintly, turning from the window and sitting down with his head in his hands. 'We had made our vows to each other, not perhaps in the eyes of the church but with our souls.' He stopped for a moment, thinking out loud. 'There is more,' he said slowly. 'This is not in Lizzie's character, why didn't she tell me herself?'

'Let's be practical about this,' said Philip, anxious to deflect the question. 'You could not have been together for years, you can never return to England until the King is restored, and besides my brother is to marry. There will be no place for Lizzie at the manor.' He watched Richard's anguished face.

Richard, a man who never flagged in his loyalties, was for the first time consumed by doubt. 'I could have gone back,' he said bitterly, banging the table with clenched fists. 'I could have asked for indemnity, turned to the Parliamentary cause, I could have claimed my Lizzie . . . don't I have a right to happiness?' he asked passionately.

'If you had done so you would not have been the man Lizzie loved,' said Philip evenly. 'You are an integral part of the

238

future of our country and the monarchy to which we are all committed, and for which hundreds of our brothers have laid down their lives. Our own happiness must take second place, we both know this,' said Philip finally.

He did not linger, but he clapped his arms round Richard's shoulders. He knew he must leave his friend to gather his courage and accept how they had both been swept along by the tide of events where the only things which kept them from drowning were their convictions and beliefs.

'We will meet in happier times,' said Philip as he left. Richard did not look up.

Richard received the letter from Lizzie a week later. Her explanation seemed glib. He knew it was not the truth, and he felt betrayed, even though deep down he knew this was not of Lizzie's doing. There was something else, something bad and far-reaching, but at least his beloved Lizzie was safe. He would not cause her more pain by writing to her again.

PART FIVE

Hinton Manor

Thirty-One

'We shall call him Benjamin,' Francis said. It was late spring and the country lay basking in sunshine. As Lizzie took her first-born in her arms, Francis's big capable hands cradled the top of his head, already covered in a soft down of dark hair. She looked up into the smiling face of her husband. Being the man he was he had been as good as his word and had taken the child as his own. No other thoughts had marred the moment. Benjamin was theirs, a new life born out of chaos.

It was only later as the child began to grow so distinctly that she occasionally let the canker of doubt niggle at her joy. Benjamin was an unusual boy, forward in everything. He learned to walk before he was a year old and developed an obsessional love for Francis who returned it in equal measure. This great bond began to worry Lizzie. What if, one day, the boy found out that Francis was not his father and she was forced to tell him the truth? For he would surely want to know. But for now she and Francis kept their secret well and the only other living people who knew the truth were Ruth and Mrs Briott, and she knew that both would take her secret to the grave.

Sir Edwin lived to see his grandson born, and it was his delight which increased her love for Francis, for he had been the instrument of her salvation.

Her father died later that winter. He told Lizzie that he felt he could leave the world a happy man, knowing she had found such happiness, and that Tom would soon move into the manor with Anne Monck whom he had married the previous month at her family home in the north. Lizzie had been unable to go to the wedding as she was once again pregnant, and the journey would be too dangerous. And neither could Mary go, as Sir Edwin was too ill to travel.

But Mathilda, Adela and Beatrice went and were maids of honour. Little Emily had come to live with Francis and Lizzie. Although she was two years older than Francis's elder daughter Mariah, the two were inseparable, and Mary decided she would be better off living with a robust young family than in the dower house.

After her father's death Lizzie gave way to all the emotions she had buried deep in her soul over the years. She was inconsolable. Grief and a sense of loss overwhelmed her. Some days she thought she might drown.

But Francis was always there. It was his sheer consistency, as if he knew she must purge herself, that kept her going. Each night she dreamed troublesome haunting dreams which left her exhausted in the morning and not fit for the waking day. Often she dreamed she was living with Richard and much as she strove to keep him from her thoughts he intruded in her nights with a cruel poignant reality.

But finally she woke one morning and decided to get on with her life. It happened as she looked out of her bedroom window. It was a sharp May day, and the air was effulgent with the promise of summer. Francis was walking with the garden steward. There had been a great deal of activity recently: he was creating a garden for Lizzie. Mary had helped him plan it. It was to be his belated wedding gift to her and, throughout the dark days of her unhappiness, Francis had found great solace in the creation of the garden. He knew that as it began to take shape and grow, it would heal Lizzie.

That morning he had on his old woollen hat. As the day was warm, he wore no jacket, his shirt hung open and his sleeves were rolled up. Lizzie could see his sun-kissed hands and wrists from her window. The previous night he had been delivering lambs and boasted as he kissed her good morning, as she drank her chocolate in bed, that they had not lost a single ewe in birth for two seasons.

She thought carefully about this. Their child was due in a matter of weeks, and suddenly she was reminded of the miracle of birth and the continuity of life. Perhaps it would be a son?

She watched Benjamin come running to Francis from the arms of the nursemaid with whom he was taking the morning air. Francis's face lit with a smile and he threw the delighted boy in the air and ruffled the top of his hair, with a love which could not be anything but genuine.

As she watched her husband and saw the respectful and admiring expression on the face of the steward, Lizzie realized that she loved this man more completely and profoundly than she had thought possible. Maybe she had married him for a safe haven, but if she were to marry him today, it would be for love as deep as any she had known.

A voice inside her said, 'You deserve to be happy. Go to him and tell him how much you love him.'

Throwing aside the covers, with Minette dancing at her heels she ran out of the room with no more that her nightdress and a shawl, down the staircase and into the garden. The steward saw her first and politely melted behind the thick yew hedge where he stayed, anxiously peering, afraid that her Ladyship brought bad news . . . but as he recalled to his wife later that night, as Sir Francis turned, his young wife had thrown herself into his arms with such force, the steward feared she might have the baby she carried there and then. Whatever she had said brought about the biggest smile on Sir Francis's face, and they had fallen to kissing each other in a way which was not seemly for the gentry. It had made the informant happy to see it just the same, and from that day on Sir Francis seemed to have become like a young lad again, and as the garden grew, so did Lizzie and Francis's love for each other.

A month later, Lizzie went into labour. It was an easy birth. Francis waited in the next room, Ruth restraining him as he heard the first cry, but he was not to be kept from the room for long. He burst in just as the child was being placed on the breast.

But Lizzie looked troubled, more than just by the ordeal of the birth. Before he could say anything, she whispered to him, 'It is a girl. You must have wanted another son,' and she held the child protectively to her as if he might not want to see it.

'My dear, what can you mean? We already have a son. I couldn't want for more than a daughter in your image, Lizzie. Shall we call her Faith?' he asked.

Lizzie nodded, smiling, and he took the baby and kissed her damp forehead with a tenderness which Lizzie would always remember.

It was Francis at his best. It was why she loved him so very much.

Thirty-Two

Mary sat in the summer house that Francis had built for the family in the garden at Hinton. She kept drifting in and out of a happy reverie. Minette sat on her lap snoring in a regular, comforting way. The dog was old now, nearly twelve. They were two old ladies together. She felt they understood each other. Minette always latched on to her when she came to Hinton.

'Six years,' she said sleepily to the little dog. She often muttered to her when they were alone. She hoped nobody ever heard her. They would think she had lost her wits.

'Six years, they've been married and all those little girls . . . and so happy,' she said dreamily. 'It's time Philip came home . . . Yes it's time,' she said before she fell asleep.

It was autumn, it had been a beautiful summer, one of birth and hope . . . although the country had been in turmoil. The King might return . . . things were getting back to normal. People wanted the old order once again.

She dreamed of Tom's sons, of Edwin. She had not thought she could be so happy and content as she was now, six years a widow, a bevy of grandchildren . . . a pity Tom's wife was such a haughty woman. She had not made the family welcome at Hatherton, but Francis had more than made up for her unkindness. Mary spent much of her time at Hinton, more than ever now that Adela and Beatrice had married. Mathilda had become a strange and lonely person, withdrawing more and more into herself. If there had been a nunnery to go to, she would have gone.

She said she would wait until the King returned and the nunneries could be restored. Then she would have a place to

246

go to and devote herself to God. Mary was in a sound sleep when she was rudely awoken by Ruth.

'My Lady, you must come at once! There's been an accident.'

Mary went as fast as her rheumatics made her able, up the long brick path between the lavender hedges she had just helped Lizzie to harvest for the linen room. It was slippery, with a scattering of autumn leaves, and Ruth had to steady her. She was losing her breath.

'Don't rush so, my Lady,' Ruth cautioned. 'You'll be needed more than ever now.' Ruth was crying into her apron. She had not said much, only that it was the master, a fall from his horse.

They had lain him on the long refectory table in the hall, a cushion hastily tucked under his head. Lizzie was bending over him, bathing a tiny wound at the corner of his temple. A thin trickle of blood snaked towards his thick crop of grey white hair.

'Oh, Lord save us. He's so white. What happened?' Mary cried.

'He fell from his horse, hit his head . . .' Lizzie faltered desperately.

The household had all gathered anxiously in the room, hearing the commotion, and each stood with his own private anguish at seeing Francis, so noble, dependable and good, with such a deathly pallor.

Each harboured their own sense of gratitude, for the many splendid things he had done for them all, and each felt a sense of impending loss on this bright sunny morning. They had all been eagerly awaiting his return. He was to have brought good news. Everyone knew he had been attending talks in London. It was rumoured the King might soon return. General Monck's army might rally for the King . . . but all this was as nothing to them now.

'It was the path, my Lady. Not the horse's fault. The path was covered in leaves and they covered the water in the stream beside the short cut his Lordship took in his eagerness to get home. The horse mistook it for firm ground and fell into the stream. It threw his Lordship. He hit his head on a stone.' It was Jacob who spoke, the flaps of his leather hood carelessly tucked up, showing his scarred head.

'Who found him?' Mary asked, encircling Lizzie with her arm.

'I did, my Lady, but it wasn't so much finding, for I'm always there watching out for my Lord Francis, in the same way I used to be for Sir Edwin before Jenny and I came with my Lady to Hinton. God rest him . . . he's been so good to us . . . As soon as I saw him in the distance, I saddled up old Ned and as he galloped down the far meadow to take the back way, I was after him so I could be there to unsaddle him after the long ride . . .' Jacob gulped back tears. 'I knew he'd be tired . . . I wish . . . I'd stopped him.' He faltered and lowered his head, and Mary saw that he was weeping.

Ruth stepped swiftly in, calling for rose water and witch hazel for the wound.

The room emptied except for Mary, Ruth and Lizzie, and the hesitant figure of little Benjamin.

Mary saw him and went and drew him towards his mother's side.

Lizzie felt the small comforting presence of her son against her. She did not cry. She looked intently at her husband, praying for a sign of life. He was still breathing but he was deathly pale.

'Dearest Francis. Speak to me,' she said huskily into his ear. She saw the blood had trickled stealthily on to the cushion. She loved Francis so very much. He was always there for all of them, a tower of strength. His love was always unconditional.

'Please, my dearest, talk to me. You're home now,' Lizzie urged again, tears beginning to tumble from her eyes. They mingled with the ribbon of blood, and she was vaguely aware of her mother's hand dabbing with a clean sweet-smelling cloth.

'My Lady, we must remove his wet clothes. He will die of cold,' Ruth said firmly, always at her best in a crisis.

'Surely we should get him to his chamber for modesty's sake?' Mary said.

'Moving him wouldn't be good. He needs to be still,' Ruth said. Without waiting for permission, she had begun to ease

Francis out of his wet clothes. Lizzie helped automatically. His skin was white and clammy. Somewhere, someone appeared with covers and a warming pan.

Minutes past and the room was silent. Suddenly Sir Edwin's precious water clock, which he had given to them as a wedding present, chimed the hour when the family dinner would normally be served.

Lizzie looked at her husband. It seemed only the other day that she had helped to dress her father in his best clothes after he had died. His body had the same marble translucency she saw now. And just as she was beginning to despair, Francis opened his eyes.

'I'm so tired,' he whispered.

'Oh, my dearest, you have come back to me,' sobbed Lizzie, throwing herself on his chest, her cheek next to his.

'Lizzie, my little fierce Lizzie, how I love you,' he said softly in her ear.

'Don't speak. It will tire you. Just let me get you warm. You were so cold.'

'Where's my Benjie?' Francis said weakly.

'I'm here, Father,' came Benjie's small voice. He had been standing quietly behind his mother.

'My boy,' said Francis feebly. 'Look at those three women. Are they not a fit guard of honour to send a man to heaven?'

His eyes closed slowly, a smile played about his lips. The three women held him, bound together on their inseparable journey through life. Francis died confident that his children were in safe hands.

Thirty-Three

Francis had been dead for two months when Ruth came to Lizzie one morning, her face incandescent with anger. Lizzie was with Benjamin, helping him with his Latin studies, which he found difficult and had neglected since Francis's death.

'What's the matter, Ruth?' Lizzie cried out in alarm.

'I should have killed him, if I'd the courage, right where he stood, but nothing good will come of it, be he alive or dead . . . My Lady, you mustn't see him. He brings evil. I feel it in my bones, and you a widow for no more than a few weeks. How dare he come here?'

Neither of them noticed that Benjamin had left the room.

'Who is it you want to kill? Ruth, speak slowly, I don't understand,' Lizzie said clearly.

'Mildmay . . . Satan in human form. You should call the servants, my Lady, and have him run off the estate.'

'Oh God,' Lizzie gasped, hanging on to the back of a chair for support.

She knew several things at once: that Mildmay had come with a purpose and would not have come if Francis had still been living.

'I must pray for guidance, Ruth. Francis will be near me. It's no use hiding. I must confront him.'

She walked slowly, and the memory of the first time she saw Mildmay so many years ago came into her mind, as clearly as if it were yesterday. She had found hidden reserves of strength and dignity then, but now she was of even firmer mettle. Mildmay had better watch his step.

But all her confidence dissolved when, to her terror, she saw him standing in the hall talking to Benjamin.

He was dressed in black and his arm was about Benjamin's small shoulders. He looked like a black crow about to fly off with her son in his claws. Ruth was down the stairs before the full implication hit Lizzie. She swept the child into her arms out of the room and down the passage to the kitchens. Lizzie could hear his protestations becoming fainter.

'So, my Lady Hinton,' Mildmay said, sweeping a low bow. 'Allow me to offer my deepest sympathy at your loss. Your husband was a fine man . . . And, as you will see, I too am suffering, for my dear wife departed this life but a month ago.' He made an expansive gesture, alluding to his black mourning clothes. 'But I,' he continued, looking pointedly in the direction that Benjamin had been removed so swiftly, 'don't have the consolation of children.'

His chin tilted as he gave her a blatant stare, and to her annoyance she could not help herself blushing in anger or shame at the knowledge he had of her.

He saw the flush in her cheeks and was encouraged to continue his remarks.

'Yes, you're fortunate, and your son told me he's six years old, and his saint's day is in November.' He looked steadily at Lizzie. 'What a joy you gave your husband. A fine son so soon after your marriage.' So far she had not spoken at all, and as Mildmay also fell silent, waiting for her to speak, he could not help but take note of her beauty. She had always been a pretty and spirited girl, but she had grown into a formidable woman, whose beauty was embellished with dignity and presence.

He had never loved his wife. He had never loved any woman, and when she had failed to give him children, he had ceased to have any feelings for her, except a kind of clandestine partnership in greed and ambition. And now she was dead, and a Restoration was quite possible. He would be left a ruined man. If the King returned, he stood to pay for his actions. He needed supporters and currency with which to buy them.

The boy was a fine lad. He had Lizzie's hair and sharp smile. But there was something in the eyes. Perhaps it was the way he held himself? When Lizzie had seen them together, it was as if she had seen a ghost . . . no, it was not his imagination . . .

'I don't know why you've come. Say what you have to say and leave,' Lizzie said evenly.

She knew exactly what he was thinking, and a dull cold fear wrapped round her heart.

'Let's go somewhere where we can't be overheard,' Mildmay suggested. He had come with a plan, but since his arrival, another and much better one had fallen into his lap.

He followed Lizzie's slim figure into a small parlour, and she took the precaution of ostentatiously standing by a tasselled bell pull by the fireplace.

'The boy is mine. There's no use denying it,' he said abruptly.

'What on earth d'you mean?' Lizzie rounded furiously. 'You don't know anything of the sort.'

251

He advanced towards her, and before she had time to pull the bell, he had her in his arms. His mouth was on her face, his words coming fast in the urgent and sensual whisper she remembered so vividly.

'I had you, my darling. You were ripe for me, and I planted that in you. It's an unexpected bonus . . . I know when you met your husband. The lad wasn't his. It was I who got there first, my little plum, and would you not like me to do it again?'

'You forget, sir,' she spat, 'that you were *not* the first, as you put it. I had no secrets from my husband, and had it not been for you, we would not have found each other, for he would have had no need to rescue me,' she hissed through clenched teeth.

His arms had her in a grip which constricted her breathing, and she felt her breasts pressed against the roughness of his coat. She felt revulsion and fear, which was in itself shamefully physical.

'So you're saying that milksop Lovell's the father of your child . . .? I think not, my pretty one . . .' His mouth moved from her cheek back to her lips. She could feel his breath mingling with her own.

'I've never forgotten you, and now you're a powerful woman. We should marry, you and I, and I'll make a man of my son. It's the right thing, Lizzie. Don't you see? I hadn't come here with that in mind, but fate has taken a hand . . .'

Lizzie could feel the anger boiling inside her. She sprang free from him, and with undisguised contempt she faced him, her outstretched arms maintaining the distance between them.

'I think you came for another reason, to get the record I keep of your thieving and mendacity carefully compiled by Prince Henry. I can assure you he speaks most movingly of the way you treated both him and the Princess Elizabeth and stole all they possessed. You thought that as my husband was dead, you could intimidate me into giving it to you . . . and indeed I might have done just so to be free of you . . . But now you've stupidly given me a reason for keeping it. Think of it like this . . .' she said menacingly, 'if ever you try to see my son or repeat the lies you told today, I'll see the list gets into the right hands to await the return of the King, at which time you'll pay dearly for your crimes. But if by retaining it

I buy your silence, then so be it, for I dare say there are plenty of others who'll have marked you, sir.'

Mildmay swung round as the door burst open. Ruth stood there still as a statue, a loaded pistol levelled straight at the captain's head.

'Doors have ears in this house, sir,' Ruth said, her voice resonant with anger. 'Now shall I kill him like the vermin he is, my Lady? I can say he was caught molesting you, when your husband was hardly cold in his grave, and there're plenty in the house who'll bear witness against him.'

The pistol moved unsteadily in her hands, and Mildmay made a move to shield himself behind Lizzie, but she was too quick for him. She darted across the floor to where Ruth stood.

Lizzie knew, and so did Mildmay, that his life hung in the balance. She had only to say the word, and this man who had haunted her for so long would be no more. But what of her conscience? How could she live with that, and just as the desire to rid herself of him swelled in her mind, she wondered what Francis would have done. She slowly put her hand on the barrel of the pistol and pushed it down.

'Now leave us,' Lizzie said.

She heard Mildmay let out a breath.

'You heard what my Lady said. Leave us.' It was a man's voice. Jacob joined the group at the door.

Mildmay had confronted his possible death more closely than at any other time in his life. It hovered before him, real and taunting. Maybe at last he had met his match. He did not need to be asked again.

As he made his decision, he knew the moment of danger had been diffused. He sauntered past Lizzie and gave her a sardonic smile.

'We shall see,' he said.

He flapped his hat against his knee and, pushing out the crown, he put it on.

'Well, mistress, you had your chance and you missed it,' he shot at Ruth.

'If there's a next time, I won't. You can depend on it,' Ruth retorted.

He gave a mocking bow and left the room, but, for all his bravado, his knees were shaking. He knew that but for Lizzie's maddening goodness, the witch of a nurse would have shot him where he stood.

They stood silently, waiting to hear the sound of his horse trotting down the drive.

'Who was that man, Mama?'

Benjamin had crept up on them. He stood small and frightened by the doorway.

'No one you need worry about. He won't come again,' Lizzie replied, taking him in her arms. She closed her eyes and wished with all her might that this were true.

PART SIX

Hinton Manor 1660

Thirty-Four

The year 1660 opened to find the country yet again in disarray. Three years previously, it had been suggested that Cromwell, now called The Protector, should become King, and the role should become hereditary.

Parliament appeared to have come round to the view that only a monarch could rule the British ... it was what the people wanted and missed.

Cromwell or Charles, that was the question. To some, Cromwell seemed the obvious choice. In Parliament he was in control; and abroad he was feared: he was the perfect choice of a constitutional monarch.

Charles watched these developments carefully from Brussels. He began mustering a rag-bag of an army: Royalist mercenaries who had been fighting for France, many hundreds of soldiers from Ireland, a country devastated by Cromwell's persecution of Catholics. And a badly-equipped contingent of soldiers tactically sent by King Philip of Spain, who was all but bankrupted by war with Britain.

'King' Charles had thought to take his men to Scotland, and march to London, but it was not to be. Morale was low; the King was at his wits' end. All Charles's plans fell apart through lack of finance, and the increasing success of Cromwell's military machine.

In 1658 Cromwell's army had a resounding victory against the Spanish, and Dunkirk was handed to the British.

Then, just as Charles had begun to see his position as hopeless, on September 10th 1658 Cromwell died.

The nation mourned Cromwell's death, but not all. Richard, Cromwell's son, succeeded to the Protectorship.

1659 was one of the bitterest winters on record. The King's troops succumbed to hardships of every kind, and the King himself could hardly afford to eat or clothe himself or get his washing done.

But factions grew. The seeds of insurrection and discontent were sewn amongst the people, tired of continuing instability, and anxious to protect the integrity of Parliament established with the waste of so much native blood.

And for all the brilliance of Cromwell's military victories the country was, as it turned out, hideously in debt.

Charles's wise adviser, Edward Hyde Earl of Clarendon, counselled a waiting game and attention focused on General Monck, the commander of the Protector's forces in Scotland. He was a man of the utmost integrity and believed in the institution of Parliamentary government, and with supreme diplomacy Charles convinced the powerful and well-respected Monck and the House of Commons of his humility to Parliament, and more importantly his conviction that the restoration of a reformed monarchy was an act of God. He would honour the concept of Godliness and tradition so important to the people.

He spoke of peace and the end to fighting abroad, a device used by Cromwell for so many years to deflect the country's opinions from matters at home.

Thirty-Five

'I am twenty-eight years old and I shall always be a widow,' Lizzie said to her mother, as they gathered early roses for Francis's grave. Mary looked at her daughter, so slim and beautiful. Adversity and responsibility had refined her looks into real beauty. She had become a well-respected and impressive woman. But for all her outward composure, Mary knew she was sad. They were so many women without a single man, except for poor little Benjie. The full weight of the running of their lives and the estate at Hinton which now supported them all, thanks to Lizzie's ingenuity, fell on her slim shoulders.

But today was cause for rejoicing. The family was to go in the barouche to the Dover road to see if they could get a glimpse of the King on his triumphal return. Jacob had decked out the whole affair in the King's colours, and just for today the children would be allowed out of their mourning clothes.

But Mary had been disappointed that Lizzie, usually so eager to make joy whenever possible, seemed so restrained. The young Prince Harry would be with his brother, the King. They would send for Lizzie. She would be rewarded for all she had done for the boy. It was a momentous time. The roads were already lined with enthusiastic crowds who were to scatter flowers in his path. This May morning had dawned perfect, with clear skies, and all around there was a sense of rejuvenation and confidence.

Despite her daughter's reserve, Mary's heart was fit to burst, for today Philip would also be home after seven long years. Would she even recognize him?

Her thoughts were interrupted by Lizzie.

'You didn't hear what I said, Mother,' she said reproachfully, for her mother sometimes failed to realize how difficult it was coping without a man. If Tom had been the slightest bit interested in his sisters and nieces, or even little Benjie, life would have been easier. But her brother was completely henpecked by his wife, Anne, who saw herself as greatly superior to Lizzie and her family in all respects.

'Dearest, I know. You think I don't understand but I do. It's less than a year since your Francis died. But Philip is coming back this very day. We've waited for so long. It's like a dream. We must enjoy it . . . And, besides, Prince Harry will be there. You may get a glimpse of him.' Mary thought the mention of the boy would lift her daughter's spirits, but it was as if Lizzie had some curious preoccupation which prevented her from wanting to share in the excitement.

'You're right, Mother . . . but it's so cruel . . .' Lizzie started to cry yet again, steering the conversation away from the King's return. 'We should have had the welcome for Philip here at Hinton, Mother. After all, he's your son, my brother. I can never forgive Anne for taking it all over in the way she has . . .'

'You mustn't take it to heart. I can understand Tom wanting to do this, and, besides, it's important for Tom to reconcile himself with his brother. There have been cross words over the years. Beatrice and Adela have both had to come to terms with Anne.'

'You're right, Mother. I know I'm being silly, but Beatrice and Adela have husbands, and somehow it makes it better. Anne doesn't treat them as she does me.'

'My dear, surely you understand the reason. You were always so close to Tom, and you ran Hatherton on many occasions. Anne Monck is very jealous of you, and she wanted to run her home her way. I think she felt she had to sever the bond between you and Tom.'

Lizzie thought for a moment. It seemed so very irrational and cruel when she had needed a brother so much after Francis had died. It would be difficult to forgive Tom such weakness.

'Well, it's Philip's day. At least Tom has made peace with his brother. I can't wait to see him. In fact, I could hardly sleep for thinking of it, and we mustn't let anything cloud it. We'll all dress in our best and go to the banquet at Hatherton, and then we shall have our own welcome for Philip.'

'And you'll come with us in the barouche,' Mary affirmed.

'No, Mother. I can wait to see the King and Prince Harry if they should send for me. I didn't tell you, but I've had a letter from Judith Briott. She's living in London with her daughter. She's asked me to visit her, and then we may go together to see Prince Harry, for it's true I would like to see him . . . but . . .' Lizzie's voice trailed away, and for some reason Mary knew not to say any more. 'As for Tom, you're right. I shall rise above it and I'm sure that one day we'll all be friends again.'

'Now that's more like it,' Mary said, but she was not convinced. Tom had behaved very badly, but then Philip had always been her favourite son. He was a force to be reckoned with and a better friend to Lizzie than she knew.

'There's one more thing, dearest,' Mary continued. 'I'm going to tell Philip he can have the dower house. He'll need a home to return to.' She hesitated, blushing slightly.

There was something she had been meaning to ask Lizzie,

for it seemed sensible. But before she could, it was as if Lizzie read her thoughts.

'Mother, that's a fine idea, and you must come to live here at Hinton, not just visiting as you do, always pretending you're needed at home, when we all know we want you here. And now that Mathilda will have a nunnery to go to, this is where your home is . . .'

Maybe, after all, Lizzie thought, she could look forward to happier times. She would have a brother again, even if she did not have a husband.

Sometimes in the dark moments of despair after Francis's death, she had thought about Richard. What was he doing? Of course, she would never know now. After all these years he would have forgotten her very existence. But she had Benjie and Emily and Mariah and Alice. Three girls more dear there could not be, and now Philip would be back, and her mother would come to Hinton. And there was little Faith. How like Francis she was. It was seeing them together before he died that used to amuse her: the same set of the eyes, something about the way the child laughed . . . She never thought about Benjie in this way. She couldn't. She could only see herself in him, and a patina of Francis who had been the father he never would have.

'Come, Mother. We've a lot to do,' she said finally.

Evening had come. They were still not back. She had begun to worry. And then there they all were. They found her in the garden. They came flying down the paths, dishevelled and flushed, each babbling out their version of the most exciting day of their lives.

'Mother, you should have been there,' Benjie cried, fit to burst with excitement. 'They came in one of the navy ships. It was *The Naseby,* renamed the *Royal Charles*, and the King is the tallest, finest gentleman, and he wore a dark suit, and he had a fine red feather in his hat.'

'The streets of Dover were full to brimming with the throng,' Emily added, so breathless she could hardly get the words out.

'And when the King saw General Monck, who'd helped him so much to come home, there were tears in both men's eyes, and a great cry went up. "God save the King" . . . And they say he'll pass this way on his journey to London.'

'Oh yes, my Lady, and young girls are gathering by the roadside with herbs and flowers to throw in his path.' Ruth had stopped, overcome. 'Oh, my Lady, it's the happiest sight I ever saw.'

Lizzie wished she could share in their joy. Richard, tall and handsome as she remembered him, would have been there . . . but that was long ago.

She dispatched the children to prepare for the trip to Hatherton in a whirl of excitement. She found herself alone and was overcome with a loneliness and sadness which was beyond her. Some time passed – she did not know how long. She sat with her eyes closed, her face towards the dipping sun. She had never felt so alone.

She heard Minette barking in a frenzy of excitement but did not open her eyes to see what had caused it, probably a fox or a rabbit.

Was she dreaming? She knew the voice, and so did Minette, for she had stopped barking and was making noises of eager recognition.

She turned with a start. She could hardly believe her eyes. There, on the steps leading to the garden was Philip. She hadn't seen him for more than thirteen years but she ran so fast that in a flash she was in his arms. Neither of them could speak. He held her away from him so that he could look at her.

'I must go to Mother. She doesn't know I'm here yet. But there's someone I've brought to see you, Lizzie. Close your eyes and don't open them until you're told.'

The voice was soft, the sweetest she could ever remember.

She could not open her eyes. If she did, the dream would fade and be gone for ever, but then different arms enfolded her.

The dream continued, the lips against hers, and her body responded in an all too human way. And then she felt a tugging at her skirt. It was Benjamin.

'Are you all right, Mother?' he asked.

He looked up at them, his face puzzled, but reassured by his mother's welcome for this tall stranger who held her so tight.

262

The stranger leaned down to him. He looked long and hard into his face in a way no person had ever looked at him before. Benjamin felt he knew him, but why, how . . .?

And then he saw his mother staring at them both in such an odd way, as if she were thinking hard. Slowly a smile spread across her face.

The stranger spoke. 'I said we would be together one day. It's taken longer than I thought.' He touched Lizzie's chin and gently lifted it. She could hardly breathe, let alone speak. The words would not come.

At last she broke her silence, fearful that she might spoil it all and it might turn out to be a dream.

'But I don't understand. How did you know I would be here?' she asked.

'Your brother Philip, he knew everything, Lizzie,' the man replied. 'He and I have watched over you. No harm would have come to you, or them.' He nodded towards the house, where children's voices could be heard carrying across the still gardens.

'Your old nurse told him everything. You were in good hands. Your husband protected you and him.' He gestured to Benjie, touching the boy's shoulder. 'Your Francis was a good man. Had he not died, I would never have come. He deserved to be happy. And I have something for you from Prince Harry. So you see I came as a messenger, unsure of what I might find.'

He handed her a small velvet pouch tied with ribbon. She carefully opened it.

Inside was a diamond pin. Her heart missed a beat. It had belonged to the little princess. She remembered it well.

There was a carefully written note, which she read aloud.

'For my dear Lizzie, my sister's pin. It is yours, for she would have wanted you to have it. Keep it near to your heart, as you always have been to mine. From your Hostage Prince.'

Lizzie's lip trembled. At this moment there were no words that could adequately express her happiness.

'You deserve this happiness and so does . . .' Richard knelt down, his eyes on a level with Benjie's. The boy smiled. Just a little. He wasn't quite sure . . . but there was something, some sort of magic in the air.

263

His mother held her breath, as if waiting for the stranger to say something important.

Choosing his words carefully the man took her in his arms again and whispered into her hair. 'How like you, Lizzie . . . how like me.'

'I never really doubted it,' she said.